Corpse in the Craftsman Cottage

by

Lori Pollard-Johnson

A Flippin' Good Mystery

Dedication

For Brian,
the OG of DIY projects
and for
Kacea and Scott and Grady and Melissa
the next generation of DIYers
and especially for
Rhiannon and Juneau
my treasured muses

Acknowledgement

Thanks to the good folks at The Wild Rose Press for believing in my book, and editor extraordinaire Dianne Rich for her insightful improvements. Special thanks to my good friends, the Witless Tiny Rhinos, who provided thoughtful critique in earlier versions, Carol Hazelwood who reviewed the final product, and especially to Judy Nill whose keen eye and cogent comments guided the earliest, later and latest drafts--you are a perfect friend.

Chapter 1

Cozy 1920s Craftsman cutie with peek-a-boo view.
Two bedrooms, one bath. Remodel includes cedar
closet, large pantry off kitchen, and detached garage.
Great starter or investment property. Huge price
reduction! Motivated Owner! Call Sam at Rainier
Mountain Realty, 260.555.HOME.

A man's pale, nearly translucent blue irises stared at me from within the coffin-size aquarium inside the closet. Technically, he wasn't looking at me—or my newly destroyed tutti-frutti pink manicure. No, he was clearly dead. Had been for some time. But his eyes were wide open, his expression steely through the murky water, and the spider web of fine silver hair around his face suggested he'd been old when he'd died.

I responded the way any normal woman would: I shrieked and jumped back, nearly tripping over the shards of seventies-era fake cedar paneling I'd stripped from the closet mere moments ago.

Scrambling backward, my spine slammed against the far wall. I slid to the floor with a thud. Clutching the dust mask from my mouth, I gasped, filling my lungs with chemical-laden air. I coughed, sneezed twice, then coughed some more. Long, esophageal-shaking hacks. My heart thundered in my chest and pounded in my ears. My stomach threatened rebellion. Despite my brain screaming, *run*, my legs froze, knees locked.

I blinked hard several times, willing my breath and pulse to slow…hoping the corpse would disappear. Slowly, I raised my head and focused my vision.

No dice. Suspended in a cloud of what I had to assume were flecks of his own skin, the corpse lay in a loose fetal curl, motionless. I took a cautious sniff. Yep. The subtle scent my best friend and business partner, Pam, and I had noticed when we first looked at the house had matured into a complete stink-fest. At the time, we assumed a strong household cleanser and good old-fashioned elbow grease would rinse it away.

We were wrong.

No amount of Lysol could remove this guy.

"Pam!" I hollered.

No response.

"*Pam*!"

I resorted to a trick I learned as a kid to measure time. One-one thousand…two-one thousand…three-one thousand.

Nothing.

Pam would have answered already. We were friends—had been since our exes introduced us twelve years ago. We'd had each other's backs through ten years of marriage, babies, our husbands' infidelities, and subsequent, not-so-amicable divorces. We'd even partnered up to create PB & J Enterprises with our divorce proceeds. It stood for peanut butter and jelly sandwich-making moms—our highest priority. But we told others it was an abbreviation of our initials: Pam Bacchus and Jan Weatherly Enterprises.

"Pam?"

Where was she? I scanned my memory. She'd been painting the wall in the other bedroom earlier. Knowing her, she was probably rocking out to '80s classics via ear buds.

I'd have to go to her...to get help...with him.

I scooped up Moxie, our eleven-year-old Chinese Crested dog we'd adopted from the animal shelter a couple months ago. We had high hopes she'd do double-duty as business mascot and guard dog. But so far, she'd slept through my yelping, her tongue hanging from the left side of her mouth.

Slowly scooting along the floor in my sweatpants while keeping an eye on the corpse, I moved halfway to the door. I don't know what I expected, but if he'd jumped out of the closet and lurched for me, I wouldn't have been more surprised...or terrified.

Moxie struggled a bit as she adjusted her bony body. She'd been reluctant to leave her pillow bed and glanced back at it longingly. No way would I leave her in there, though. Not alone with a dead guy. I tucked her firmly under one arm and eased onto my knees. As I waddled across the floor, Moxie lifted her stringy head and sniffed the air. No doubt her elderly nose had finally picked up the noxious scent. She wriggled, trying to get free, her hairless legs seeking traction in the air.

"No, Moxie." I crossed the threshold and jumped to my feet, then galloped down the short hallway. Chemicals cascaded down my throat as I swallowed. My lungs' response was to hack up thick, sour phlegm. I knew bile couldn't be far behind.

Rounding the corner to the second bedroom, eyes burning, I pinched my nostrils closed and massaged the sides. The air here tasted much better, but the stench from the other bedroom lingered in my nasal passages. I definitely knew that stink but couldn't place it. Something from high school, nearly twenty years ago.

I shook my head and focused through watery eyes. There, three rungs up a ladder, a blurry Pam painted to the faint strains of Van Halen's "Jump."

"Pam!" My voice registered an octave above David Lee Roth's shrieks, which isn't easy to do for a woman my size. We have naturally deep tones.

Clad in size two denim overalls and pink running shoes, Pam twisted on the rung and faced me. She pulled out her ear buds. The sounds of Roth imploring me to release my cares and catapult myself into the air grew louder. As if on cue, Moxie hurled herself from my arms and raced across the room. She began running circle-eights through the ladder legs.

Pam lowered the volume on her ear buds. "Hi, Janny. Did you finish stripping the paneling already? Man, you're fast!"

I shook my head and wiped my eyes, finding myself unusually tongue-tied. "No."

"Do you need some help?" Pam began climbing down the ladder.

That was Pam. Always ready to lend a hand. Her energy could be exhausting sometimes, but at other times, like now, I welcomed it.

"Help," I repeated, trying to form more words but failing miserably.

Pam reached the floor and picked up Moxie. She walked toward me, cradling the dog in one arm and giving her a belly scratch with the other hand.

"What's the matter, Janny? You look like you've

seen a ghost."

I slipped off my head lamp and looped it over one wrist, trying to find the right words. How do you tell your best friend that you'd just found something that could easily destroy both your financial futures? Something neither one of you could have anticipated or planned for during the long nights dreaming of our own house-flipping business?

"Are you all right? Are you coming down with something?" Her nose wrinkled. "Hey, what's that smell?"

I fiddled with my head lamp, flipping the switch on and off a few times. The light cycled through the low, medium, high, and red functions. "Um... There's something you need to see."

"Wait a minute." Her eyes lit up. "Did you find something? O...M...G. I knew it! I knew we were going to find treasure in this old house!"

Pam's excitement skyrocketed. She believed all older homes had antiques and memorabilia hidden in the walls and under the floorboards. All she had to do was find it.

She swept her blonde bangs to one side, painting her hair with a swath of the Santa Fe Tan she'd been painting the walls with. "Is it super old? Is it an antique? Oh, my gosh...oh, my gosh...oh, my gosh!"

"Antique?" I envisioned the graying skin and shock of white hair. He *was* old enough to be an antique...of sorts. I shook my head to dispel the image. "No," I said. "It's a, uh, a..."

Pam squealed and squeezed past me. She sprinted down the hallway, tiny blonde pigtails flapping with each step.

"No," I called out. "Pam, wait!"

She stopped short and twirled around. "What?"

I nearly toppled over her. "Man. Dead man. Dead man floating. In a fish tank." I spilled everything in gusty exhales.

She squinted. "What?"

I eased past her and held my arm across the door. "There's a dead guy in the closet."

Pam cocked her head to one side, clearly confused. A split second later, a smile spread across her face. "Oh, Janny. It's probably just shadows in this creepy old house…that will be fresh and new when we get done with it." Her grin broadened.

That was Pam. The eternal optimist. I'm not exactly a pessimist, but next to her, even a preschool teacher would be a Debby Downer.

"No." I shook my head. "A very dead, very buoyant man is in a big fish tank a few feet away."

Pam glanced from me to the closet and back. I dropped my arm from blocking her way. "Brace yourself."

She gave me the side eye and handed Moxie over. As she entered, she covered her nose with one hand, then tiptoed over the paneling pieces on the floor.

She glanced back. "I know that smell. It's formaldehyde." She paused and placed one foot inside the closet, followed by her whole head. A moment later her scream pierced the silence, and she barreled past me, through the living room, and out the front door.

I chased after her to the sidewalk, Moxie clinging to my forearm. When I caught up to her, she was bent over, hands on her knees, head hanging low between them. Gurgling sounds rumbled in her throat. I reached out to hug her.

She waved me off. "Stand back. I'm gonna toss my cookies."

I stepped outside the splatter zone and patted her back as she heaved and retched. After several minutes of producing nothing but spit, she straightened, still clutching her stomach. She stared at the house, then took a slow 360-degree turn, staring at each pastel-colored house along the tree-lined street of perfect, white picket fences. Without a word, she focused her blue eyes on me.

"You okay?" I asked.

She grimaced. "Why didn't you tell me he was naked?"

Chapter 2

"What are we going to do?" Pam asked, shaking the bangs from her worried eyes.

I scanned each gray, tan, and yellow bungalow that lined the street. Aside from a lone cat atop a red, white, and blue mailbox, eyeing something in the grass below, not a soul seemed to exist. It was like a ghost town. I shivered.

"I don't know," I replied. "What do you think we should do?"

Pam stared at the softly sprinkling sky. "We need to call the cops." Her teeth chattered. "You do it."

I nodded. "Yeah. I guess so. They'll know what to do, right?"

I handed Moxie to Pam and pulled out my cell and punched a few digits.

The operator picked up with a tired, "Nine-one-one. What's your emergency?"

I gave her a condensed version of the man swimming in his own soup. An awkward pause ensued, but finally she placed me on hold. A few anxious minutes later, she returned and asked if I knew the consequences of filing a false report. I gulped and admitted that I didn't, but there was definitely a body in the closet. She confirmed that an officer was dispatched and ended the call.

"I think she thought it was a prank," I said,

pocketing my cell again.

"Geez Louise. Who would kid around about a dead person?" Pam squeezed Moxie close.

"Beats me."

The misting had changed to the more traditional Seattle drizzle. I held out a hand and caught a few drips. Fat splashes pooled in my palm. Overhead, a gray sky promised a full-fledged shower.

Moxie began to tremble. Each tremor sent tiny ripples cascading down her bare sides and legs. Her crest lay flat like a bad comb-over and she began to whimper. Pam rewrapped her arms around the dog and held her tight. Moxie sighed and nosed her way into Pam's armpit.

"Do you think we should wait in the car?" Pam asked, her pigtails drooping.

I frowned. "My car keys are in my purse."

"And the purse is in the house with the dead guy." Pam finished the logical sequence, her shoulders quaking.

"Yep."

She cast a sideways glance toward our Craftsman and straightened her back. "I can wait."

"Me, too."

Rain pooled in my hair and dripped onto my shoulders. Pam and I huddled closer. We waited in silence for several minutes until a black and white rounded the corner. It pulled to a stop at the curb.

The lone officer killed the engine and took a good look at us through the dashboard windshield. No doubt he noticed my stoic exterior. My ex always said I should have been a professional gambler...or a lawyer. The truth, however, was that I'd become excellent at camouflaging my frustration and anger toward him in front of our kids.

The officer mouthed a few words into his shoulder mic but didn't seem to be in any hurry. They must see this kind of thing all the time. Or at least more often than we did, which was never.

Pam's quivering drew my attention. Silent tears made their way alongside her nose, nearly indistinguishable from the rain drops. Someone who knew her less well would assume sadness, but I knew these were tears of defiance. Defiance in the face of true challenge.

I put my arm around her shoulders. She leaned in for a short moment, then wiped her face free of emotion and stared at the police car.

The officer exited his vehicle and eyed the neighborhood. I wasn't sure what he was looking for, but when his gaze fell on me, I figured I didn't fit the bill. Not surprising. After a morning of demo work and then standing in the rain for nearly half an hour, I had to be one sorry-looking lady.

I couldn't help but stare back at him. He was tall, maybe six feet, and built my side of height-weight proportion. Not exactly chubby, but capable of weathering a night on a mountain. His close-cropped hair was the color of salted caramels, and his eyes were somewhere between blue and green.

Pam shifted her weight, and I pulled a whimpering Moxie toward me, covering my midriff. I stand an even five-ten in my work boots, and weigh in at 180 when I'm not retaining water. Pam's a shade over five feet and has never weighed an ounce over a hundred pounds. In contrast to her overalls with the cutesy

10

appliqués and the pink bra straps peeking out, I wore a white T-shirt over an old nursing bra I couldn't quite justify throwing out, even though my youngest was seven years old. Complementing my ensemble was a pair of elastic-waist, black sweatpants. With my hair drawn back in a rubber band and the accumulated dust streaked with rain, I passed for a true construction worker, not a former housewife trying to forge a new life for herself and her kids and to stand on her own financially.

I straightened my posture and finger-combed a few brown locks into the holder they'd escaped from.

The officer, clad in navy from head to ankle, stopped a few feet from us. "I'm Sergeant Daniels," he said. "Dispatch says you found a *body* floating in an *aquarium* in a *closet*?"

I nodded. Green. His eyes were definitely green.

Pam replied, "The bedroom closet."

Daniels pointed at Moxie. "What is that?"

I frowned. Sure, Moxie was unattractive on her best day. Her tongue lolled from the corner of her mouth at all times, and her eyes bugged. To top it off, only the comb-over and a few bristles of hair on her tail graced her body.

"She's a dog," I replied.

Daniels cocked his head. Moxie drew in her tongue, revealing all three of her front fangs. A low growl-hum rose from her throat.

"She's missing a few teeth," he said.

"Her breed has dental problems," Pam explained.

He tore his focus from Moxie and back to the house. "So, in the bedroom closet?"

Pam pointed at the open front door. "First door on

the right."

"Okay. Let's get started." He fished a notepad and pen from his front chest pocket. "How old's the body? Any chance it might be about forty years old?" He winked.

"Oh, no," Pam said. "He looks closer to seventy…when he was alive, that is." She turned to me. "What do you think, Janny?"

"I didn't get that good a look. But he's got white hair, so I think seventy is a good guess."

Daniels smirked and ran a hand over his head. "Very funny. And I suppose he's wearing his birthday suit, right?"

"He *is* naked," Pam whispered, her eyes widening. "How did you know? Jan, you didn't tell the dispatcher that, did you?"

Before I could answer, Daniels grinned. He spun around to peer behind him. He replaced his notepad. "So where are they?"

Confusion spread over Pam's face, and I felt my own brows pull together. Something was wrong. Maybe the dispatcher hadn't believed us after all. Moxie's growl-humming grew louder.

"There's only one body," I said, my words slurring due to my numbing lips and clenched jaw. "And he's in there."

Pam put her hands on her hips and stepped forward, glaring up at Daniels. Any minute she would begin tapping her index finger on his chest. "And none of this is funny," she said.

He stared at us in turn. "You mean Jackson's not here?"

In vain I searched for anyone—a curious neighbor,

kids on their way home from school. Where's an Avon lady when you need one?

"Who's Jackson?" Pam forced through chattering teeth.

Moxie's humming grew to a strong vibrato.

"Whose house is this?" he asked.

I shuddered. "Ours. It's our house, Pam's and mine."

"Yeah. This is *our* house." Pam's voice broke when she continued. "We're flipping it so we don't have to take money from our lyin', cheatin' exes, and if you don't get in there and do your job, I'm calling your boss!"

Daniels paused, his gaze ping-ponging from Pam to me and back again. I felt the blood drain from my face. Pam's abrasiveness wasn't going to help. I cleared my throat in a desperate attempt to calm everyone.

His grin flattened. "Is this for real?"

"Yes, sir," Pam and I said together.

Daniels's expression screamed skepticism. "I'll go take a look. Why don't you wait inside? It's pretty cold out here."

"No," Pam said, a little too loudly. "We're okay. We'll wait here."

"I'll go take a look." He headed up the concrete path that bisected the lawn into two patches of overgrown grass and dandelions.

"Go through the front room to the hall," I said. "Then turn right." I knew that he couldn't get lost in the eight-hundred-square-foot home, but I wanted to hurry him along.

Daniels nodded and disappeared through the front door. Neither Pam nor I moved a muscle as we waited for his return.

When he reappeared on the porch, he paused and spoke into his mic. Then, he jogged back to us, his steps finding mini-puddles on the asphalt and splashing water in all directions.

"Sorry about the confusion earlier," he said, coughing. "My partner, Jackson, likes to throw surprise birthday parties, and the dispatcher, well, she sounded skeptical."

My shoulders released. "That's okay."

"No, it's not!" Pam yelled. "It's super scary, not to mention a total budget buster!"

I glanced at Daniels. If he was surprised by Pam's outburst, it didn't show.

"We'll get this going right away." Daniels checked the time. "I'm going to call for the crime lab and the M.E. The local fire unit will be out, too, but that's just a formality. There's no one to revive in there." He cast a look around the neighborhood. "Everyone should be here within an hour. It's not high priority because the victim is, uh, clearly deceased." He refocused his attention on us. "That must have been quite a shock for the two of you. I apologize for my department's confusion, all 'round."

Pam and I bobbed our heads.

"Do either of you have to be anywhere soon?" he asked.

"I need to pick up my kids from school by four," I said.

"And I have to pick up my baby from daycare no later than five." Pam checked her cell for the time.

"We carpool, so we need to leave together," I added.

"Okay. We'd better get started." He reached into his pocket and withdrew the notepad and pen. "I'll need a statement from both of you. And I'll need your contact information."

Chapter 3

As Officer Daniels took our information, the rain ceased and the sun broke through a cloud. Another police car arrived. No lights. No sirens. Two officers, a tall Black man and a short Latino woman, got out.

"Officers Sanchez and Adams." Daniels motioned them toward our house. "First door on the right. Check the closet."

Sanchez and Adams nodded as they strode toward the house. At the front porch, they paused. As if on cue, they wrapped their arms across their faces, burying their mouths and noses in their bent elbows. The odor must have spread.

"Oh, yeah." Daniels glanced back. "Forgot to tell you. There's a strong smell in there."

The two waved at Daniels, who grinned at his notepad. He began reading our information to us: home addresses, phone numbers. When we confirmed, he cocked an eyebrow. "So you two live next door to each other?"

"Yes." Maybe it was the way he said it, or maybe I was being super sensitive right then, but I felt a need to explain that we were capable adult women who could stand on our own two feet, but that living next door made us feel safe. I wanted to say that being married for ten years had made me used to having another adult around, and that I sometimes felt lonely for someone other than my children. I wanted to tell him that Pam and I needed each other for moral support. But I didn't say a word. The stress of the day had left me feeling weak and weepy. Talking about it would produce waterworks. And crying in front of him was something I would not do.

"Our exes are best friends," Pam said, her tempo racing, words blurring. "The marriages didn't last. But our friendship did."

To everyone else, her spilling of private information would seem like awkward flirting. They would be wrong. When upset, Pam developed verbal diarrhea.

"They cheated on us…after ten years of marriage…and when my baby was just a few months old." She caught her breath and clamped a hand over her mouth then exhaled before continuing in a neutral tone. "That's why we're here, doing this, flipping this house. We're trying to make some money. So we don't need anything from their lying, cheating asses."

My smile weakened. Her narrative left lots of loopholes that only I had the map to navigate.

Daniels's expression remained neutral and professional. He nodded sympathetically. Then he jotted a few more notes on the pad then wiped the rain off and flipped it closed. "I'm guessing from the lack of furnishings in the house that no one lives here. Is that right?"

"No," said Pam. "We told you we we're fixing—"

"Rehabbing—" I corrected.

"Flipping it." Pam's amended statement sounded like a clumsy sales pitch.

Daniels paused, shifting his focus toward the house

and then back to us. If he thought we were scattered and biting off more than we could chew, he wisely kept quiet about it. I wasn't sure how much longer it would take for Pam to truly explode. I expected at least some questions about financial risk flipping in a craptastic market. But when he opened his mouth, all he said was, "I'll need a key."

"It's in my purse." I nodded toward the house. "In the kitchen to the left when you go in. But it's the only one we have. It goes to the front door and the door in the kitchen that leads outside. We were going to get copies made today, but didn't get a chance."

He crooked a finger. "Follow me. I'll have to escort you in so we don't contaminate the scene."

I stifled a laugh. Contaminate the scene? Hardly.

Reluctantly, we trailed behind him as he headed for the house.

As we neared the front door, my heart began to beat faster. It may have been fear of returning to the scene of the crime, so to speak, the stench that made my stomach churn and throat burn, or simply nerves taking over. Whatever the reason, I felt shaky and sick.

Gritting my teeth, I straightened my spine, pulled Moxie closer, and walked in. I had a key to get, a corpse to avoid, and a business that needed a smart and speedy backup plan.

Cars sounded in the distance. Another black and white appeared. It coasted down the street and parked. Two officers got out, both white men in their thirties, both sporting tight crew cuts. They looked comfortable in blue jeans and flannel shirts, their pace unhurried. Clearly, they weren't here for the investigation. They hustled past us, issuing a quick "ma'am" to each of us, and slowed only momentarily to stare at Moxie. Moxie's grumbling began anew.

"Jackson, McDonald," Daniels said in acknowledgment.

"Thought we'd help out so you can get on to other things," one said to Daniels. "Happy fortieth," said the other under his breath.

Daniels shot him a look, then glanced in the direction of the bedroom. "Follow your nose."

They headed down the hall and a moment later someone exclaimed, "What the hell?" Laughter erupted. Pam and I exchanged horrified looks. How could anyone think this was funny?

"Sorry about that," Daniels said. "I think we're all a bit surprised by this incident. It's not exactly textbook."

I found my voice. "We're going to need our jackets."

"Moxie needs her coat, too," added Pam.

"The dog has a coat?" Daniels asked, a half-smile forming on his face.

"She's hairless!" Pam said, indignation in her voice.

Any trace of smile disappeared from Daniels's face. "I'll grab the coats...all of them. Where are they?"

My heart sank. "They're in the bedroom with the corpse next to Moxie's bed."

"Okay. No need for the two of you to go in there. It may not be safe. I'll grab the coats and you get the purses. We'll meet on the front porch."

"We need Moxie's bed, too," Pam called out as Daniels rounded the corner, nose buried in his elbow.

Daniels stuck his head out the doorway and

uncovered his mouth. "Got it."

As he retreated, Pam and I dashed for the kitchen, grabbed our purses, and high-tailed it all the way to the sidewalk. When Daniels joined us, our jackets hung over his arm, and in his hands he carried Moxie's pink bed.

Pam took the bed, and I took the coats, sniffing each. I hoped the fabric hadn't absorbed the odor. I didn't think I could stomach that stench in my washing machine. Fortunately, our nylon raincoats smelled of spring rain.

"Thank you," we said in unison. I handed him the key.

"Tell you what." Daniels pocketed it. "Take some time to get your bearings before picking up your kids. This must have been a shock for you. Our confusion didn't help."

"Sounds good." Pam sniffled. Gone was the little firecracker I knew her to be.

I pumped my head up and down in agreement. His kindness touched me, and I couldn't help but soften a little, too.

"I may need to fill in a few blanks on your statements, too. I'll contact you as soon as the scene is cleared."

"Okay," Pam and I replied, one right after the other, already inching away from the house.

Moxie whimpered and leaned toward Pam, and more likely, her pillow bed. I passed her over. Pam wedged the dog's bald butt into the front of her overalls, and we picked up our pace along the concrete path, her tennis shoes making squishy sounds. At the sidewalk, I turned around. Daniels watched us from the porch.

I shot him a half-smile. "Happy birthday," I called out.

He gave me a lopsided grin before Pam yanked my arm and hurried me across the street.

"What's the matter with you?" Pam asked as we neared the car.

"What?"

"You are flirting with that cop."

I swiveled around to make sure no one had heard her before replying. "No, I am not."

Pam rolled her eyes. "Fine. It looked like flirting to me, but what do I know? Clearly, I flirted with the wrong guy for a very long time."

"Oh, Pam."

"But if you were flirting, it would be a bad idea. A very bad idea."

I glared her direction, but she conveniently ignored me. I popped the Kia's hatch. I threw in the coats, and Pam placed Moxie and her doggy bed down. Moxie gladly attempted settling in, but Pam wriggled the dog's squirrelly body into the dog coat first.

Once Moxie lay curled in her bed, and her food and water dishes were replenished from the supplies we kept in the car, we hurried around and got in.

"What do you think will happen?" Pam asked from the shotgun seat.

"They'll probably clear out and then go celebrate Daniels's birthday." I inserted the key.

"No, silly." Pam yanked on her seatbelt and clicked it closed. "I'm talking about the house…and the body. What do you think they're going to do about that? And how long do you think it will take?"

She reminded me of my wide-eyed seven- and eight-year-olds the day I explained that their daddy was moving out. Their faces had reflected a mixture of apprehension and confusion. A gush of sadness overwhelmed me. The divorce was still too new, too fresh, even after a full year of living apart and reminding myself daily I had made the right decision.

"I don't know," I said. "I just hope they hurry."

Pam gulped. Worry lines appeared between her eyes. "That's my biggest fear. What if they can't get him out? What if it takes months to clear the house?"

My checkbook flashed before my eyes. It didn't hold months of reserve. Weeks would be a better guesstimate. "I don't know."

"What if they *never* clear it?" Pam's voice dropped an octave. "We'd lose everything."

I fired up the engine and pulled away from the curb. "I know. I know."

Silence filled the Kia as we wound through the neighborhood. I pulled onto the main road, my heart too heavy to quicken from anxiety.

"Hey, what goes well with worry?" I asked, eyeing our favorite ice cream shop looming ahead.

Pam followed my line of vision. One corner of her mouth turned up. "Chocolate?"

I nodded and switched on my turn signal.

Chapter 4

I pulled into the lot and parked under the giant swirl ice cream cone, partially shielding us from the sprinkling rain. After killing the engine, I checked both the exterior temperature and a soundly sleeping Moxie. Pam cracked her window open. We hurried across the asphalt, entered through smudged glass doors, and ordered: chocolate milkshake for me and a hot fudge sundae with two cherries on top for Pam.

We carried our goodies to a booth with red plastic seats and slid in. After shredding the paper from my straw like a heroin addict craving a high, I took my first sip. Yummm…rich and creamy. Chocolate Heaven.

Already, I felt a little better.

From across the table, Pam snapped off the clear top of the sundae bowl and tossed a whipped cream-frosted cherry into her mouth. Her eyes rolled back and she muttered, "Mmmmmm…"

We indulged in chocolatey silence for a solid two minutes before Pam's eyes widened larger than usual when she had an idea. "Oh!" she said.

"What?"

She dabbed at her lips with a napkin then leaned in. Her words came out in a hushed whisper. "Do we have to tell people that we found a body in the house?"

My heart sank. "You mean buyers, right?"

Pam nodded. "Buyers—realtors—bankers—

escrow."

The extra layer of dread settled onto my shoulders that even the most decadent ice cream concoction couldn't budge. "I've heard that ghosts are a net zero—as many people like the idea of ghosts as don't. It doesn't affect the time a house stays on the market. But a dead body? I don't know."

Pam inhaled deeply. "I'll call the realtor. He'll know." She punched a few numbers into her cell, looked around, then ended the call before speaking. "I'm going to wait to call Sam until we have some privacy. No sense telling everyone within earshot our house boasts a cadaver until we absolutely have to."

"Oh, I don't know," I said. "Everyone's got a skeleton in their closet."

Pam laughed, which sent a little whipped cream spittle flying from her mouth. It landed with a splat next to my elbow. She dabbed at her lips with a napkin.

"Very funny." She raised an eyebrow. "I thought my closet was cluttered."

Halfway through a swallow, I felt a giggle bubble up. Essence of dark semi-sweet chocolate filled my nose. Not a completely unpleasant sensation.

Pam smirked. "We really need one of those closet organizing systems to make the competition for our house *stiff.*"

I replied, "That *remains* to be seen."

Immediately, my guilt-o-meter registered mean. A man was dead. "Okay," I said. "Now I feel guilty."

We were quiet for a moment. Questions sparked in my brain. Why was he put into an aquarium? Who put him there? How did he die?

"Do you think he was murdered?" Pam asked. "He

must have been murdered, right? I mean, why keep a body otherwise?"

I shook my head to clear my thoughts. "Well, I doubt he killed himself, but I would think if a killer wanted to hide a body, he would throw it in the ocean, or bury it in the woods. Why keep the body so close to where you sleep? That's super creepy." A chill coursed up my spine. I doubted it was from the ice cream. "Do you think the owner of the home knew about it?"

"Who else could have stashed him there?" Pam asked, stirring her sundae into a light brown soup. "Maybe it was the contractor who did the remodel."

I pushed my milkshake aside. It was a horrible thought, but I had to admit, it would be a perfect plan. "Some people leave town when they're having work done on their house," I said. "It wouldn't be the first time a foundation had a little extra filler."

Pam fished the second cherry from her sundae, then threw it back in. "How professional was the workmanship on the cedar planking?"

"Not good," I replied. "In fact, I think it was a do-it-yourself job. And a hasty one at that. No pattern to the nails and no furring strips anchoring the paneling to the wall." I thought a moment. "Wait. There was no drywall."

"That doesn't surprise me," Pam said. "A lot of homes built back then used paneling in place of a wall. It was cheaper. No one worried about the lack of insulation because heating costs were cheap."

"Hmmm…"

"It had to be the owners." Pam retrieved the cherry once more and popped it in her mouth.

"Or a very incompetent carpenter," I said. "Or a

shady subcontractor. We can't rule out anyone at this point."

"I agree. Too many to account for." Pam snapped her fingers. "I know why they used formaldehyde."

"To preserve the body?"

"Right, but that's not all. It would also cover any other odor," Pam scrunched her nose. "Decaying odor."

My stomach heaved remembering the scent. "I bet you're right."

"One thing's for sure," said Pam. "Whoever put the body in there wanted it hidden for a long, long time."

"Okay." I paused a moment before continuing. "But that doesn't help us. The killers could have escaped to South America, or stayed there, or simply kept the door closed. We haven't narrowed down the list of suspects at all."

"Oh, oh!" Pam's eyes grew round, and her head bobbed up and down in agreement. "We should tell Daniels what we've figured out. We can help him on this case!"

I frowned. "What can we tell him? It's all speculation."

"Darn it. You're right. We need facts." She chewed on her red plastic spoon. "Did you see any blood in the tank? Any bruises on his, uh, body?"

I shook my head. "No, but I wasn't looking that closely. I was so freaked out, a freight train could have run through the backyard and I wouldn't have noticed."

Pam rubbed her chin. "Me, too. Still, if there are any clues that we can dig up that would help Daniels solve the case, we need to at least try. It could help us get back into the house sooner."

"What kind of information?" I asked. "All we

know about the house is the names of owners and what we can glean from county parcel searches."

"That's a start." Pam nodded. "We could also check permitting—if they filed for permits."

"That's a long shot. Only reputable contractors get permits before beginning a project, and not every project needs one—" I held up my hands and made air quotes. "—'only significant structural changes' in this county. Do you think a bedroom renovation would require a permit?"

"Nah," Pam replied. "Contractor rule of thumb: No plumbing, no electrical, no permit."

"Plus, any contractor who planned to bury a body in the construction isn't worried about filing for a permit," I added.

"Back to square one." Pam's shoulders slumped. "Still, county records are a good start. The only thing we know for sure is that whoever did the remodeling knows something about the body."

"So what do we do now?"

"We start by talking to the previous owner. What was his name—Morrow?"

"Morford," I said. "He's old. He lives in a rest home up north as I recall. Sam, our realtor, had to drive all the way up there to have him sign the papers, remember? That's why the process took an extra day."

"Maybe we could go talk to him. See what he knows. We need to know how long he owned the place."

"I can check county records for a complete history," I said. "Maybe do a little cross-referencing between dates and owners."

"It's a start." Pam stuffed her napkin into the half-full sundae cup. "Now—brave faces so the kids don't freak out. They're like wild animals sensing fear."

"Right." I stood, my knees weak but brain determined, and propelled myself forward.

Halfway across the parking lot, Pam said, "I know what will help us get in a happy mood." She fished into the kangaroo pocket of her overalls and pulled out her iPod. Raising it in the air, she hollered, "Beastie Boys! 'Cause we really gotta fight for our right to party now!"

Chapter 5

We trooped through my condo's front door, Annie, my eight-year-old, leading the way. Following her were my other daughter, Emily, age seven, and Pam with fourteen-month-old Gabriel riding on one hip. I brought up the rear, Moxie under one arm. The girls ran toward their rooms, and Pam set her diaper bag atop my overstuffed mint-green couch before settling into the cushions. I followed suit, plopping into my tan leather recliner that sat kitty-corner from the brick fireplace, purse still on my shoulder, and released Moxie. She promptly chased after the girls, her toenails clicking on the hardwood floor.

Pam's purse slipped off her shoulder, and she wriggled free of her running shoes. "It's days like these that a pass-through door would come in handy."

"Between our condos?" I kicked out the footrest and rested my calves. "Where would we put it?"

Pam pointed toward my hall closet next to the front door. "Right there."

I followed her finger's trajectory. Our condos were mirror units, so her closet backed up against mine.

"We'd lose closet space," I said. "But with the amount of time we spend going back and forth, it would be worth it."

"Plus, the kids would always be in earshot."

I nodded. "That will become more important as

Gabe gets older."

"That's what I was thinking." Pam wriggled Gabe's coat from his relaxed body. "It would be good for security, too. If one of us needed help, the other would be right there without having to worry about unlocking a door." She lowered her voice. "I still feel a little uneasy about the you-know-what in the you-know-where."

I clamped my jaw shut to stave off a quiver. The dead man had been at the back of my mind as we hustled through school pick-up lines and day care sign-outs and daily summaries of feedings and poopings. I felt fairly certain he'd make a reappearance in my dreams that night. And, after a year of sleeping alone, I still missed Jim, or at the least the warmth of another adult, when I woke in the dark.

I sighed, struggling to free myself from memories of what he and I would never have again, and pushed myself up off the chair. "Why don't you stay for dinner?" I blew dust from the numerous picture frames atop the mantel. "If Daniels calls, I can go meet him and you can hold down the fort until I get back."

"Good idea," Pam replied.

Gabriel's eyes fluttered open. He echoed, "Good de-uh," the words clogged by his pacifier.

We laughed and headed for the kitchen. I replenished Moxie's water and emptied the last of the dry dog food into her bowl. I wrote *dog food* on the grocery list, then opened the fridge door and searched for dinner ideas. Nothing looked appetizing, probably due to the late afternoon milkshake.

The girls always had ideas, though. I called down the hallway and a moment later, a tiny thunder of padded feet stormed my way.

"What do you want for dinner?"

Annie yelled, "Lasagna," and Emily shouted, "Tacos." Gabriel simply shrieked, one fist raised in the air.

I winked at Pam. "How about enchilada casserole?"

The girls were silent a moment, checking each other's expression. "Okay!" they agreed.

"Good. You girls entertain Gabe while Pam and I make dinner."

Gabe immediately squealed and began fidgeting. Pam set him on the floor, and the trio crawled under the dining room table, creating a play fort with toy blocks left there from the night before.

I pulled out a bag of tortillas, cans of beans and enchilada sauce, and set to work. The kids giggled in the background, Gabe releasing excited squeals at regular intervals.

Pam and I paused a moment, watching from the doorway. Nothing buoys my mood like the sound of children at play.

Pam turned to me, her eyes moist. "I'm so glad we have each other, Janny," she whispered. "I can't imagine what Gabe's life would be like without the girls. He'd be so lonely with just me."

"Oh, Pam." I gave her an awkward hug, an opened can of enchilada sauce in one hand and can opener in the other. "And I'm glad the girls and I have you guys." She squeezed once, then released me. "And you *are* enough," I said. "Gabe is lucky to have a mom like you."

Pam sniffled. "Thank you. I'm just glad we're in

this together. I never dreamed I'd be a single mom. Never imagined I'd be divorced, either."

"Life is full of surprises." I poured a little sauce into the bottom of the casserole dish and swirled it around, coating the entire bottom surface. "Some good and some not so good."

Pam drew her shoulders back, then grabbed the cheese from the refrigerator. A cup and a half of grated cojack later, she said, "After the kids go to bed, let's crunch some numbers. A couple of ideas on how to trim the budget just bounced into my head."

"Sounds good to me." I turned the oven to preheat, then began layering tortillas into the dish. "You know, at times like these, I'm grateful you're the accountant. I wouldn't know where to begin."

Pam swung the refrigerator door wide and pulled out tubs of salsa, sour cream, and guacamole, a head of lettuce, and two large tomatoes. "Well, we've got to start somewhere."

"Agreed."

After dinner, cleanup, homework, and bedtime books, Pam and I retreated to the living room. We were well out of earshot of the kids, and Gabe had been settled into the spare crib in the girls' room. Moxie sat in front of the unlit fireplace, staring at the tiny blue gas pilot light. Daniels still hadn't called.

We nursed fizzy mocktails of cranberry juice and seltzer, relishing the silence. After ten minutes, Pam set her glass on the coffee table and flipped on the lamp beside her.

She reached into her purse and pulled out her calculator, a small legal pad and pencil, and after adjusting her glasses, spoke. "Let's look at the numbers. I'm going to start by assuming we'll be set back by one week. That's a nice whole number and it gives us something to work from."

"Good," I said. "That's one-quarter monthly mortgage payment, plus insurance, plus utilities."

Pam wrote down some figures. "I'll have to guess at the electricity, but since we're almost into summer, it won't cost too much to heat. The power will be limited to tools and light. Water will be next to nothing, probably just a service fee. What else?"

I racked my brain. "Garbage—yes, but no phone, no internet. Oh, interest on the business Visa for materials and supplies we've already purchased or ordered."

Pam chewed the eraser end of her pencil. "Let's see. We bought replacement light fixtures, paint, and some tools—"

"Ladder, stand-up fan, some lawn fertilizer and weed killer," I added. "We've also ordered the carpet and paid for the first half. The rest is due at the end of next week when it arrives."

"That doesn't leave us much time." Pam frowned.

"Maybe we can put it on hold," I said.

"We don't want to put anything on hold or pay late." She shook her head. "Word travels fast. If we don't pay on time or don't accept delivery, no one will want to do business with us again. That's all we need right when we're starting out."

This was news to me. When we worked for our exes' construction company, Pam had done all of the accounting and I had helped out with scheduling and coordinating work time frames. Occasionally, I'd do a little demo work and meet installers at worksites to let them in. Once the babies came, ours and later Gabe, I stayed home with all of the kids and Pam continued the administrative tasks. My ex, Jim, and her ex, Marcus, had done everything else...and *everyone* else, as we later came to find out.

"It's a good thing we didn't order the toilet, sink, and cabinet for the half-bath we planned," Pam said.

"Right. That can wait."

"It'd be a shame if we had to redline that whole addition." She chewed on her lip.

I nodded. An extra bathroom would command a higher sales price, and homes with two baths sell far faster. "Let's wait to nix the extra half-bath. Maybe they'll get him out of there by the end of the night and we can start fresh tomorrow."

"We can always hope," she said.

I took a sip and swallowed. "I hate to ask, but how long can we go without selling?"

"Reasonably? Two months." Pam removed her glasses. "But that has to include all the time it takes to close."

I envisioned my bank account dwindling under the dual drains of personal and business expenses. "I'd hate to do it, but in a pinch, I could go to Jim for a loan."

"I will never go to Marcus for help." Pam jutted her chin. "I will live on crackers and water before I ever ask him for anything."

I understood Pam's feelings well. I'd felt the same way at the beginning. But for whatever reason, I'd let go of the anger sooner. Maybe it was because my kids were older. Maybe Jim had apologized in a way that made it easier. Maybe Pam had never suspected the affairs. But I had to admit, I had. Little things that seemed suspicious but got dismissed with the demands of everyday life. Then again, I don't know what I would have done if I'd found out earlier. Would I have left? Would we have worked it out? I would never know.

"It's okay if it's for the kids, Pam," I reminded her, my words gentle. "It's not taking if it's a loan. And even though we don't like what they did to either one of us—and it was wrong, no two ways about it—they're still part of the kids' lives. They'll always be a part of ours, too."

Pam took a deep breath and released it slowly. "I know in my head you're right," she said. "I'm just not able to forgive him yet. He shouldn't have gone outside our marriage. He shouldn't have ignored me. He shouldn't be so detached from Gabe now."

I listened. Venting in small doses prevents an eruption later.

"It's just that the anger makes me feel powerful, you know?" she continued. "I know it's bad for me. I try to let it go. And then I get mad all over again because I'm the one who has to do all the work to get through this, and he doesn't seem to be bothered by anything at all." Pam trembled, tears forming in both eyes.

"I understand."

"Sometimes it feels like as long as I stay mad, he'll never get close enough to hurt me again."

I nodded. "Resentment feels like a fortress. But it also locks us away from anyone else and the joy we'd get from another relationship." I scratched my head. "Forgiveness is weird. It feels like we're giving in. But it actually gives us more control. It's like deciding that his actions won't bother you. Like you're above it."

She uncrumpled her napkin and flattened it on the arm of the sofa. "You're probably right."

"It'll take time," I said, "for both of us. And we aren't on any schedule."

"I know." She set her accounting tools on the table. "I know." A few more minutes passed as we finished our drinks. Finally, Pam sighed and checked her cell. "Daniels has to call us no matter what time his team finishes, right?"

"I think so," I replied. "What time is it, anyway?"

"Nearly ten thirty. I'm beat." Pam rubbed her forehead.

"Me, too." My back ached from stress and hard labor. I stretched, arms overhead, and yawned. "Why don't you stay over? When he calls, one of us can stay with the kids while the other picks up the key."

Pam rubbed her toes, then swung her legs onto the couch and fluffed a pillow behind her head. "This couch is super comfy. I'll just nap a little until then."

"Sounds good."

I double-checked the front door locks, then scooped up Moxie, who still stared at the motionless cement logs in the fireplace. "Night."

What seemed like a heartbeat later, a series of short quick beeps woke me. In a stupor, I checked my cell on the bedside table. 11:57.

My pulse quickened. Unknown number.

In a flash, I remembered. The cottage. The corpse. Daniels.

I sat up, cleared my throat, and answered.

"This is Sergeant Daniels," he said. "I apologize for the late hour. Things took longer than expected. Would you like me to come over? I'm five minutes away."

"Yes," I said. "Thank you."

I switched on my bedside light and blinked hard. Before lying down, I had stripped to my granny panties and that's still all I had on. I needed a bra, clothes, and to rouse Pam, and in that order. And I had to do it all on-the-double, without waking Moxie or disturbing the sleeping kids.

I eased out of bed, pulled on my blue robe with the yellow moons, and tightened the belt. At some point, Moxie had joined me in my bed, and now, she lay sprawled, tummy-side up, at the foot of my bed, half-covered by my comforter. Still asleep, still softly snoring. Good.

Stubbing my toe just once on stray toys in the hallway, I made my way to the living room. I hit the light and adjusted the dimmer to low. Pam was asleep on the couch, wrapped in a fleece blanket. Her overalls lay draped over the coffee table.

"Pam," I whispered as I drew near to her.

She didn't respond.

I gave her shoulder a little nudge. "Pam, Daniels is on his way."

She opened her eyes one at a time, then squinted my direction. "Daniels?"

"He'll be here any minute."

Pam stretched and swung her legs over the edge of the couch. In one motion, she grabbed her overalls and pulled both legs through, then hiked them up. I twisted the dimmer to medium, then folded Pam's blanket and patted my hair, hoping there were no eye boogers—or worse—on my face.

A soft knock came at the door as Pam hooked her

overall straps. She yawned and I opened the door.

"I've got news." Daniels's voice was husky. "Can I come in?"

Chapter 6

Daniels stepped inside. His eyes were alert, but his five o'clock shadow had crept across his cheeks and chin, revealing a long night. He'd loosened his tie and rolled up his sleeves, making him look like a teddy bear in a cop costume. The mic at his shoulder and gun at his hip told a different story, though. I shook free the image of officer Beanie Baby and ushered him to the recliner next to the fireplace.

"I hope you don't mind that I came by so late." He sat. "I didn't want to do this by phone."

My heart sank. It had to be bad news. Pam's stony expression revealed nothing, but her shoulders slumped forward.

I pushed down my fear and settled in next to Pam on the couch. "What happened? Did you get him out?"

Daniels rested his elbows on his knees and interlaced his fingers. "Sorry to disappoint you both, but not yet," he said. "We haven't even tried."

"Why?" Pam asked.

"This is a very complex project." Daniels's forehead wrinkled. "We've sent out a sample of the fluid and we have a tentative plan on how to remove the aquarium—and the body—given certain, most probable lab results."

"Good," I said, glancing toward Pam. "That's good, right?"

Pam's head bobbed up and down.

"I wish that was all it would take," he said, rubbing his chin. "But you need to be prepared. This project may take a while. And if the results don't come out the way we hope, it could take a lot longer."

"How long?" Pam's voice sharpened.

"Let me explain. We expect the liquid to be embalming fluids. That would be good news. It will require specialty officers, of course, but we know how to handle that." He cleared his throat. "But if there's anything else in there, we'll need to do more in-depth testing prior to removal."

I clenched my teeth and held firm. I would remain logical and emotionless—a true businesswoman—at least on the outside.

A door squeaked. Small footsteps trudged down the hall. From the cadence, I knew it was Emily, probably headed for the bathroom. Listening carefully, I heard the door open and then close. A split second later, Gabe called out, "Momma."

Pam jumped up. "I'll be right back."

"Take your time," Daniels said. "I know you've all had a long night. I can wait."

Pam headed down the hall, her footsteps receding as tiny clicking noises grew louder. I heard her whisper, "Heya, Moxie," and a jangle of collar later, Moxie tip-tapped her way into the room. She blinked hard at the light and emitted a loud canine yawn that ended on a high note. After a quick slurp from the water bowl in the kitchen, she came in and sat at my feet. I picked her up and held her on my lap.

Daniels smiled, twin dimples gracing his cheeks. "I'm hoping it will take only a week," he said.

"Unfortunately, I don't have control over the schedule. There are a lot of people who'll be involved in this one. I would plan at least a month's delay."

A punch in the gut would have had less effect. I struggled to breathe…and remain composed.

Moxie's head perked up. One ear straightened and she focused her gaze Daniels's direction. She probably hadn't heard him earlier. She definitely couldn't see him from this distance and in the subdued light. I scratched behind her ears in an attempt to distract her.

"Anything more than a month could put us out of business," I said.

"I understand." Daniels frowned. "I've put a rush on everything. But there are lots of processing challenges, like lab analysis, logistics, furloughs—"

I held up a hand. "Could we wait until Pam comes back before you say more? I'm only going to remember half of what you said. She'll be able to remember the other half."

"No problem." Daniels shifted his focus to Moxie. "That's some dog. What breed is she?"

Moxie's nose twitched in Daniels's direction. She attempted to wriggle free of my arms, but I snuggled her closer.

"Chinese Crested. She's probably the only Chinese Crested that thinks she's a guard dog." To Moxie, I whispered, "It's okay."

Moxie whined but stayed put. Down the hall, the bathroom door squeaked again, and Emily plodded back to her room.

"She doesn't smell good," I said and laughed. The tension in my back eased a little. "I mean, she's lost her sense of smell. It's on account of her age. The shelter

41

couldn't tell us exactly how old she is, but their best guess is at least ten. This breed doesn't live much longer than fifteen."

Daniels grinned. "Dogs that old probably lose their sense of smell because they smell bad. My beagle was fifteen when he passed last year. He couldn't hear and he had to wear a diaper in the house. But I couldn't see putting him down—not as long as he could wag his tail and enjoy a good scratch behind the ears."

My heart softened, and a giggle bubbled up at the thought of this big, burly police officer diapering anything, especially a dog. "A diaper? I didn't know they made dog diapers."

"'Fraid so," he replied. "Not cool. Dogs don't lie on their backs like babies. You have to catch them when they're standing still and preoccupied and feed the tail through an opening. I usually timed it with meals."

I nodded. I couldn't help but think of Jim's attempts at diapering our girls. He had changed—at most—a dozen diapers between both girls. I couldn't imagine him having the patience or the dedication to change a dog's diaper. "Wow."

He held my gaze, but I looked away. My emotions teeter-tottered between the unexpected connection I felt with this kind-hearted man and the bad news he brought with him. The gravity of the situation took over, however. Visions of bills piling on the desk and an empty bank account raced through my mind. I sighed.

At times like these I resented Jim the most. If he'd kept his pants zipped, our kids wouldn't be trying to sleep through a police visit, and neither Pam nor I would be up late worrying about a corpse or how we were going to make a business work in this economy.

Swallowing hard against the lump in my throat, I willed myself not to cry for the second time that night. Fatigue...the circumstances...everything conspired against my ability to control my emotions.

It hit me all at once, though. My eyes welled and I tilted my head toward Moxie in an attempt to hide my reaction.

Moxie, sensing my full attention, flipped onto her back. I smiled despite myself and rubbed her tummy. Immediately, she began cooing. Long, drawn-out "ooohs"—a sound I'd never heard from a dog prior to adopting Moxie. Her eyes closed to mere slits and her tongue slipped between her teeth and hung to one side.

Daniels laughed. "That's a great dog."

My emotions in check again, I kissed Moxie's head. "She sure is."

Pam returned, Gabe held snug to her chest and a green and yellow blanket wrapped around both of them. He'd fallen back asleep, thumb firmly in mouth. Pam eased onto the couch again and glanced at each of us.

"It could be as short as a week or as long as a month," I whispered.

"A month?" The words came out hushed, but her gaze shifted frantically from me to Daniels and back again. "We can't be out a whole month."

Gabe opened his eyes and surveyed the room.

"It's okay, Gaby-baby," Pam cooed, commencing her rocking. She turned to Daniels, lowering her voice. "Please do whatever you can. We can't wait as long as a month. It's too expensive."

"I understand," he said. "The trouble is, we may not have a choice. The tank is, uh, cumbersome at best.

To remove it without draining first would require removing a wall from the house and some big equipment brought in. But to drain the tank means identifying all of the contents, so no workers are endangered. And then, there's the consideration of forensic evidence. We need to be sure we retain, uh, everything."

Pam's grimace mirrored my own disgust. Everything Daniels said sounded logical. But it was also the worst news we could get. I weighed our options in a flash, my heart racing. We could work nights to catch up on lost time so long as the guys agreed to watch the kids. But replacing a wall, especially an external one, would seriously damage our budget. It could mean complete rewiring, new materials, new window, maybe even new exterior paint. It would definitely mean cutting back on other necessary changes…or finding money elsewhere…or losing money on the property…or giving up.

I took a big breath. None of those options were acceptable. They all led back to asking Jim and Marcus for a bail-out.

I exhaled and asked, "Can we do anything to help?"

Daniels shook his head. "The best thing the two of you can do is focus on your kids, that dog, and all the money you're going to make once we've cleared out and you finish your rehab."

It would be nearly impossible to sit and watch as our house was torn apart. But what choice did we have?

Pam kissed the top of Gabe's head. "So what's next?"

"We've taken a sample of the fluid through the

caulking that's holding the tank together. It's brittle, and appears close to failing, but we withdrew enough to send to the lab."

"Failing?" My voice rose and Moxie scrambled to all fours, loosening my robe.

Daniels's eyes drifted down to my lap, then immediately rose to my face again. I looked down. Sure enough, my knees and a solid four inches of chubby thigh were exposed after Moxie's re-adjustment. Criminy! The last thing I needed to do was provide proof that I hadn't shaved my legs in a week and that cellulite ran rampant in my family. I pushed Moxie off my lap and gathered my robe around me.

Without skipping a beat, Daniels answered, "No one knows for sure, but it is reasonable to assume that a slow leak would form first, and then a larger leak and eventually…"

Pam's expression changed, reflecting amusement. Clearly, my accidental flashing, courtesy of Moxie, had pleased her. As happy as I was for her momentary diversion, I attempted to glare her into focusing on the problem.

"What a mess," Pam said, trying to keep a straight face. "Those are original floors…"

Daniels continued, "We're trying hard to avoid any damage to the existing structure. We're pretty sure the chemicals are formaldehyde, methanol, and ethanol—standard embalming fluids. There may be other toxins, but our chemicals guy said those were his best guess, given the condition of the body and the amount of time he'd been in there. He's pretty well, uh, preserved. Still, we need an analysis, a plan, and signatures all round. That's going to be a minimum of one week."

Pam asked, "But we can still work on the other rooms while you're doing your work, right?"

Daniels shook his head. "Sorry. Absolutely not. We need to protect the integrity of the scene. Plus, it could be dangerous for anyone to be in there with the chemicals, let alone work with the corpse next door." He allowed a moment for that to sink in before continuing. "Until we can get the tank removed, we'll be babysitting our John Doe."

"Babysit?" Pam said. "Who would kidnap a dead body?"

Daniels's eyes twinkled, but he answered with a straight face. "It's highly unlikely that someone would take the body," he said. "But it's against the law to leave dead bodies unattended. Disease and other things can spread quickly in situations like this. Not that I've seen anything quite like this before."

"Could we sign a waiver to allow us in to work?" I asked. It didn't sound like a good idea, but I wanted to explore all of our options.

Daniels shook his head again. "Sorry," he said. "No can do. The department would never allow that. From now until we release the scene, we're responsible for everything."

"How about the exterior," Pam asked. "Can we work outside?"

"Sorry," he repeated. "No access until the scene has been released. I know it seems a little strict, but this protects the scene, our personnel, and the two of you."

"Which means we can't get in until he's out," I said.

"'Fraid so. Sorry." Daniels looked from me to Pam and back again. "Can I answer any other questions for you?"

I glanced at Pam. She shook her head. "I guess not," I replied.

Daniels rose from his chair.

"Thank you for coming over in person," I said. "You'll call as soon as you know something, right?"

Daniels nodded. "I'll leave another card." He rooted out a small rectangular card and a key. "I had a deputy make a copy of your key, so you can have this one back. I'll return our copy when we release the scene."

I nodded, fatigue and worry rising from my gut and sitting in my throat like bile. I swallowed hard, but sour filled my mouth. My upper back and shoulders throbbing, I saw him to the door.

Once on the welcome mat, he turned. "Try not to worry too much. And don't hesitate to call me with questions or for updates. I'll call whenever something significant occurs. Leave everything to us, and the process will go as quickly as possible."

I locked up and returned to the living room. I stood next to Pam who stared into the fireplace a la Moxie. Gently, she patted Gabe's back, seemingly transfixed by the same pilot light that had mesmerized Moxie. Despite the doo-doo storm we were currently in the middle of, Pam seemed peaceful.

I followed her and Moxie's gazes. A sense of tranquility from the unwavering pilot flame calmed me, too. Within seconds, my breathing came easier and my back relaxed. I made a mental note to remember this spot next time Jim showed up.

"Should we brainstorm tonight, or wait until the morning?" I asked.

"Let's wait. Things always seem more manageable in the morning."

"I hope so." I scooped up Moxie and held her close. "I hope so."

Chapter 7

I woke with a start, my heart racing and cold sweat coating my body. The chill spread quickly as I remembered the events of the day before. The body. The tank. The formaldehyde. I held my queasy stomach for several minutes, breathing slowly, as Moxie licked the backs of my hands. When I felt certain I wouldn't vomit, I rose, shrugged into my sweats, and cinched the drawstring of the sweatpants tight. The minute my feet hit my slippers, I began moving toward the kitchen. I could have used some grown-up talking time, but Pam and Gabe had returned to their condo after Daniels left late the night before. I sighed and started planning meals for the girls. Motherhood doesn't stop, even when the world collapses.

I set coffee to brew for me and savored the earthy scent while I packed lunches for the kids. A fold-over turkey and lettuce sandwich for Annie, two cheese sticks and a mini-muffin for Emily, plus a juice box and small red apple for each. Then, I called to the girls and made warm bowls of oatmeal for each as they readied themselves. While they ate, I combed their hair and twirled it into ponytails.

Like clockwork, Pam let herself into my condo, Gabe riding shotgun on her hip, and we were all ready to go. We made the carpool loop to school and day care, then returned home to find Moxie still curled in front of the fire-less fireplace.

After refilling the coffee maker with a chocolate-infused cache of beans and water for two, I flipped the switch and sat across from Pam at the kitchen table. The coffee bubbled a happy, irregular tune as we brainstormed.

"What's the first thing we need to do?" Pam asked, pencil and yellow pad at the ready.

"Call the realtor, Sam, at the office," I said. "Let's find out if we have to disclose a body in the closet. We might have to reduce the price, which may determine what we can and cannot do with our renovation plans."

Pam wrinkled her nose and jotted the note, labeling it with a big "1." "You know what?" she pulled out her cell phone. "I'm going to do that right now. It'll be easier to catch him before he starts his day. It's almost impossible to get a hold of him after ten."

She punched Sam's number on her speed dial and whispered, "That coffee smells heavenly." A split second later, she spoke into the phone. "Hi Sam. It's Pam Bacchus." Pause. "We're okay. You?" Another pause. "Well, we had a bit of a surprise with the house."

A few tense moments passed as Pam explained the situation. I searched the fridge for good dunking material to go with the coffee. Seizing a pair of blueberry muffins with a sugary crust, I returned to the table and set one in front of Pam. She rolled her eyes heavenward and mouthed her thanks.

"Yes, it was a shock, and yes, we've called the police. They're investigating as we speak. We're hoping they'll finish quickly and we can get back to work," she said. "What we're wondering about, and hoping you can answer, is whether or not we need to disclose this, uh, discovery, to potential buyers once the house is renovated and ready to sell."

Pam's brows knitted together as she listened. "That explains it very clearly," she responded. "Thanks, Sam. I'll keep you posted when we're ready to list it for sale."

"So?" I hovered near the coffee pot as the percolating slowed.

"Technically, we don't have to disclose that we found a body. He said it falls under the category of 'due diligence,' similar to any kind of death or even murder or suicide—it's up to the new buyer to ask the right questions and do their own research. But he also said it was a good idea to disclose. He called it good, honest practice." She air-quoted the last few words before continuing. "It also saves the hassle of problems later on, when and if the new buyers find out."

I grimaced but had to agree. If I were a new buyer, I'd want to know if the house had been a crime scene. And if I hadn't been told, I'd wonder what more I didn't know.

"So we'll disclose," I confirmed. "Probably not in the ad copy, but in the seller's statement papers."

The coffee maker pinged. I poured the rich dark brew into mugs, and by the time I set them on the table, Moxie had meandered in. I gave her a dog biscuit, then retrieved a carton of milk and a container of brown sugar and set both on the table.

Pam drew the mug toward herself and breathed in its aroma. "Ah, sublime." She picked up her spoon and set it at an angle in her cup. "Disclosing is the right thing to do. And I agree it can be done in the seller's statement." Her face cracked into a smile. "But I'd love to read the ad that includes that info."

I grimaced, picturing Sam's wording in the advertisement. "Bungalow once held body," I said, affecting a sales pitch.

"Cute Craftsman with corpse," added Pam, smirking.

I wrinkled my nose. Again, with the guilt. A man was dead, probably murdered, and we were making jokes. I refocused on the task at hand and spooned brown sugar into my mug.

Pam swirled her concoction to a cocoa brown. "One task crossed off our list. On to task two: find out everything we can and turn it over to Daniels."

Pam's positive spin buoyed my spirits. I doubted there would be anything we could discover that the police wouldn't think to check out, but it would be better than sitting around worrying.

"What do you want to do?" I asked.

"Research ownership for starters." She tested her coffee with a short noisy slurp. "We'll be able to narrow down the possibilities of who lived there when the body was sealed in."

"We might even get lucky and find info on the dates of remodeling—if they filed a permit."

"Good point." Pam set the mug down and began scratching notes on her pad. "We might be able to find out the name of the contractor—if there was one."

"Oh." I swallowed a lump of muffin. "That reminds me. What if the contractor hired a subcontractor? Maybe he or she was responsible."

Pam pinched the spoon between her lips in thought. "It's completely possible. Contractors should go out and check the progress every day, but some don't. A lot of people assume the contractor has everything under control and leave the house in their care. It's easier that way—no mess, and a renovated living space when they return."

"They could have hired a contractor in between sales." I swigged my coffee. "An escrow account may have covered the expense."

"Anything's possible," Pam said. "It's noisy and a hassle, but I would never leave anyone alone in my home. Besides theft and breakage, I'd want to watch for errors."

She fed the remaining muffin to Moxie, who had been waiting patiently at our feet. "Maybe I've been watching too many crime shows, but it wouldn't be the first time someone buried a body in a foundation."

"Ick," I said. "And you are watching too many."

"Yeah. But most of the bodies go undetected for years. It works pretty well, actually."

We fell silent as we considered this new possibility. I savored the sweet blueberry muffin. When all that was left was the sugar-crusted top, I speared sections of it with my fork and dunked each morsel in the remaining coffee before bringing it to my lips.

Pam pushed her plate away. "So we'll do research and bring it to Daniels, right?"

I wanted to help in any way, but I couldn't help remembering Daniels's warning from the night before. "Wouldn't that be interfering with the investigation?" I asked. "Daniels seemed pretty clear about us steering clear of the house and removal process until he gave us the go-ahead. I'd hate to make a mistake and then have the, uh, extraction take longer than it has to."

Pam shook her head and took her dishes to the

sink. "I don't see it that way. Daniels said we couldn't go in the house or the yard. He didn't say we couldn't research our own house."

"Hmmm." I didn't feel completely convinced, but she had a good point. "It seems like splitting hairs."

"Don't be such a fraidy-cat, Janny. We aren't doing anything illegal."

"Well—" She was right, of course, but it still seemed like we'd be doing the exact opposite of what Daniels had asked.

"I know what you're going to say. We're still meddling. But we actually aren't." Pam leaned against the counter. "Everything that we will look up is public knowledge—it's on the internet. Anyone could do the same. At any time. From anywhere. Us included."

She was right, of course. Our research wouldn't affect the progress of the police. She must have sensed me softening, because she continued before I could object.

"Plus, who knows if we'll find anything significant? If we do, we'll simply be saving Daniels and his crew some time."

She was right. County records research was perfectly legal and moral—so long as we didn't disturb anyone or go onto the property. It's just factual data…that we may or may not decide to turn over to the police, depending on its importance. I felt a small rush of adrenaline at the thought of seeing Daniels again, but quickly pushed it back down.

Wiping my hands on my napkin, I said, "Okay. I'll do the research this morning."

Pam placed her mug in the dishwasher. "I'll go look at comps that are currently on the market. Since we'll probably be ready to sell within a week or two, current sales stats will still be valid…and a good way to know what price will attract the most home buyers. I'd been wanting to do that anyway." She shrugged into her jacket before speaking again. "It will also help us figure out the cost of dealing with our surprise visitor. And I'll burn up some of this nervous energy, which I have plenty of."

I knew exactly how she felt. Anything was better than sitting around waiting for more bad news. "Meet back here this afternoon?" I replaced the sugar in the cupboard.

"Perfect." She returned the milk carton to the fridge, then turned and winked. "This will be over quickly. I feel sure of it."

I crumpled the plastic wrap from the muffins and tossed it into the garbage can. I wished I could share Pam's optimism, but I couldn't. It wasn't just that her reassurance felt like false bravado. I simply didn't believe a problem this big could be solved in such a short amount of time.

When I honestly reflected, I thought a month would be a more likely time frame. That may be considered quick to law enforcement, but it doubled our already meager budget. And going over budget meant no income. No groceries. No gas for the little Kia. It meant admitting failure.

Chapter 8

An hour later, deep into a county parcel search, I remembered. Today was Daddy Friday. Directly after school, the girls and Gabe would leave us to spend the weekend, and hopefully some quality time, with Jim and Marcus.

I groaned and bookmarked the web page.

To the kids, Daddy Friday meant two and a half days of carefree eating, sleeping in their clothes, and bathing irregularly, possibly brushing their teeth. For Pam and me, it meant an entire weekend without the kids, and an overwhelming feeling of failure. We should have been able to make our marriages work…somehow.

I sighed, logged off, removed a warm Moxie from my lap, and headed for the girls' room. I struggled with tears as I laid out tan capri pants, bright red shorts, and a pair of jeans for each. It seemed so unfair that Annie and Emily had to be shuttled from home to home as if they were birdies in some crazy badminton game. Anger rose in my throat and lodged like a lump as I matched new white and blue T-shirts to the pants and grabbed a small stack of underpants. I folded all of the clothes neatly, then packed them in their tiny twin suitcases, throwing in swimsuits in case of sun and hoodies in case of rain. Combined with the clothes they wore to school that day, they'd be set for the weekend.

Rolling the suitcases down the hall, one in each hand, I wondered how long this would continue. The divorce docs specified forever, but I knew that as the girls got older and entered puberty, everything would change. They would start menstruating and eventually begin dating. Would they want to leave me, their mother, when all of that was happening? Would they be uncomfortable asking their father if they ran out of toiletries?

I stopped short at the bathroom. The girls would need their toothbrushes, a tube of toothpaste in case Jim ran out, hairbrushes, and a couple of ponytail holders. I threw in some freshly laundered washcloths and towels, said a quick prayer that I would get them back on Sunday, and hoped Jim had everything else they might need. I stepped into the hall and then doubled back. One more thing. I located a spare roll of toilet paper and wedged it into Annie's suitcase.

I set the suitcases near the front door where we couldn't miss them when we returned home and allowed myself another minute to mourn the picture-perfect family I thought I'd created. I remembered Mom and Dad, and how my brother and I always had both of them nearby. Fresh tears stung my cheeks. Divorce is exactly the opposite of what I had planned for my children's lives...or my life, for that matter.

A vision of myself, lying on my bed, comforter soaked with tears and sleeves streaked with mascara formed in my mind. I'd spent a lot of Daddy weekends drowning in sadness. And I'd woken many mornings since the divorce with a damp pillow. I couldn't let myself fall into that pattern again. It's too hard to break through.

I closed my eyes and began my silent pep talk: I am strong. A strong woman with good friendships, great kids, and a loving family. A strong woman with a savvy business sense and a great little cottage nearly ready to flip.

Three mighty breaths later, I pulled my sweatpants a little higher and tugged the drawstring a little tighter. Then I returned to my computer and committed to scanning property records.

The history read in reverse chronological order, spanning the past sixty years. Anything earlier than that would have to be ordered from the county. No problem there. All I needed was the last fifty years of ownership to cover the time of the remodel.

Since the title transfer had occurred only a week ago, the property still showed as being owned by Silas Morford. It would take a while longer before PB & J Enterprises showed up as owners of record. The change might not be reflected until after we re-sold it.

I scrolled down, noticing the changes in ownership. Silas Morford received title from Thaddeus Huntington, who in turn received title from Silas Morford. I took another look. Could I be reading it wrong?

I glanced over the listings carefully, correlating the grantor and grantee names and dates. Sure enough. Silas Morford took possession of the property via quit claim deed only a couple of months ago. The grantor was Thaddeus Huntington. Prior to that, Morford had owned the property until 1992 when he quit-claimed the deed to Huntington.

So the property changed hands from Morford to Huntington in 1992, then back to Morford earlier in the year.

Morford, in turn, had taken possession of the property way back in 1978 from the previous owner, Gerald Jones. Jones owned the home from 1950 to 1978.

I printed a copy and pored over the relevant time period:

G. Jones 1950-1978

S. Morford 1978-1992

Then Huntington in 1992 and back to Morford a couple months ago.

As confusing as it all was, one thing was clear. Only two people owned the house when the paneling job had been completed: Jones, and then Morford. As odd as the Huntington tradeoff was, it may have had nothing to do with the dead body.

Moving on, I scanned through the various tabs, looking for any additional information. Nothing. No permits filed, no denials, no approvals.

No surprise there. Some people don't realize they are required to file for permits, and others don't want to be bothered with a county headache. A few know it's easier to say, "Sorry," and pay a fine later than to get permission beforehand. And chances are the county may never discover the improvement.

It all boiled down to one thing: Either Jones or Morford had to know something. If I could narrow down my search to a particular year, I'd know which one.

I printed a second copy for Pam, then began a search of paneling. If I knew when the paneling had been manufactured, I might be able to determine the installation dates. That timing would further reduce the number of possible owners. I didn't have much to go on. I did, however, have a distinct visual memory of what it looked like during removal…or rather splintering apart.

An hour later and with only a few pictures to show for my efforts, I logged off. Faux wood paneling didn't hold much interest for anyone anymore, other than a couple of websites that featured "before and after" renovations on "ugly homes" websites.

Frustrated, I rose. I'd learned very little about wood paneling, aside from the fact that it was made of knotty pine or particle board and came into fashion in the '50s and '60s. By the '70s, it had already gone south in the minds of interior designers, but some homeowners continued to use it as a cheap substitute for drywall, plaster, and paint.

Then it dawned on me: Whoever installed the "cedar" closet had to have cut into the wall, possibly into the wall in the living room adjacent. That would create a space for the aquarium that hadn't ever existed, because the home had been built prior to the paneling craze. It also explained the oddly shallow closet space on the opposite side of the wall. At the time of original building, way back in the early twentieth century, homes didn't have closets. People used armoires or wardrobes to hold all of their clothing.

I leaned back in my chair. All this information was interesting, but it didn't reduce the number of suspects. It was still Jones and Morford in the right place at the right time.

My research had hit the proverbial wall. I could attempt to date the nails, but none of the ones that flew off as I stripped the paneling looked different from any I'd ever seen. Then again, I wasn't exactly a nail expert.

If I could get a sample, I might be able to find out a little more, but I doubted Daniels would allow me inside the house to collect one. They might even be considered evidence.

Stumped, I decided a cup of spicy tea would re-energize me.

I grabbed Moxie from the foot of my bed and headed for the kitchen. After setting a mug of water in the microwave and giving Moxie a nibble of leftover chicken, I made a list of everything in the room with the faux cedar closet. Paint, light fixtures, paneling, nails, framework that the nails attached to. What else? I racked my brain.

As the microwave beeped, my thoughts cleared. Of course! The aquarium!

I dunked the tea bag into the steaming water. Immediately, the twin scents of orange spice and ginger filled my nostrils. I raced back down the hall to the computer, Moxie hot on my heels. She released short bursts of high-pitched barks as she ran. I sank into the chair, wiggled the mouse, and the computer, still warm, hummed to life. As I waited, I scalded my tongue on the tea and drew a picture of the tank. I guesstimated at the dimensions: five x two x two.

Soon, I was surfing the web in an attempt to find large home or business aquariums. I quickly discovered the difference between glass and acrylic aquariums, and after a scroll through the history of aquariums, noted that acrylic hadn't been used until the '70s. Of course, our aquarium was glass. Sealant had been used, but it had begun to deteriorate. After additional research, I found that tanks as large as the one that held the body hadn't been commercially produced at that time. That meant it had to have been custom made. Maybe the aquarium builder knew something about the body. Then again, it would be almost impossible to find him—or her—unless there was an identifying company mark on the glass or frame. And if he or she were still alive. A lot can happen in that many years.

I made a note to myself, then surfed for information on glass. One website gave tips and facts for the do-it-yourselfer, including weight. I calculated the estimated weight of the aquarium and water together: Approximately eighteen-hundred pounds. Good Lord. That was almost a ton! Add in the weight of the cadaver, and the tank would easily surpass a ton.

Wait a minute. A ton? How could one person manage all of that?

Easing into my chair, I sipped my tea and considered. The weight alone would require two, or even more people to accomplish. It might even require special equipment to complete such a large and cumbersome project.

That left me with only one conclusion: There were at least two people who knew something about the corpse in the cottage.

At least two.

But which two?

Chapter 9

Pam returned at three o'clock sharp. In one hand she held a stack of computer printouts of sales and listing comps, in the other, a cup of raspberry tea. Glancing at the girls' suitcases, she groaned and dropped the papers onto a nearby chair in dramatic fashion. "Crap. It's Daddy Friday, isn't it?"

She plopped onto the living room couch and gave Moxie a quick scratch behind the ears. "I hate Daddy Fridays."

"I know." I stepped into the kitchen and made another cup of ginger tea for myself.

When I returned to the living room, Pam and her cup of tea were still steaming. I planted myself next to her.

"What gets me is how nice we were to them," she said. "We played fair, helped them build their business. Now they're off playing bachelor most nights of the week and we're left to build a new business."

"Yeah. I know. It sucks."

I blew across the surface of my tea, sending little wisps of spicy steam curling into the air. I was angry, too. Even now. I couldn't help it. But I had found a way of letting it go. Well, letting a lot of it go. I'd found that if I focused on what I'd learned along the way, I felt happier. And happier is always better.

I tested my tea, then spoke. "The way I see it, or at

least *try* to see it is we practiced on their business. We found errors, smoothed out bumps, and learned from all of their mistakes. When we divorced, we got a portion of that company to start our own. Our new and improved company with our improved understanding of what works."

Pam eyed me over the top of her cup. "I've never thought about it like that. I always think about how much we put into making the company a success and how they don't respect us. Then I get pissed. Not just garden-variety pissed—super pissed."

"I understand." I sipped. "But we could have opened our own business when we were still married to them, right? We chose not to. We chose to work as a team."

Pam sat in silence a moment. "I guess we could have gone into business ourselves when we were still married to them," she said. "I guess nothing stopped us. It never occurred to me, though. I always thought of the four of us as a team. I guess I was a little naïve."

"We both were naïve. But we were also loyal."

"Loyal to a fault." She harumphed.

"Loyalty is loyalty. We did good things as a team."

"But they repaid our loyalty with betrayal."

"You're right. They did." I kicked off my shoes and tucked my legs under me. "We played fair, and for some portion of that time, they did, too. I don't know how long that was. And then, they got a little too comfortable…made some poor decisions…and ended up betraying us."

"Don't forget Gabe and the girls," Pam said. "They got screwed, too. Their whole lives got screwed up, and all because of *them*."

I paused, sensing Pam needed a moment to process. When I began again, my words were soft. "They made some very big mistakes. Mistakes they won't be able to undo. Someday, they'll probably regret those choices—if they don't already." I sighed. "But we held fast to our beliefs and acted with integrity for the sake of the kids. I don't think it benefitted only the girls and Gabe, though. I think it made us stronger. Don't you?"

"Maybe you're right," Pam said. "I feel like I can take on anything nowadays. Well, almost anything. This whole dead guy in the closet has me questioning everything."

I took another drink of the cooled tea. "We picked ourselves up, moved the kids to a safe place, and started up our own business. That's a pretty good example of making lemonade from lemons if you ask me."

Pam grinned. "That's what I love about you, Janny. You always make sense. You always give everyone the benefit of the doubt." She paused a moment, swirling the contents of her cup and staring into its depths. "You're right. There's always two ways to look at anything. I need to focus on us. Us and the kids."

I winked at her. "Atta girl."

"Okay." Pam drained her cup. "I'm over it. They're idiots. We aren't. End of story."

We both knew she wasn't over it. Probably wouldn't be for a very long time. Maybe never. Sometimes, though, it helped to remind ourselves that the road ahead had to be easier than the one we've traveled. We're smarter and have learned to avoid some of life's potholes.

Time to turn to the important stuff. "Okay. What

did you find out?" I asked.

Pam shuffled the printouts. "I drove by ten houses," she said. "Of those, three were solid comps—similar square footage, similar style, similar quality." She slid some photos across the coffee table toward me. "Then, I checked the info from county records and came up with a realistic sales number."

I looked over the pictures. All of the houses exuded the charm ours promised. To the buyer's eye, there wouldn't be much of a difference.

"We need something special so ours will stand out," I said.

Pam raised one eyebrow. "You mean instead of coming with its own cemetery?"

I smirked. "Yeah. I'm thinking more along the lines of something that would add value."

Pam took a pencil from her purse and nibbled on the eraser. "How about raised flower beds in front and a garden in back? That's something we can do ourselves, cheap and easy."

"I like it," I said, envisioning petunias in reds, yellows, and purples lining the front path. "It's the perfect time of year for planting annuals. What else?"

She removed the pencil from between her teeth and tapped it against her forehead. "How about new appliances?"

"Those are big expenses, especially for a house in this price range. Then again, it would definitely increase the value and desirability." I thought a moment. "What if we swapped out the stove and dishwasher with brand new ones? That would draw a lot of interest."

"Good idea," said Pam. "I'll check the plumbing."

She scribbled a few notes then set her pencil down. "Your turn. What'd you find out?"

"I got the names of ownership back to the fifties. Lucky for us, there are only two owners during the seventies: Gerald Jones and Silas Morford."

"But what if the paneling came later?"

I shrugged my shoulders. "I guess there would be one more: Thaddeus Huntington." I sipped before continuing. "There's something else, though."

"What?"

"The conveyance is a little weird. It may be nothing, but my gut tells me it's a little odd."

Pam cocked an eyebrow. "Go on."

I started from the beginning. "Jones and Morford owned the home during the seventies, so one of them has to know something about the body." I pulled out my notes. "But there's something else that bothers me. Morford quit-claimed the house to Huntington, and Huntington quit-claimed the house back to Morford just this year. That's when we bought it."

She frowned. "Are they related?"

"There's no way of knowing by looking at the data, of course. The last names aren't the same. But nowadays, that doesn't mean anything. There's step-children and adoption and blended families."

"It's odd, though," Pam said, "but not really cause for alarm. They could even be father and son-in-law, grandfather and grandson. What else ya got?"

I gave her the run-down on the wood and hardware roadblocks. "Material research is a dead end. But I did discover one thing. There's no way one person could have built that aquarium and entombed the body on his own."

"How do you know?"

"The weight. The sheets of glass would have been too heavy for one person to lift into place."

"Now that's interesting." Pam leaned forward. "How much weight are we talking about?"

I did some mental aerobics, guesstimating the load of the glass and its cumbersome nature, less the equipment. "I think it took two men. At least two men."

"So he had an accomplice. That changes everything."

"It might," I said. "But what it changes, I don't know." I checked the time and stood. "What I do know is it's time to pack up Moxie, pick up the kids, and deliver them to their daddies."

Pam rolled her eyes. "Ah, crap. You're right. Give me a few seconds to throw Gabe's bag together. I'll meet you out front."

Within minutes, we'd stowed the suitcases and diaper bag in the Kia. After settling Moxie into her car bed in back, Pam and I piled into the front. We headed for the school, daycare, and the pre-arranged kid exchange place. Before picking up the kids, however, we went over our plan for keeping quiet about the body.

"Marcus and Jim might ask questions," Pam said. "Just be non-committal."

"Right."

"Nothing about bodies or police or money or nothing."

"It'll be easy." I slowed as we pulled into the school zone. "We just have to keep our mouths shut."

Annie and Emily climbed into the back seat and after a quick kiss, noticed the suitcases.

"It's Daddy Friday," shouted Emily.

Moxie, sensing excitement, leaped over the backseat and licked the girls. Annie and Emily pulled Moxie between them and created a three-way hug. I felt the familiar ripping of my heart. Even though I wanted them to be close to their dad, it saddened me that they had to be away from me to do it. Making it worse was that they were happy, even without me.

Pam glanced my way and rubbed my arm. I gave her a brave smile and pulled out of the parking lot. Another few minutes of chatting about their day, and I'd eased the Kia into the drive-through of the day care.

"Be right back," Pam said, unbuckling. When she returned, a very happy Gabriel rode on her hip. Once Gabe and the girls had exchanged hugs and he'd been sat squarely in his car seat, we headed straight for Juicy Burger and the guys.

"Are we going to eat dinner here?" asked Emily as we pulled into the restaurant's parking lot.

"I hope so," said Annie. "I want to eat in the car."

"I want a car picnic, too," Emily said.

"I don't know about the car picnic," I told them, "but as for eating here, I hope not."

"Oh, Mom," said Annie. "You always want us to eat healthy."

I smiled at her in the visor mirror. "You're right. I do."

"So do I," Pam chimed in. "We want you to grow up big and strong."

I reversed into a convenient slot, out of the way of incoming traffic, and shifted into park before shutting down the engine. We prepared to wait.

But it wasn't necessary.

A brand new, bright red, very tall F350 truck with

big all-terrain tires pulled to a stop directly in front of the Kia, blocking our way.

"It couldn't be…" whispered Pam.

I stared through the windshield at the tinted passenger side window. Vaguely, I could make out the profile of a man. The window rolled down, and Marcus gave us a two-finger wave. Sure enough, Jim sat at the wheel next to him.

He'd bought a new truck—an expensive one, by the looks of it.

White hot anger started in my gut and spread at lightning speed through my body. My pulse jumped into overdrive and sweat formed in my armpits. Here we were, trying to figure out how to survive, and he went out and bought an expensive new vehicle to park in the garage of his new house. A vehicle a year ago we'd decided was too expensive for our combined budget. I couldn't help but wonder how he'd managed to pay for it along with child support. Their business must be doing really well. The thought pulled my mouth into a solid frown.

I peeked at Pam. Her mouth had pulled into a straight line and her eyebrows formed a perfect V.

"Daddy!" the kids cried at once, unbuckling. Annie swung her door open and the two scrambled out.

I released my own seatbelt, intent on getting the girls' suitcases out of the Kia and into the truck as quickly as possible, when I felt Pam's hand on my arm.

She leaned toward me with a grin. "I double-dare you to suggest a car picnic in their new truck."

Chapter 10

I giggled. Leave it to Pam to lighten the mood. Bracing myself for anything, I slid out of the driver's seat. Even though we'd started the kid-exchange when we were newly separated, it still felt uncomfortable. I still had to force a smile on my face every Daddy Friday.

The girls raced to Jim and he hoisted them high in the air, one in each arm. He planted kisses on each of them, then nodded my way.

I gave a little wave and tried not to stare. Jim was wearing a pale-yellow short-sleeve shirt, which suited his tanned complexion. It also revealed strong spheres of biceps. I gulped. He'd been working out. He'd also shaved his head and grown a goatee. All the markings of a divorced man on the prowl for a good time. I hoped he didn't use this weekend to seek out that fun. The girls don't need any more confusing situations. And I didn't need any more confusing situations to explain.

I turned away. "I'll get the bags." As I rummaged in the back of the Kia, double-checking the girls' backpacks for necessary homework items, Moxie began growl-humming. Jim's silhouette caught my attention from the corner of one eye.

"Let me help." He grabbed the girls' suitcases, then shifted both cases to one hand and reached out with the other toward Moxie.

Her growling erupted into a bark—a sound that had never come out of her mouth. She bared all three teeth and shifted her bulbous-eyed gaze from me to Jim and back again.

"It's okay, Moxie," I said, grabbing everything, and then closing the hatchback. Immediately, she pounced against the glass, snarling at Jim.

"Wow." Jim took the backpacks in his free hand. "That dog hates me."

"She doesn't know you well enough to hate you."

His face fell. Immediately, I regretted my words. I hadn't meant to hurt him, but I had to admit, Moxie's reaction reflected my own feelings on occasion. Sometimes I wondered if I had ever really known Jim at all.

"Never mind. She's like that with everyone for a while, being a stray and all." I brushed a hand through my hair. "So, the girls have reports due Monday. Annie's researching Thomas Edison and Emily's learning about giraffes. Make sure they do their homework. Scan the docs, then email them to me in case they lose the printouts." I searched my memory for anything else. "I think that's all. Just be sure they brush their teeth. They both have dental appointments next month."

"Got it." Jim strode toward the truck and tossed the suitcases into the flatbed.

I lingered, waving to the girls, not ready to say goodbye.

Pam watched over Marcus's shoulder as he settled Gabe into his car seat. This was always a multi-stage process as Marcus completed the task and Pam checked and rechecked his work, reminding him of the multitude of straps and adjustments at every step.

"So how's the flip going?" Jim took the backpacks and stashed them with the suitcases.

Without so much as a glance between us, Pam and I replied, "Great!" Mine came easily, but Pam had to tear her focus away from Marcus and his mistakes for a moment.

Jim cocked his head and stared at each of us in turn.

Inwardly, I sighed. He knew something was up. I could tell by the look in his eyes. He knew me better than I liked to admit. It was one of the hazards of being married for ten years to someone you thought was your best friend. I pasted on a smile and made light of the situation.

"All good," I said.

Satisfied that Gabe could weather a tornado in his car seat, Marcus turned around and faced us. He, too, had grown a goatee. But he hadn't stopped there. Inside the goatee, just below his lower lip, he'd shaved everything but a hairy triangle. A soul patch, as I recalled. In addition to looking ridiculous, the thing must have taken a ton of time to shave around every morning.

"I thought you were painting this week," Marcus said. "Where are your painting clothes?"

"Maybe we didn't paint today." Pam's words dripped sarcasm.

Gabriel's eyes sought out his mother and held her gaze. Clearly, he felt anxious. Pam took a deep breath, smiled at Gabe, and continued in a lower, sing-songy tone. "What I mean is, we completed the painting yesterday and moved on to other things."

"Like what?" Jim swung his attention back to me.

Great. Now he wants to talk about how my days are going. That never happened during our marriage. My mind whirled, fighting resentment and searching for something to say.

"Little things," I said. "Stripping the cedar paneling from the closet." I'd never been a good liar, so I stuck with something that was at least half-true.

"Why would you strip cedar from a closet?" Jim asked. "People love cedar closets. It drives away moths."

"We know what cedar does," Pam replied, her tone sharp.

Confusion spread across Jim's face. Usually, Marcus bore the brunt of Pam's snippy comebacks. Jim looked to me.

Damn.

"Uh, this paneling was faux cedar. Not pretty and not utilitarian. Mostly an eyesore." I shook my head. "It had to go."

Marcus picked up on the interrogation. "Uh-oh. Paneling can be covering a whole host of other problems—drywall issues, plumbing leaks, even dry rot. Have you checked out everything?"

I shuddered at his pinpoint accuracy. Neither Pam nor I had thought about the paneling from that angle when we first viewed the house. We'd noticed the mild scent and assumed the wood had held an accumulation of odors from many years. Marcus's unwavering stare provided more proof of their expertise…and our inexperience.

"Oh, no." I gathered my thoughts. "This paneling had been nailed directly to the framing. No wall issues."

"And you stripped it?" Marcus's voice was incredulous, and I understood first-hand why Pam occasionally got rude with him. His tone mocked us, as though we were simple-minded children making unbelievably stupid errors. "You don't strip old paneling, especially the type they used in place of drywall. You paint it."

Of course I hadn't known painting was the best solution when we began. Neither had Pam. Had we known, we would have bought more paint. Then again, we would have been sealing in the dead guy for the next owners. I shuddered at the thought but held my tongue.

"Are you sure there aren't any leaks?" Jim asked. "I have a guy who works cheap. I can get you his number."

"No," Pam's response resembled a shriek. "No leaks. No problems. Everything's fine."

Jim searched my face for answers. I shifted my focus to the rapidly filling drive-through lane. Marcus's eyes narrowed, a sure sign he had something he wanted to say. But he didn't open his mouth. Thank heaven for small favors.

Pam broke the silence a split-second later. She leaned her head into the truck and planted a kiss on Gabe's cheek. "Bye-bye, baby," she caroled.

"Bye-bye," Gabe called out, clenching and releasing his fists.

"Bye, Momma," the girls shouted to me.

I walked around the other side and kissed and hugged them in turn. Their faces mirrored excitement. Daddy weekends always held surprises...for them, and, when they returned home with bellyaches or lost shoes, for us. I couldn't help but smile at their joy.

Pam and I plodded back to the Kia. Halfway there, she turned. "Be sure to put the night rail up on the crib. Gabe's been climbing out."

"I know," Marcus said. "I'm his father, you know."

"I know you know," Pam replied, anger sparking. "I'm just reminding you so Gabe doesn't get hurt. That's *my* top priority."

Marcus rolled his eyes and Pam glared back. Both fell silent. I shrugged and nudged her along.

At the car door, Pam called back. "My cell phone will be on."

"So will mine."

Beside me, Pam stiffened. She took a deep breath and exhaled slowly, then dove into the Kia.

My emotions tumbled like socks in a dryer. My stomach churned and my heart bounced around in my chest. Since Jim's new truck blocked our way, we had to wait until the guys pulled away before we could escape. I busied myself with car gadgets, adjusting heat, vents, radio…anything.

Just as the guys' truck roared onto the main road, Pam's cell rang.

She glanced at the screen. "Daniels," she whispered, punching the answer button.

Chapter 11

"He's got an update." Pam turned and punched the speaker button on her cell phone and held it up so we could both listen.

I killed the engine and removed the key. Setting my keychain in my lap, I eased back in the driver's seat, closing my eyes in concentration.

"I've got some good news and some bad news again," Daniels began, his tone professional, yet relaxed. "Let's start with the good news. The lab determined the contents to be exactly as we expected: standard embalming fluids. The better news is we know how to handle these toxins, although in large quantities, it'll take quite a bit of time."

My heart lifted and I opened my eyes. A breath I'd been unaware of holding released. Okay. Everything would be okay. The police knew what to do. All that was left was to do it. I shot a smile Pam's way.

"Awesome," said Pam. "So what's the bad news?"

"It's going to take more time than we'd anticipated. More time than I estimated."

"How much more time?" I asked, my heart sinking a bit.

His voice became cautious, almost weary. "It depends. There are a lot of factors, and I don't want to get your hopes up. First, there is the removal of the body. We have two options to accomplish that. One method is to drain the tank at the site and then remove the aquarium and the deceased. The challenge with this option is maintaining the integrity of the scene. In case this becomes a homicide investigation, we need to keep all fluids and materials as evidence. Like we talked about, that takes time, resources, money—which neither the department nor you have to spare."

"In case?" I said. "How could it not be murder?"

"We don't like to make any assumptions," Daniels said, his words measured.

Pam's mouth turned south at both ends. "What's the second option?"

"The other entails removing the entire aquarium all at once." He cleared his throat. "The challenge with that is finding an opening big enough to get the aquarium out of the house. It's clear it had been built on the premises with raw sheets of glass, silicone caulking, fluids. It didn't arrive to this house like it is now."

Mentally, I envisioned the doors and windows of the home. Front door, back door, living room, kitchen, and bedroom windows. The door frames were wide enough for the oversized aquarium to squeeze through, but the weight would prohibit carrying, unless they had a lot of strong people doing the heavy lifting.

"Sergeant Daniels?" I said, "Even if we did have an opening large enough, wouldn't you need equipment for heavy lifting? I did some calculations, and the weight of the tank with its, uh, contents must be nearly a ton."

"Absolutely, Jan. Very good. That's exactly what we're up against. Our preliminary discussions have determined that we would need to take out the bedroom wall. Then we could use a forklift."

Pam's and my mouth dropped open at once. Take out a wall? Forklift?

"A forklift? In the bedroom?" Pam squeaked in disbelief.

"I'm afraid so," he said. "But nothing's set yet. Like I said, I don't want to get your hopes up. We're keeping our fingers crossed for an easier solution."

Visions of torn-out walls and forklift-shaped tire dust prints on the hardwood floors filled my mind. Cash registers dinged in my ears.

"That's not in the budget!" Pam's voice broke.

"I understand," Daniels said, his tone softening in response. "We all understand. Truly. That's why we're leaning toward the slower, but less intrusive method. There's an additional concern about the, uh, coffin bursting or breaking during transport. We can bind it and wrap it, but we can't promise that everything would hold. Then, we'd be back to square one with fluids possibly spilling onto the floor. That wouldn't be a great outcome, either."

He paused a moment, perhaps allowing us a chance to speak or ask questions. Pam and I simply stared at each other. She appeared bewildered. I couldn't even wrap my head around the magnitude of the problem yet.

"I hate to bring this up, but we're also going to need to double-check the structure, too," Daniels said. "Our initial calculations put it at about the same weight as a large waterbed, but a bed's spread out over more area. This weight is concentrated. Super concentrated. We'll need to get under the house, too. Make sure the foundation is holding. There are a lot of variables. We haven't made a final decision which way to go yet."

"I know I sound like a broken record, but how

much time are we talking?" Pam asked.

"I have no idea. I wish I could tell you a week or two, but there are so many variables, either way could create more of a delay. This is an unprecedented, unpredictable situation. That's why I want to keep you informed so you can weigh in with thoughts and ideas as well. I hate to say it, but I don't see how we're going to get this removed without some additional expense renovating or refurbishing what gets destroyed. I wish it were different."

"Will the department pay to clean things up?" Pam asked.

"Sorry." The muffled sound of shuffling feet came over the line. "We don't pay for any cleanup. However, our personnel are as careful as they can be. I'll also give you the numbers of victim assistance groups that may be able to come up with some compensation."

Silence stretched between us and Daniels. I was lost in thought. If we opted for the first method, it would take significantly more time. We'd pay more in holding costs, not to mention the possibility of the market value spiraling south, also decreasing values. Plus, by his own admission, Daniels had predicted some level of rehabbing the room. Everything added up to breaking the budget.

On the other hand, replacing a wall would cost a lot more than we had in reserves. There might be electrical or plumbing that would need re-working. Plus, we'd have to hire that out. Pam and I didn't have that level of expertise. And then there was the possibility of needing a building permit…all of which would take even more time and money.

I sighed and rubbed my eyes. Everything seemed

too big at the moment. I needed a cup of tea and Moxie on my lap. Pam's blank expression revealed that she felt the same way.

"Could we give you a call a little later?" I asked. "Pam and I will discuss the situation and get back to you."

"I understand," Daniels said. "Here—let me give you my other cell number. I'm off this weekend, but I have a hunch I'll be updated on this case anyway."

I jotted down the number. "Thanks. Do we have a deadline for input? How late can I call you?"

"We probably have until Sunday night. By Monday, the powers that be will want a decision and a plan. And you can call me anytime. My cell's on twenty-four seven."

I pictured him in blue jeans and a soft flannel shirt, maybe a baseball cap, clean and fresh like he had been that first day. Quickly, I dispelled the image. "Okay, we'll crunch some numbers and get back to you."

"Sounds good," Daniels replied. "And there's one more thing."

My shoulders drooped. What more could there be?

"What is it?" Pam asked.

"There's some, uh, concern about the rest of the house."

"What do you mean the rest of the house?" Pam's frown deepened.

"I don't want to alarm either of you," he began, "but it's clear that this, uh, aquarium was well-planned, and pardon the expression, executed."

"So?" Pam's voice reflected impatience. She brushed her bangs to the side and stared hard at the cell phone.

"I don't know how to put this, exactly, but there's speculation that there may be more bodies in the home."

"What!" Pam and I exclaimed together. Clearly, that was something neither of us had considered.

I gasped, a sharp intake of air. This could not be happening.

"Holy shit!" Pam said, before slapping a hand over her mouth. "Pardon me."

"No problem. If it's any consolation, I don't think there are. But I can't promise you that they won't look because I don't have the final say in these things."

Pam took a deep breath, exhaled slowly, then spoke. "What do they want to do?"

"It's a little premature to go into all of that right now." Daniels's words conveyed cheerfulness, but his pause spoke volumes. Clearly, he didn't want to further unnerve us. I didn't think that would be possible, however. One more nudge and I'd be over the edge.

"Give us a general idea," I said, "so when we are looking at the numbers we'll know what to account for."

Daniels cleared his throat. "It would mean checking all walls, attics, and possibly floors. The attic will be easy. We'd send a technician up there to look around. The walls will be a little more difficult. We might have to bore holes into each, but more likely we'd bring in an x-ray machine to get a look inside without damaging the paint, plaster, or drywall. The floors will be the most challenging. That process will require someone crawling around underneath with a hand-held x-ray wand—and that's after we check the integrity of the foundation."

"What if they find another body?" Pam braced an elbow on one knee and rested her forehead in her hand.

"Any body, or bodies, that we find will have to be exhumed," he said. "But I think we should wait to cross that bridge when we get to it."

Visions of holes all over our flip, ripping our plans to shreds, filled my head. I tried hard not to panic, but this was as close to a financial catastrophe as anything could be.

A moment passed before Daniels said anything. "Try not to worry. I'll give you regular updates. And I'll make sure everyone knows what this means to the two of you."

I struggled to find my voice, and when I did, the words came out shaky. "Thank you. I'll call by Sunday."

"Sounds good." His tone returned to the confident one we'd heard at the beginning of the conversation. "Sorry for all the bad news on a Friday afternoon."

"It's okay." Pam shifted her gaze to the window. "We know you're doing what you can."

"I am," he said. "We all are."

Pam and I faced each other. She still clutched the phone to her chest long after we'd said our goodbyes and hung up.

What would we do now?

Chapter 12

I zipped out of the Juicy Burger parking lot and headed straight for home. Neither of us said a word about being child-free mothers for the weekend or Daniels's phone call. We were both too overwhelmed to say anything. By the time we'd reached the condo parking lot, however, I was ready to reevaluate our plans.

I killed the engine and turned to Pam. "Do you still want to go see the previous owner, Silas, up at the convalescent center tomorrow?"

"Absolutely." Pam nodded her head vigorously. "What time?"

I considered it. "Not too early, but not too late. Maybe right before lunch?"

Pam whipped off her seatbelt. "It'll take about an hour to get there, and maybe half an hour to talk to him. Why don't we plan on having lunch afterward?"

My spirits lifted. "Maybe Mexican? I've been craving nachos."

"And I've been craving margaritas." Pam wiggled her eyebrows.

I chuckled, despite the stress, feeling relief flow from my shoulders to my toes. Normally, I dreaded Daddy weekends. Too much time to think...and worry...and play "what if." Now, with financial obligations and potential disaster on the horizon, I'd have even more time to dig myself a pit of despair. With plans for Saturday, however, my mood perked up. One day down, one day to go.

"Sounds good," I said. "Let's each come up with a list of questions tonight, then meet up tomorrow morning after breakfast."

"Deal," Pam said, swinging the door open.

After a quiet evening catching up on sitcoms and having a makeshift dinner of popcorn and diet soda, I turned in early. The next thing I knew, I was waking to the chug-chug-chug-wheeeeew of Moxie's snoring.

I pulled her closer and she laid her head atop my chest, blinking first, then gazing deep into my eyes. I tucked the blankets around her and stroked her nearly hairless head. She sighed, content, and closed her eyes again.

Twenty minutes of snuggling later, we got up and wandered into the kitchen. Moxie ate half of a leftover hamburger and I savored a chocolate chip muffin with my coffee. By the time Pam arrived, I had grabbed a small bag of food and a bottle of water for Moxie's travel dishes. Carrying the dog like a football, I was ready to go.

On the way, we made a quick trip through the local java juice kiosk. I got a drip blend, and Pam ordered a caramel macchiato with real whipped cream. Moxie jumped into the front seat and placed her paws on my door, fixing the barista with a hard stare. After confirming Moxie's so-ugly-she's-cute status, the barista placed a dog bone in Moxie's mouth. Despite her lack of teeth, Moxie took it, then bounced into the back of the Kia. Munching sounds ensued.

Back on the road, Pam consulted her GPS app.

"Get on the freeway going north," she said. "Take it all the way to Renton." She placed the phone between us. "Let's go over our notes."

I merged onto the freeway. "Good. You go first."

"I want to ask about the relationship between Morford and Huntington," said Pam between sips. "That seems like the most obvious place to start."

"Agreed." I switched to the far-left lane to allow ramp traffic to merge in. "I think we should also ask why the title transferred back to Morford." I sipped the heady, rich brew of an Americano sweetened with Splenda and sugar-free hazelnut syrup. "What happened to Huntington? Did he die? Become incapacitated?"

"Maybe they're dad and kid," Pam said. "Dad gifts the house to the kid and then something happens to the kid and the dad takes it back. I don't know. Maybe the kid died? That would be sad. I can't imagine losing your child, no matter how old you are."

"But why the different last names?" I asked.

"Hmmm…maybe Huntington was Morford's stepson?" Pam said. "Or maybe adopted son? Or maybe one of them changed their name for some reason."

That opened up all kinds of possibilities I hadn't thought of previously. "Maybe they were brothers, or cousins, even. My hunch, though, is that they have to be family of some kind. I mean, who else quit claims deeds nowadays? It's such a loose way of transferring title. Too many loopholes."

"I know. Usually people use it for inheritance. Or to divvy up monies in a divorce," Pam said. "My gut says they had to be related."

I thought back to the property records. "Look at

that printout and see if there's a record of dual ownership. I don't recall any women's or wives' names on the titles."

Pam scanned the page. "That's funny. No women. Not even '*et ux*,' so no spouse, either."

We rode in silence a moment. I stared out at the gray asphalt ahead. It wasn't that strange. Plenty of men own homes on their own. And there have certainly been many women who have owned homes on their own—us included.

"It could have been a family friend or a nephew," I said. "But I agree, something feels a little off."

"I'm going to put a question mark next to relationship." Pam shuffled her papers. "On to the next question: Who did the remodel and when was it done?"

"It might be too obvious if we ask about the remodel directly, but if we know who lived there during the paneling, it would be a huge lead."

"Right. It is possible that the homeowner hired out the work, and the contractor's responsible. We talked about that." Pam covered her mouth. "Oh!"

"What?"

"Maybe no one who lived there ever knew the body was in the closet."

I shivered, thinking of the implications. If the body had been there nearly fifty years, any old house could have a body between its walls. I gulped. Could one of the houses I'd lived in have held a corpse and I'd never known it? A shiver snaked up my spine.

"This is all so creepy." I turned to Pam. "Do you think there could be someone in our condo closets?"

"Not living," she deadpanned.

A giggle bubbled up before I could speak. I could

always count on Pam to lighten the mood. "Really? Do you think it's possible?"

She shook her head. "Nah. The odds of that are astronomical…I think."

"Yeah," I said, not quite convinced. "You're probably right."

"Plus, we're on the third floor. If someone buried a body in our building, it would have been done on the ground level."

I snorted and a little coffee went up my nose. "Fantastic. I feel so much better."

Pam grinned. "Plus, an aquarium like that would have crashed through the floor years ago. I'm surprised it hasn't at the Craftsman."

"Well, they're known for being built really well. Maybe that was its saving grace." I exited the freeway. Following the app's directions, I pulled into the circular entrance of Evergreen Convalescent Center behind a row of bright yellow cabs. The cabbies waved us forward, one by one, until I had exited the circle and entered a large parking area.

I selected a slot labeled "Visitor," and took a look around. The facade of the ECC had been brick originally but appeared to have been painted white long ago. Normal wear and tear, and a good deal of rain, had stripped the paint, though, so that red brick peeked out in so many places it appeared styled in shabby chic. The columns, once a matching white, had yellowed slightly with age and revealed an ornateness rarely seen in today's buildings. Cobwebs and a fair amount of moss had gathered in the nooks and crannies. The lawn and shrubbery, however, appeared healthy and well-manicured. I could only hope the residents experienced the same level of attention as the living things in the yard.

"I've never liked these places." Pam peered out the front window. "They put me on edge."

I nodded. "I know people come here to get well, too. But it seems like mostly people come to these places to die."

Pam unsnapped her seat belt. "Okay. Let's get in there, get our questions answered, and get out again. Before I lose my nerve."

I grabbed my purse and locked the doors. Together we hiked across the lot to the front entrance.

The foyer furniture consisted of a worn brocade fainting couch in gold and cream and two crushed velvet chairs, also in tones of gold, circa 1975. A waist-high wrought-iron partition separated the sitting area from the beige reception desk.

We headed for the tall counter. When no one showed, we wandered down to the far end and paused at the door. After a quick conversation debating whether we should just walk in or knock, I tried the handle. Unlocked. I twisted it and entered, Pam hot on my heels.

In front of us stretched an oversized hallway with off-white linoleum that covered the floor and crawled up each wall several inches. Easier for clean up, I presumed. Several doors led off of the corridor, but not a soul, wheelchair, or walker, was in sight. The scent of urine assaulted my nasal passages, however.

"There." Pam pointed to a small table. "We need to sign in."

Sure enough, a "Guest Book" lay open. Next to it, an old-fashioned feather pen stood at attention in its holder. Pam signed first, and I scrawled my name. After a quick survey of the area, we marched forward, our shoes squeaking on the floor.

Midway down the hall, we came to a nurse's station. A lone bored-looking girl of about twenty played solitaire on her computer. She wore light-blue scrub bottoms and a blue-and-white top patterned with clouds. She brushed her bleached ponytail over her shoulder, revealing her name tag: Allie.

Allie raised her blue eyes. "May I help you?"

"We're here to visit Silas Morford," Pam said.

Allie cocked her head. "Silas Morford? I don't think we have a Silas or a Morford here. Let me double-check our guest list."

After minimizing her game to the bottom of the screen, she typed in the name and a few variations. "I don't see anyone here by that name." Her eyebrows furrowed. "Could it be Morton or Simon? Something like that?"

Pam and I exchanged glances. Maybe we were in the wrong place.

"Is this Evergreen Convalescent Center?" I asked, showing Allie the address Sam had given us. "Are we in the right place?"

Allie glanced at it, then back to me. "That's us," she said, "but there's no one here by that name. There are only eighty guests here, and I know every one of them. I also know all of the nicknames, and we don't have anyone who goes by Silas here."

It took a moment for me to gather my thoughts. How could Silas Morford have signed a paper here one week ago and now be non-existent?

Then I remembered what kind of place this was.

"How long have you worked here?" I asked. "Is it possible he could be, uh, deceased?"

Allie pursed her eyebrows. "I've been here nearly a year. I would definitely know if someone named Silas Morford had died here."

"Where are all of the guests?" Pam asked.

"They're down in the activity room." Allie lowered her voice to a conspiratorial whisper. "There's a magician performing in there. He does sleight-of-hand stuff. He's not very good, but if half the audience has cataracts, who's to know?"

I tried hard to smile. I couldn't decide if Allie had simply seen it all or if she were slightly callous to the guests' medical conditions.

"And you're sure there's no Silas Morford here?" Pam persisted.

"Yep. Sorry." Allie enlarged her game of solitaire. "Is there anything else I can help you with?"

"Could you take my number?" I asked. "In case someone remembers a man by the name of Silas?"

"Sure thing." Allie drew a piece of scratch paper from beneath the counter.

I recited the number. She wrote it down and read it back. With nothing left to do, we said goodbye and headed back down the long corridor.

"What now?" Pam slid into the passenger seat.

"I don't know," I said. My gut told me this was no coincidence. "But something is very wrong."

Chapter 13

I merged onto the freeway, then drove ten miles before feeling the first hunger pang. I checked the time. "Let's stop for lunch and talk this over."

"Great idea, Janny."

I pointed the Kia in the direction of our favorite Mexican restaurant, *Mis Amigos*. Within moments, we'd parked, checked that the exterior temperature was cool enough for Moxie to stay inside the car, gave her a quick potty break, and topped off her food and water dishes. Moxie settled back into her bed, and I closed the hatchback. Ahead, the neon marquee promised, "Live Mariachi Bands on Weekends."

"Oh, good," Pam said. "I prefer live mariachi bands to dead ones."

I giggled, she smirked, and we sat at a table in the bar. We ordered nachos and drank skinny, half-the-alcohol, ice-cold margaritas. After our initial giddiness, Pam grew pensive. I could tell by the way she stirred the green fluid in the glass and toyed with her nachos that something bothered her.

"So what do you think happened to Silas?" Pam asked. "Where is he?"

I shook my head. "I have no idea. Maybe we got the wrong Evergreen Convalescent Center? Maybe we got his name wrong? Maybe Allie behind the desk was confused? I just don't know."

"Those are the same things I've been thinking. But how could there be more than one center named Evergreen? And we looked his name up on the closing documents. As for Allie, she seemed pretty sure of herself."

I sipped my margarita, enjoying the bite of lime. "The only thing we can do at this point is go back over everything."

"I could call Sam, the realtor. He might know more."

"Good idea."

Pam pulled out her phone but then repocketed it. "I'm going to wait until we're not in a public place."

"Another good idea."

More salsa arrived, and we sat in silence a long while, each of us scooping cheesy chips into bean dip, sour cream, salsa, and guacamole.

"So what else is eating you?" I nibbled a toasted brown chip.

"Oh, I dunno." She met my eyes, then dunked a chip into the guacamole. She set it on her appetizer plate without eating.

"C'mon," I said. "I know when something's bothering you—you stop eating."

"Besides the fact that Silas disappeared, there's a dead guy in our flip, and our life savings are on the line?" She removed the straw from her drink and set it on her napkin. A small green pool formed below each end of the straw. "It's that place."

"The convalescent center?"

"Yeah. It makes me wicked sad."

"It does seem kind of dismal there, doesn't it?" I replied. "I know the staff does the best they can with decor and a positive attitude. But in the end, it's where you go…at the end."

"It's not just that. It makes me think they're—the people who live there—they're all alone. Like they don't have anyone, you know?"

I nodded.

She swallowed hard. "Don't they have kids?"

"Maybe." I shrugged. "Maybe not. Why does that bother you so much? After all, you have Gabe."

She cast her gaze downward toward her lap. "It makes me wonder what happens to people like us. You know, divorced people." She looked up and her eyes had welled with tears. "What happens to divorced people when they get old?"

I angled my fork across the edge of my appetizer plate and dabbed at my mouth with a fresh napkin. "I don't know."

"I don't want to be alone." Pam's voice broke and her face contorted in emotion.

In the past year, I'd occasionally considered what would happen to me if I never remarried. Would I get lonely? Bitter? Adopt a lot of cats once the girls moved away to college?

But then, I'd taken a good, honest look around. Some of the loneliest people I knew were married. And some of the single people I knew were constantly busy with friends. They went to movies, hikes, out to dinner. They traveled, went bowling and golfing. They swam and volunteered to head up fund-raising campaigns. They didn't complain.

"Being alone doesn't necessarily mean being lonely," I said. "And there's nothing worse than feeling alone when you're married."

"That's true." Pam nodded, clearly weighing my words. "But what if no one ever wants me again? What if I spend the rest of my life divorced? Will I end up in one of those places?"

I sighed. Maybe. Maybe we would both end up there. "I don't know. I don't think it matters if a person is married or not. I think what matters is how much care a person needs and who's available to give it. We can't predict that. If we could, we'd all choose our spouses with that in mind."

The mariachi music grew louder and the band stopped in the bar. After a lively "La Cucaracha," Pam and I applauded loudly. They bowed their sombreros, then retreated to the main dining room again.

"You're probably right," Pam said. "Spouses care for each other as long as they can. But there could be a car accident and they could die together. I guess someone has to be left alone in the end. Then, it's up to the kids to step in."

"Right, so long as their help is needed. But some people, a lot of people, live independently their entire lives."

Pam exhaled gustily as if relieved. "Oh! Wait! It could go the other way. We could end up taking care of a spouse." She shook her head. "I'm not taking care of Marcus. That's for damn sure."

"Really?"

"Not now." She straightened in her seat. "Maybe a couple of years ago I would have. Not now."

We sat without speaking, each of us pushing olives, onions, and tomatoes around our plates with our forks. I thought about what it would mean to be a burden on my children and how I wouldn't want that to happen. What if the tables were turned and one of my children, or even Jim, needed care? Would I be willing to set aside everything and provide the level of care they'd need? In my heart I knew the answer was yes. Definitely for my children…but even for Jim, so that he wouldn't be a burden to our kids.

"Janny?" Pam interrupted my train of thought. "Do you think you'll ever, you know, fall in love again?"

I rolled my eyes. "It would be nice to be in love and experience all those feelings again. But I don't know. I don't think I have the energy for all that anymore. It's kind of exhausting, you know? How about you?"

She shook her head. "It's different for me now. I'm different. I don't think I could love someone completely anymore. Only Gabe. He's the only guy I think I'll ever truly love."

We stared at each other. I understood perfectly. While a man's actions could change the way I felt for him—even make me want to divorce him—my love for my children would never die. Nothing they could ever do would make me want them out of my life.

"Maybe that's the way it's supposed to be," I said. "Unconditional love rules all."

"I'll drink to that." Pam held her glass high, and we clinked. Afterward, Pam dabbed at her mouth with her napkin. "One thing I do know is that I'd take care of you. That won't ever change."

Tears sprang to my eyes. "Thanks, Pam. We'll take care of each other."

"Good to know." She drained her margarita without using her straw, then wiped her mouth with the back of her hand. "Enough with solving all of our problems. Let's save some for tomorrow."

"Cool beans," I said, laying down PB & J plastic to pay the bill. The least we could do was treat ourselves to lunch on the company dollar. We did, after all, talk about work.

Chapter 14

Late Sunday afternoon, after a full condo cleaning, Moxie hot on the vacuum's wheels, Pam rushed over. Sam, our realtor, was holding on the line. No sooner had Pam set the call to speaker phone than a pounding sounded at my front door. Jim and Marcus had arrived home with the kids an hour early.

"I'll take this in your bedroom," Pam whispered. She cast a longing look at the door. I knew she was eager to welcome Gabe back and give him a snuggle, but she hurried off down the hall, phone in hand.

Once I'd tugged my leggings up and oversized T-shirt down over my rear, I pasted on a smile and swung the door wide. Immediately, Moxie and the girls reunited in happy squeals and the tip-tapping of many feet. After gracing me with a quick hug each, Annie and Emily raced to their room. Moxie chased after them, new life in her old legs.

"Where's Pam?" Marcus carefully lifted Gabe from his shoulders.

A waft of strong, musky cologne hit me full in the face. I resisted the urge to cough and took a step back. Marcus wore a tight pink T-shirt that stretched across his chest and shoulders. His hard nipples jutted out in a way that looked painful. Below he wore colorful Bermuda shorts and slip-on tennis shoes. Jim, on the other hand, was a little more subdued. He had on a green polo shirt and a pair of khaki cargo shorts. He also wore the tire-soled sandals I had convinced him to buy two summers earlier. One thing was certain: They were dressed for an outing.

"She's on the phone. She'll be out in a minute." I smiled, holding out my hands to Gabe. He climbed into my arms and squeezed tight, his breath hot on my ear. "Momma's got important PB & J business," I sing-songed, my words directed toward Gabe. "She'll be here soon."

"Okay." Marcus dropped the diaper bag onto the floor, then turned to Jim. "I'll be out in the truck, catching some rays." He slipped on his reflective sunglasses and turned on his heel. He walked down the corridor without a backward glance.

I fought against the urge to roll my eyes and turned away from the scented trail. Instead, I grinned at Gabe who had found my yellow flowered earrings. He examined them closely.

Jim waited for Marcus to disappear, then swiveled back to me. "Who'd be calling on a Sunday?"

I shrugged. "Just business stuff."

He eyed me, but I diverted my attention to Gabe once again. I hoped he'd leave without any additional conversation or questions, but no. He wanted to talk again. Swell.

"What's going on?" He stepped closer.

I swallowed hard. "What do you mean?"

He stared straight into my eyes. Defiant, I jutted my chin forward. *No words shall cross my lips unless I allow them.*

"Look, Jan, I'm not trying to meddle." He was close enough so that I could smell his breath. Minty

99

fresh. I wondered who that was for. "I'm just concerned that something has happened with the flip, and you're not telling me."

"Well," I said, my voice sweet as sugar, so as not to alarm Gabe, "I don't have to tell you everything anymore. In fact, I don't have to tell you a single itty-bitty thing."

Jim's shoulders hunched, and for the first time I saw a wistfulness in his eyes that had been absent during the last years of our marriage. I couldn't help but soften a little. It had been good once. Very good. For a long time. A pang of regret stabbed my heart. Those memories were hard to let go.

"I know you don't have to tell me everything, or even anything." His voice was steady, but his words were enunciated. "I'm just trying to help. I know how to fix things…solve problems…I've been at this game a while."

I nodded but said nothing. As much as I would like help solving this rather large problem, there was nothing he could do, even if I did confide in him. The solution lay in police hands now, specifically the very capable hands of Sergeant Daniels.

After a moment of silence, he spoke. "Okay. I'll back off. Will you promise to come to me if you have a problem?"

At first I didn't respond. Why should I? He was the one who caused our divorce. He was the one who played house with his realtor, not me. He was the one who refused to come to me when he was unhappy.

I paused, a sudden realization.

He had been unhappy. Truly unhappy. Why else would he have gone outside of our marriage?

For the first time in a very long time, I met his eyes without anger or frustration. Had I always been willing to listen to him? Had I been too preoccupied with the kids? Had I shown the same level of interest in him as he currently showed me?

The pang shifted lower, into my gut this time, and twisted. Maybe the divorce wasn't all his fault.

I took a deep breath and promised myself some soulful reflection later. For now, I would be kinder. Clearly, his attempts at a healthy relationship would be good for the kids...and it would be good for me, too.

"Thank you." I allowed the corners of my mouth to turn up in a half-smile. "I'll keep that in mind."

Another moment of silence passed before he called goodbye to the girls and headed back the way he had come. Closing the door behind him, I felt the stabbing replaced with a heaviness of regret that slumped my shoulders. Maybe heartache never goes away completely.

I carried Gabe into the kitchen and together we searched the refrigerator for dinner. As we were debating the merits of baked chicken versus turkey burgers, my bedroom door opened. Pam padded down the hallway, and Gabe's head swiveled in response. As she entered the kitchen, he shrieked and thrust himself at her. Pam crossed the kitchen in a single stride and eased him out of my arms. She smothered him with kisses, holding him tight and twirling. When she stopped, Gabe planted one hand on each side of Pam's face and kissed her hard. She giggled and settled into a chair at the table, holding him close.

"Here's my little man," she cooed. "Here he is."

Gabe squealed, kicking his legs in excitement.

"What'd Sam say?" I pulled out a package of chicken and a casserole dish.

"He said that was the right address. Told me he'd gone there himself, room two eleven."

I paused and stared at her. "What? When?"

She shook her head. "Same time frame. It's as if Silas Morford simply disappeared."

I sprinkled salt and pepper on the chicken, then laid a few rosemary sprigs across the top before placing the dish into the oven. "Could he have been transferred to another facility? Is there another wing we don't know about?"

Pam frowned. "I don't think so." She went to the pantry and grabbed a small handful of circle-shaped cereal. She set the pile onto the table and held Gabe as he studiously reached out and pinched one after another with his forefinger and thumb, grinning each time one made it into his mouth.

After measuring rice and water into a second casserole dish and setting it in the microwave, I asked, "None of this makes sense—how can someone just disappear? What about the title? Did he know why it was transferred back and forth?"

"He told me the house had only recently come back into Silas's possession," she said. "But we already knew that."

"Did he know why? Did he know what the relationship is, or was, between Huntington and Morford?"

She shook her head. "He didn't know. He said only that Silas had never expected to own the property and had no interest in owning the property, or even renting it out. He just wanted to get rid of it. It sounded like an inheritance or something, but Sam was vague. When I pushed it a little, he said it wasn't his business to ask questions. He was probably happy just to get the listing." Pam grabbed a piece of the cereal, tossed it in the air and caught it in her mouth. Gabe squealed with delight and began throwing the few remaining pieces of cereal in the air, none of which landed in his mouth. Cereal fell to the floor like confetti, clearly delighting him.

"Sorry, Janny." Pam laughed and rose from her chair. "I'll sweep."

"Don't bother until he's finished. It'll keep." I poked around the freezer for a bag of vegetables. "An inheritance would make sense. Did Sam say anything else?"

"No." Pam's expression changed from puzzled to thoughtful. "He was in a hurry, though. He wrote up two more Purchase and Sale Agreements this weekend. Things are picking up a little."

"That's good," I said. "Maybe prices will rise enough to cover the cost of our delay. Maybe this is all excellent timing, and the end result will be more profit when it sells."

"Maybe." She smiled.

We were quiet as I filled the steamer with green beans and listened to its hum. It wasn't until much later, after the kids had been fed and down for the night and we'd poured ourselves a glass of Moscato, that our worries returned. *What if we ran out of money? What if our home flipping business fails? Who could we go to for money if we ran out, other than the guys? What if...what if...what if...*

Chapter 15

"We have to go back there," Pam said from her corner of the couch, wine glass balanced on her knee.

At first I couldn't believe she was serious. Even Moxie's ears pricked up.

"To Evergreen Convalescent Center? Again? Why?" I forced the recliner back while holding my own wine aloft to keep from spilling. "We already know he isn't there."

Pam sipped the sweet wine before responding. "But now we have a room number."

"Why don't we just call? It would be faster and easier. We'll just ask for the room number. What'd you say, two eleven?" I raised the footrest and kicked off my shoes.

"Because, that receptionist—Allie—might answer," she said. "And I think she might be lying."

I frowned. That seemed highly unlikely. Allie had appeared bored, not deceptive. "What motive could she have?"

"Maybe she's in on it."

I cocked my head. "In on what?"

"The murder." Pam wiggled her eyebrows.

"Pam, Allie hadn't even been born when John Doe died. I doubt she knows anything about it. Besides, she seemed sincerely confused."

"I know. I know." Pam rubbed her chin. "But if we

just show up there, we can take them by surprise."

I took a drink, allowing the sweet bubbles to dance across my tongue and the apple scent to fill my nose before swallowing. "Who are we trying to surprise?"

"Anyone," she replied. "We need to trip someone up. Get them to tell us something."

I shook my head. Chasing after old people and playing detective was not like Pam at all. Then again, we were both a little out of our element.

"Say we go back," I said. "What could we learn that the police can't?"

Pam sighed and drained her glass. "I don't know. Maybe we should let Sergeant Daniels handle this. But I feel so useless. Plus, I'm really, really curious. How can an old man be there one week and not the next?"

That had been bothering me, too. The whole point of convalescing is having someone else take care of you because you can't take care of yourself, right? How could a resident simply up and disappear? Wouldn't they need help to do that?

None of it made any sense.

I set my wine glass on the coffee table. "Do you think this could be dangerous? What if Silas is a murderer? Are we really the right people to go chasing after him?"

Pam shook her head. "Nah. After all, he—Silas—is old. And we're young and strong. And maybe he doesn't know anything about any of it. And even if he does, he doesn't know we know what he knows. And...and...and..."

"But that doesn't mean he didn't have an accomplice who is also young and strong. Remember, it took at least two people to build that aquarium. Who knows who the other person is. Maybe the same person helped him escape from the ECC."

She leaned forward as if telling me a secret. "But his accomplice, if he had one, would also be retirement age."

I picked up my glass and drank, pondering her words. She had a point about Morford. His age and condition couldn't pose a threat to either of us. That is, if he actually was involved in the body's interment, and it's entirely possible he wasn't, whoever helped the murderer would be much older than Pam and me. He— or maybe even she—couldn't hurt us now.

Even if this turned out to be a wild goose chase, and I suspected it would be, I would rather feel as though we'd done everything we could to get back into the house. Back to work. Back to the independence we wanted—no—needed.

I sipped again, feeling the bubbles dance on my tongue.

Maybe our questions would help the investigation. It couldn't hurt, could it?

"I'll make you a deal," I said. "We'll call Daniels tomorrow afternoon before the end of his shift. If he doesn't have anything new to tell us, we'll find Silas ourselves."

Pam saluted me, then picked up her glass. We toasted the decision, then drained the wine and said good night.

The next afternoon, as we began the pick-up loop of school and daycare, my cell phone rang.

"Daniels," I said, reading his number on the screen. I handed the phone to Pam and continued driving.

"Hi, Officer Daniels." Pam set the phone to

speaker. She loosened her seatbelt and turned toward me. "We're in the car, but we're listening."

"More good news and bad news," he said.

"Bad news first," Pam replied.

"Okay. We're going with the drain method. It'll take at least a week."

"A whole week? Is everyone on vacation or what?"

Daniels paused. When he continued his voice sounded tired but professional. I imagined his green eyes softening. "Actually, yes. The head of that unit is on vacation. She's asked us to wait until she gets back. She wants to make sure it's done right."

"Will the seal hold that amount of time?" I asked.

"We think so." Sirens screamed in the background, and he paused until they passed.

"Sorry about that," he said. "Yes, we think it will hold. It's held the past forty years or so, so we figure it's good for another few days. If it starts to leak, we'll course correct. We'll proceed, just earlier. She'll then make the call to come home early or not."

"So no leak means we wait for the person who's calling the shots to come home?" I asked.

"Looks that way," Daniels said. "She wants to oversee every aspect. I understand her reasoning. This is a unique case—it's an opportunity for field training. We won't get second chances with this one."

I couldn't help but feel dejected. Sure I wanted to help the police learn as much as possible, but I also wanted them to hurry the process. "So what's the good news?"

"Sorry, but I have more bad news first."

Pam's eyes met mine. Her shoulders slumped and I felt my own droop forward in mirrored response. Up ahead, the light changed to yellow and I slowed down.

"Give it to us," she said.

"Chief wants a complete scan of the house," Daniels said. "We need to ascertain that there are no additional bodies hidden anywhere on the premises."

Pam slapped her forehead. "Good grief! What's next?"

A moment of silence passed. I glanced her way, frowning. Pam's tone had been sharp—too sharp. I understood her feelings. But I also believed Daniels held our best interests at heart. Besides, he didn't have any reason to want this investigation to take longer than it had to.

"Sorry, Sergeant Daniels," I said. "We're both under a lot of stress. All of this is a surprise."

"Yeah. Sorry." Pam's voice lowered. "How long will that take? Can it be done at the same time?"

"No. Essential personnel only until body's removed." Daniels cleared his throat. "It won't take long. We won't have to drill any holes. We can use an x-ray device. It penetrates drywall, even. Odds are against any more bodies. Walls were framed at sixteen inches back then. That's not big enough for a body."

"That's good," I said. "Right?"

"It is good," he confirmed. "And if we get a high-level dog, we can sniff out the yard rather than a backhoe."

"Backhoe?!" Pam's mouth dropped open.

"Yeah, well, like I said, we'll get a high-level dog. Their noses are good for thirty years of decomposition or so. Granted, the remains could be older, but that's the captain's call."

"Anything else?" Pam had calmed down a little.

"Actually, there's good news."

"Go on," I said.

"I got the okay to procure the x-ray machine."

Visions of wait lists and out-of-stock messages and shipping delays marched through my brain. "How long do you think it will take?"

"My best guess is a week," Daniels said. "But that works out pretty well. By the time the body's out, the requisition should be in."

I glanced at Pam and shrugged. That was probably the very best that they could do. It really did sound like he was working the problem as quickly as possible.

"Once the body's removed we can get in to begin work, right?" Pam asked.

"Sorry. Investigation complete before civilians go in or out. Until then, we're still babysitting the corpse."

His answer didn't surprise me. The police had the ball now, and they had procedures to follow. If they broke their own rules and someone got hurt, or worse, they would be liable.

There was nothing more that we could do now…except wait.

"Any more questions?" Daniels asked. "Jan, Pam?"

Something about the way he said our names made me believe he really cared. It shook me a little. It had been a long time since I'd felt important to a man. I struggled to think of a question just to keep him on the line, to hear his soothing voice.

Finally, I blurted out, "Do you have any ideas about who killed him? I mean, do you have a suspect list?"

Daniels chuckled. "Things don't move quite that fast. And, without all of the details, I won't hazard a guess. What I will say, however, is that we're not sure this is a homicide. The circumstances are odd. But there aren't any obvious marks. Of course, he's been sitting in embalming solution, and none of us are experts on body decomposition in that situation. We'll know more once we get him to the lab."

"How could it be anything but murder?" Pam asked. "He didn't seal himself in there."

"True," Daniels said, his speech cautious. "But we can't jump to conclusions. There may be plenty of reasons someone would, uh, hang onto a body after death."

I felt my face scrunch up. "Why would anyone want to keep a dead body around?"

"There are a lot of reasons people do that kind of thing. Most of them revolve around money. Right now, I'm more concerned about getting him out of there."

"Wait!" Pam said. "Since we found the body will we be suspects?"

A short bark of a laugh came over the line, but Daniels camouflaged it by clearing his throat. "No. That body's been dead longer than you and Jan have been alive. No need to worry about that."

I giggled a little, and Pam joined in. It eased the tension, and I felt my back relax.

"I guess I've been watching too many detective shows," Pam admitted, removing her glasses and rubbing her forehead. "This is getting to me."

"No problem. I understand," Daniels said. "This can't be easy on either one of you. It's a strange, strange case. Definitely one of the strangest I've experienced in nearly twenty years of law enforcement."

"We understand, Sergeant Daniels," I said.

"Bye, Pam," he said. "Good-bye, Jan. I'll be in touch."

"Bye-bye." As my mommy tone spilled out, I clasped a hand over my mouth and rolled my eyes.

Pam ended the call and laughed out loud. "Girlfriend, please. You've got it bad."

I waved her off. "No, I don't."

Pam's eyebrows twitched. "You know what I'd say—or rather what Robert Palmer and I would say." She began searching pockets and her purse. "We'd say you're *Addicted to Love*."

Heat rose in my cheeks. "I don't know what you mean."

"Sure, you don't." She pulled out her iPod and scrolled through her playlist.

Soon, Robert Palmer's warm tones filled the car. I couldn't help but sing along and sway in my seat. Once we were in line at the elementary school, Pam turned the volume down.

"You know what else this means?" Pam said.

"What?"

"The police think a serial killer may have lived in our house."

I laughed. "You really have been watching too many crime shows. Daniels said he wasn't even sure it was a homicide."

"I know. But why else are they searching for more bodies?"

I gulped. She had a point. I'd heard stories of neighborhoods completely shocked by the arrest of one of their own. I'd watched television reports of decades-long relationships questioned as police dug up the backyards of next-door neighbors. And I'd seen the devastation and confusion as their friends were convicted of murder. The common thread was that they never knew, never suspected, someone from the block party or Fourth of July BBQ to be capable of murder, much less hiding it right below their noses. Maybe I'd been watching too much television, too. Still, the idea sent a shiver up my spine.

"Do you think that's possible?"

Pam shrugged. "I'd believe anything at this point. You know what else this means?"

I wasn't sure I wanted to know.

"It means we're heading to Renton to interrogate one Silas Morford first thing tomorrow." Her voice had taken on the gravelly tone of an old-time detective.

I hesitated. Heading to the home of a potential serial murderer didn't seem like such a fantastic plan without a glass of sweet white wine making me brave.

I frowned. "Do you think that's smart?"

"I think it's a better idea now than before," Pam said as students began pouring out the elementary school's double doors. "Remember, Daniels also said John Doe may not have been a homicide. No murder, no murderer. No murderer, no danger."

I followed her leapfrogging logic but doubted it was a good enough reason to get involved. It didn't matter, however. I'd already promised to go. And if it satisfied Pam and kept us busy, so be it. There was always a chance we might find out something. Then, we could see Daniels again…just to give him the additional information, of course.

"Okay," I said. "First thing tomorrow morning, we surprise the elusive Mr. Morford. Tonight I'm going to dig up a little dirt."

Chapter 16

Bright and early, after tucking Moxie into her dog bed in front of the fireplace and dropping off the kids, Pam and I headed straight for the Evergreen Convalescent Center. In the light of day, I had few qualms about our independent investigation. What could be dangerous about an old folks' home? Still, all the talk about serial killers and our house being a mass burial site unnerved me.

During the drive up the freeway, I updated Pam on what I'd learned about Silas Morford, Gerald Jones, and Thaddeus Huntington, the three owners of our little Craftsman.

"I used one of those people search engines and splurged for the full report," I began. "Just as we suspected, they're all related. It was easiest to find information on Gerald Jones. Silas Morford had the least amount of information, even though he's the oldest. There was a fair amount on Thaddeus Huntington, too."

"Well, that makes sense, sort of." Pam wrinkled her nose. "What could their relationship be?"

"I can't be sure, but I discovered that they're really far apart in age, like twenty or twenty-five years each. They could even be grandfather, father, and son."

"They could also be cousins, if the parents were far enough apart in age. Two of them could be brothers, but

I doubt all three are brothers."

"Babies forty-five years apart?" I grimaced. "That hurts just to think about. I don't think that's even possible." I pointed to my purse. "Pull out that yellow legal sheet."

Pam retrieved the notes. "Oh my gosh. I can't believe how much info there is online about people. Their addresses? Emails? Phone numbers? What if someone is trying to get away from an abusive spouse, or they testified against someone who just got out of prison? Anyone could get this information."

"I know." It was scary to think about the ramifications of trying to hide and not be able to. Being newly single made me think about security in a whole new way. "Refresh my memory on the ages of each."

Pam quieted as she read the information. "Silas Morford. Ninety-two years old. Good Lord! No wonder he's in an old folks' home."

"Yeah," I agreed. "But there's a couple other things in that report. Look at when he first deeded the property."

"Hunh."

I changed lanes to allow speeding traffic to pass. "The way I figure it, he would have had to have been in his seventies."

"Probably mid-seventies," Pam said. "Maybe seventy-four or seventy-five. But that doesn't seem so unusual. Lots of people get sick or disabled in their seventies."

"That's not what I'm talking about. The thing I'm wondering about is where he moved. Where did he go?"

Pam frowned. "Probably the ECC. Why else would

he have moved from a great low-maintenance house like that?" She gasped. "Oh my gosh! He's been there nearly twenty years. How horrible!"

I nodded. "Right. But there's more that bothers me. If he can't live independently, how'd he survive that long?"

"Maybe it's something that isn't so bad, like an amputation."

I shook my head. "I don't think so. Amputees live on their own all the time."

"Maybe it's a super slow debilitating disease, like Crohn's or something."

"Pam. Take a look at the addresses for each and the time frames that they lived there."

She shuffled the papers back and forth, running her fingers along the dates on the county records and matching them to the dates on the personal information.

"See anything unusual?"

She raised her head and peered through the windshield. "I don't get it. It shows that they were both living there at the same time. They were both there when the deed was conveyed back and forth."

"Yeah. It's weird." I slowed as I exited the freeway. "It makes me think that they're not only related, but that they must all know about the paneling remodel."

"Then they're all in on it! They have to know who's in there! Wait!" Pam gasped. "Do you think the John Doe is one of them?"

I squinted in confusion. "That's what I'm wondering. But how could it be? They're all recorded as still alive." I hung a left into the parking lot.

"Well, I'll be sure to ask Mr. Morford about that."

Pam folded the papers and stuck them back in my purse. "We'll show him the facts if he tries to deny anything."

I parked, then sat with the engine still running. The facts didn't add up. Too many inconsistencies and unexplained relationships. "You know. It's not too late to change our minds about going in there."

Pam unbuckled her seat belt. "Why? I'm more curious now than I was before."

"I don't know. It's just that something doesn't feel right. I feel queasy." In addition to skipping breakfast in yet another attempt to lose weight, I felt uneasy about interrogating an old man. That is, if we could even find him. Plus, it definitely bled into meddling territory, which Officer Daniels specifically told us not to do.

"I'll make you a deal," Pam said, holding out one palm. "If things get weird, we'll high-tail it out of there. Of course, that means we leave everything in Daniels's hands. Our sanity, our financial futures, our kids' financial futures. Everything."

Touché. I may be afraid of a lot of things, but being unable to provide for my kids topped my reluctance to confront an old man.

I shook her hand to seal our pact. "Let's go."

We swung through the big glass door. As before, no one greeted us, so we breezed through the interior doors that led to the long sterile hallway. After signing the guest book, we stood at the end of the corridor and surveyed the activities.

Fresh from a solid night's sleep and breakfast, the residents buzzed everywhere. Women in housecoats eased down the halls, walkers in front. Tennis balls had been attached to the legs of the walkers, muffling their approach. A few wheelchair-bound folks brushed past us on their way up and down the hall, their tires squeaky on the clean tiles. Occasionally, someone shuffled past, one hand on the wall, tracing an invisible line from where they've been to where they're going. The scent of urine from our first visit had been replaced with the aroma of institutional breakfasts—hot meat patties and potatoes, and an occasional whiff of melted cheese. My stomach gurgled in response.

Pam swung round to me, her eyes accusatory. "Did you eat this morning?"

Chagrined, I shook my head. Pam often chided me about my weight loss attempts. She knew whenever I went without my morning meal, I was trying, once again, to reduce.

"Starving yourself isn't good," she reminded me. "You'll just get over-hungry for lunch. Remember, they fatten up Sumo wrestlers by denying them breakfast."

Palm to forehead. The last thing I wanted to resemble was a Sumo wrestler. She was right. Going without a meal felt torturous and punitive. It always ended with me giving in to a large, early meal anyway.

"Okay," I said. "I'll pick up a granola bar on the way home. Now let's find room two eleven, talk to Morford, and get out of here."

"Good." Pam slipped on her glasses, and together we strolled down the hall.

Several residents stopped and stared at us, and a few nursing assistants smiled as they hurried from room to room. Nothing seemed out of place, but the more we walked amongst these people, the more anxiety started a slow crawl up my spine. Compounding my discomfort, the hunger in my tummy sent a surge of nausea into my throat. Who knew what we would find in room two eleven?

"One hundred fourteen, one hundred fifteen," Pam recited as we passed rooms. Her step quickened.

I, however, slowed, my tension mounting. My pulse raced and my head felt light. I really should have eaten breakfast.

Pam kept up her fast-paced stroll. "One hundred sixteen, one hundred seventeen, one hundred eighteen." I lagged behind, the distance between us increasing.

She turned at a utility closet and urged me forward. "C'mon, Jan."

I motioned her back. "It may be hunger, but I have a bad feeling about this."

She pulled me over to the wall, out of the way of traffic. "What are you afraid of?"

I fidgeted. "Everything. I'm nervous. What if we find out something we shouldn't know? Something that puts us or our kids in danger?"

Pam cocked her head. "Like what?"

I thought about everything we'd learned in the last year and how blissfully unaware I had been until then…and how sad some of the lessons had made me. "Maybe it's best that we don't know. Do we always need all the answers?" I was speaking in riddles, and of course, they all alluded to the affairs, that led to the divorces, that led to us trying to flip a house, that led to us finding a body, that led to us having a heated, hushed discussion in the hallway of an old folks' home.

Pam's face softened. She stepped closer. "I understand," she whispered. "Sometimes I wish we hadn't found out about the guys, too. But it wouldn't have changed anything."

I felt the familiar itchiness of tears begging for release. I breathed deeply.

She frowned a moment before continuing in a low whisper. "Sometimes, I conjure up all kinds of scenarios if we hadn't found out: health issues, more babies, you name it."

A memory of a frantic doctor visit after learning about the affairs and the relief I'd felt when given a clean bill of health flashed through my mind. I frowned. Pam was right. Nothing would have changed. Things would have gotten worse. Possibly much worse.

"Okay." I squared my shoulders.

"The way I see it," Pam said, "either we find the answers, or we wait for the police to find them. And they're a little busy right now." She peeked inside the nearest room. "I'd rather help them. We'll only be helping ourselves."

The tension in my body eased with this new resolve. We may not want to do all this digging, but somebody had to do it. And it was our house, so it may as well be us. "Let's go," I said.

"Forward." Pam led the way.

I allowed myself one quick glance back toward the door we came through, then swiveled and propelled myself ahead again. I caught up with Pam, and we walked side-by-side for several steps.

"Where is it?" Pam swiveled her head from side to side at the end of the hallway. "Do you think room two eleven is upstairs?"

"I doubt they have an upstairs in a convalescent home." I scanned the hall for stair signs. "Residents in wheelchairs wouldn't be able to go up and down flights during a fire...or earthquake...or tornado."

"We're not in Kansas, Dorothy." Pam scratched her head. "But you're right. Room two eleven has to be here somewhere."

"Maybe it's in a different wing."

"I'll ask." Pam scampered down the hall to the nurse's station, me lagging behind.

Allie's chair was empty. To the right of the desk, an older woman sat in a wheelchair. Her snow-white hair had been anchored in place with a pink barrette. I strongly doubted she worked here, despite her proximity to the station. She met our eyes and smiled, resulting in a crinkling in her full face that connected the crow's feet at her eyes to the laugh lines at her mouth. It was an inviting smile.

"May I help you?" she asked, her voice surprisingly strong.

"Can you tell me where room two-one-one is?" Pam asked.

Her pale eyes shifted to the left along another long hallway and her lips turned slightly downward. "What do you want with Jerry?"

"Jerry?" Pam said. "No. We're looking for Silas. Silas Morford."

The woman paused, eyeing us with clear caution. "There's no Silas that lives here."

Surely, this lady, although well-intentioned, had to be mistaken. We now had a name and a room number, as well as a confirmation of both by Sam the realtor. I scanned the area for a staff member or nurse. There, at the far end of the right corridor was a very large, very tan, very bald man in white top and bottom, wielding a mop.

I raced his direction, footsteps slapping on the wet

floor.

The man turned. "Careful, ma'am," he said. "Floor's mighty wet."

I slid to a stop just in front of him, leaving me teetering. Reaching out, I braced my hands against the most solid surface available: his chest. His ample, well-developed chest. I could feel his strong pecs just below his shirt.

"Oh!"

I righted myself and jerked my hands back to my sides. Then I cocked my head back to meet his eyes. He was tall—maybe six-six and solid muscle. "Sorry," I said.

"No problem." He swished the mop inside the bucket, loosening the strands, his biceps bulging. "Where's the fire?"

"No fire," I said. "I'm looking for a resident, Silas Morford. He's in room two-eleven."

He faced me, revealing a name tag just above his heart: *Antonio*. "Who?"

I repeated myself.

Antonio scratched his head, again making his upper arms bulge. Just below his sleeve the tattooed image of a pair of breasts shimmied. "We don't have a Silas. But room two-eleven's just down the hallway. Turn left at the nurse's station where Hazel's sitting."

"Hazel? You mean the lady in the wheelchair?"

He smiled, revealing a too-perfect set of teeth. They had to be dentures. "She's our unofficial greeter when staff are on break. Not bad at her job, either."

I thanked him, and noting the still-wet floor, tip-toed back down the hallway to Pam.

Pam winked as I approached. "Nice catch back

there. If I didn't know you better, I'd think you stumbled into him on purpose."

I rolled my eyes, thanked Hazel, and pulled Pam alongside me. "Let's go. Antonio says there's no Silas there. But someone in room two-eleven has to know something."

"So you're on a first name basis with Mr. Clean already?"

I yanked her arm. "Come on, you."

A few steps later, we were at the doorway of room two eleven, peering in. I'm not sure what I expected to see, but this wasn't it.

Chapter 17

A smallish man in a large motorized wheelchair sat at a child-size plastic-coated table. He had salt-and-pepper hair, which seemed surprising at his age, and the delicate, nearly translucent skin of the elderly and the newly born. When he turned to face us, he smiled, his blue eyes twinkling.

Pam entered first, extending her hand. "Hi. My name is Pam. This is my friend Jan."

The man took her hand, but instead of shaking it, he flipped it over so that Pam's wrist lay exposed. Gently, he bent down and kissed it. "*Enchanté*," he said, before looking up at me.

Reluctantly, I proffered my hand. He repeated the gesture, leaving a minor amount of spittle that oozed into my palm. I smiled but wiped my wrist on the back of my pants. It wasn't just old people's spit that bothered me—it was anyone's.

"How do you ladies do?" He motioned for us to sit.

"Fine," Pam drew a chair from the corner of the room and sat. "We're looking for Silas Morford."

"*C'est moi*," he said. "What can I help you with?"

I perched on the edge of the only sitting surface left—the bed—and stared at him. Here he was, in his ninety-two-year-old flesh. How could everyone not know he was here?

"We're the new owners of the Craftsman you just

sold," Pam said.

Silas didn't speak, but the muscles just below the slack skin of his jaw hardened slightly. "Yes. How can I help you?"

"We're doing a little research." Pam's words bounced out of her mouth, a clear indication she held her true motive back.

"And?"

"Since you've owned the home twice, we're wondering what renovation projects you've already done. We want to restore it to its original glory. Maybe you could give us some tips." She rested her right elbow on the armrest and braced her chin on her fist. The chair squeaked in response.

She appeared relaxed. I, however, could feel my heart thundering in my chest like a Midwest electrical storm. Something about misleading the elderly felt not only disrespectful, but nearly evil. I pasted a smile on my face.

Silas's eyes shifted quickly to me and then back. "Of course." He settled into the wheelchair, adopting the pose so many old folks do as they begin a long story. "My stepbrother sold me the property in the seventies. I did a little work to it at that time. When his stepson, my nephew, graduated from college, I sold the property to him. He allowed me to continue to live there until I came here. He didn't do much to the house, either, is my understanding."

He paused long enough to make me question if he were going to continue.

"Honestly, trying to renovate a home of that workmanship can't be done. You can never replicate the original handiwork. Besides being almost impossible to match surfaces and wood types, you'd pay a fortune if you could find the materials." He paused again before continuing. "Then, you'd have to find a master-level craftsman who could mimic the style. Nearly impossible. It's best to make it your own in other ways. Leave the old stuff alone and build additions. That's what we did. That's what I'd recommend to you as well."

Pam's question came a split second later. "So how did the house come back into your possession?"

Silas cleared his throat. "My nephew passed away a few months ago. He willed the home back to me."

"Didn't he have a wife? Or kids? Maybe a cousin or niece or nephew?" Pam's questions bubbled up and spilled out of her mouth without filter.

Silas's demeanor changed. When he spoke, his voice had become raspy. "I appreciate your...concern. But I don't see how that is any of your business. The home has been conveyed correctly each time, including this time. You now own it."

Pam remembered her manners. She pulled back and apologized.

Silence filled the room before a trio of fully ambulatory women padded in. All sported tunics: one bright red, another orange, and the last a striking pink. More interestingly, each wore lipsticks to match. Black leggings and flat-heeled shoes completed their attire. What stood out most about their appearance, however, was their teased and bleached blonde hair that rose atop their heads in a style reminiscent of the '60s beehive. That, and the scent of roses they'd doused themselves in before arriving.

Silas flashed them a wide, toothy grin. "Ladies.

You've arrived! Is it time for our bridge tournament already?"

The women took turns glaring at Pam and me. Clearly, they didn't appreciate the disruption we'd caused.

Finally, the tallest one spat words from her fuchsia-tinted lips. "We didn't realize you had *company* when we traipsed all the way over here from Willows."

"Never you mind, Margaret," he said, his tone congenial. "These ladies were readying themselves to leave."

Margaret glared our direction, her mouth puckered as if holding a lemon.

Pam and I rose at once. Clearly, Silas wanted us gone, with or without answers to our questions. That in itself seemed suspicious, and a little intimidating, at least to me. I gulped, forcing myself to remain calm and not run straight to the Kia.

"I shall bid you both *adieu.*" He blew kisses our way. The sweet little old man had returned.

Pam and I said our goodbyes, then slipped between the ladies and out the door. Just as we turned the corner, I heard Margaret ask, "Well, well. Looks like you've been doing some flirting, haven't you, Jerry?"

Chapter 18

Pam and I met each other's eyes as we race-walked down the hall, but we didn't break stride. We passed the nurse's station and picked up speed once we were outside. Pam didn't even crack any jokes as we passed Antonio, who was replacing bulbs in the lights that lined the sidewalk. Once in the parking lot, we broke into a run, locking ourselves in the Kia before exhaling.

"What on earth is going on?" she asked. "Why did he tell us he was Silas and the rest of them call him Jerry? And why doesn't anyone know him as Silas except for the realtor and us?" She paused for a breath. "And man, what did that guy eat and drink to make him look that good at ninety-two?"

I laughed, feeling an immediate release in my shoulders. Being in there, quizzing the elderly, had rubbed me the wrong way. I was glad to be back in my own familiar territory.

"I can't tell if it's just a strange set of circumstances or if it's suspicious," I said. "On the one hand, some people have nicknames. Or they go by their middle names. On the other, if he goes by different names with different people, there must be a reason for it."

"And the reason may be because he's hiding something." Pam snapped her seat belt into place. "And given that there's a dead body in the house he used to own, I bet he's hiding a lot."

I revved the Kia's engine and followed the exit arrows through the lot. "I don't want to assume anything, but I don't want to ignore facts, either."

Pam shuddered. "Don't be so logical. This is some weird shit." We merged onto the freeway and she added, "Let's stop and get some food. We can talk over everything we know then. Maybe there are more clues in the printouts. We need to bounce everything off one another."

"Good idea." I scanned exits for coffee shops or grocery stores, tummy rumbling. "Breakfast and a cup of tea will calm us down and help us think straight."

Fifteen minutes later, in a strip mall coffee shop, we settled into easy chairs. We quenched our thirst with fruity herbal iced tea and filled our tummies by sharing a banana and slice of low-fat cinnamon bread. Throughout our gobbling and slurping, we discussed our options. Should we keep the multiple names and family relationship to ourselves? Or should we call Daniels immediately to tell him what we'd discovered?

Then it hit me. "Pam!" I set my glass onto its coaster. "Give me those printouts on the county records."

Pam licked her fingers clean and dug the papers out of her purse. "What are you looking for?"

I scanned down the short list of owner names. There it was: Gerald Jones. I slapped the paper down and scooted it toward Pam.

"Gerald Jones." I pointed to the name.

Pam shook her head. "So?"

"*Ger*-ald Jones. *Gerald*."

Pam frowned and cocked her head. Slowly, her

mouth opened as realization poured in. "Oh! Wait! Gerry. *Gerald* is *Gerry*! All this time, I've been thinking Jerry with a 'J.' But it's not. It's Gerry with a 'G.' "

"Exactly."

For a moment we simply stared at each other. True, it could be yet another coincidence. But it was quite a coincidence, given that they were brothers, or stepbrothers. But why would one person pretend to be two people?

Pam's eyes grew wide and she clasped a hand over her mouth. "Are you thinking what I'm thinking?"

"That depends. Are you thinking that Silas Morford killed Gerald Jones and stuck his body in the aquarium to hide the evidence? That he then took over his name for some reason?"

"Exactly. Or, Gerald Jones killed Silas Morford," she said. "And Gerald took over Silas's name."

I glanced over the docs again. It would be impossible to know who killed whom from the dates listed. "But why kill your own stepbrother?"

"Beats me. Why does anyone kill anyone? According to all the crime shows, it's usually money." She frowned. "The house is one source of money, but not enough to kill over, right?"

"But you're talking from the point of view of someone who would never kill anyone else." I closed my eyes, imagining that frail old man wielding a weapon. I refocused my gaze on Pam. "He's someone who did. Maybe it started out as anger. Then after one killed the other, the remaining one took the house."

Pam's eyebrows rose higher than usual. "That's one way to keep a secret."

I nodded.

"Wait," Pam said. "But who helped him? If the aquarium took two people to build and install, and one of them is in it, that leaves only one." She slapped her hand on the table. "Thaddeus!"

I scanned the printouts again and did a little mental math. Thaddeus would have been young—maybe fifteen. "I don't see him helping in any way due to the family relationship or his age. The dead man would be his dad or his uncle."

"Stepdad, or step-uncle," Pam corrected me.

"Oh. Right."

Pam slid the paper between the two of us and we reread the information. "What if someone promised him a house in exchange for his help?"

I shook my head. "I don't know. Would a fifteen-year-old care about a house?"

She leaned back. "Let's go back to the start. Gerald signs over—or more likely his signature is falsified—to Silas, right?"

"Right."

"Silas takes ownership of the house and entombs Gerald in the closet during the remodel."

"Right."

"Thaddeus, Gerald's son, also Silas's nephew, may or may not have helped Silas entomb Gerald."

"Right."

Pam drew a diagram of the relationship on a napkin. "I know what you mean about Thaddeus. Too young. But it is fishy that he was given the house later. It could have been a payment."

"Or maybe extortion," I added. "Or maybe Thaddeus had nothing to do with it and Silas felt guilty for killing Thaddeus's dad. Guilty enough to will the victim's son the house."

Pam shivered. "Ick."

"Icky, yes. But possible."

"And repulsive. Cray-cray level repulsive." She paused a moment before continuing. "Then again, people have weird ideas about morality. And kids can be talked into anything by an important adult. Who knows? Maybe the whole thing was an accident."

"This all sounds very Shakespearean. Twists and turns…which is how it stayed hidden for so long."

"I think we should call Daniels," said Pam.

"I think you're right."

She nominated me to call and I happily agreed. I dialed his cell. Part of me wanted to hear his voice. Another part wanted to run as far away from the warm fuzzies I got when near him as my solid thighs would carry me. These feelings made me feel guilty. Like I was cheating on Jim. Or breaking my marriage vows. I sighed.

I wasn't completely over the marriage yet. Or, more likely, I wasn't over the divorce.

Would I ever be?

"Good morning, Ms. Weatherly." Daniels's voice interrupted my thoughts. His tone was pleasant, and I imagined him sitting at a desk strewn with paperwork. "What's up?"

"Good morning," I replied. "Pam and I have something to, uh, tell you."

"Hmmm…could it be that you're interfering in my investigation?" His voice conveyed nothing. He didn't sound irritated or happy.

Heat flushed my cheeks. How would he know we'd

been to the ECC? Is that what he considered *interfering*? Oh, boy.

"Um…" I began, "well…" I fumbled with my words, then gulped and plowed forward. "What do you mean?"

"Seems you two have the same questions for Mr. Morford that I had," he replied. "Can't say that I blame you. If it were my house, I'd probably do the same thing—try to get some answers, maybe speed up the investigation."

"It's not that we don't trust you to do your job," I stammered. "It's just, uh…" I looked to Pam for support. She mouthed the word *curiosity*. "We're just very curious."

Daniels cleared his throat. "Come into the station. We'll share what we know."

Apprehension toyed with my emotions. It was as if I were half-kindergartener who'd been sent to the principal's office, and half-sixth grader assigned to square dance with a cute boy. My body filled with prickly anticipation.

"What time do you want us to come in?"

"This afternoon's good. Maybe one o'clock?"

"Let me check with Pam." I held the phone away from my mouth and updated her. She nodded enthusiastically.

"We'll be there."

He recited the address, and after I read it back, he said, "Looking forward to it."

That time I actually did giggle. Quickly, I ended the call.

"Oh, sister." A full-tooth smirk formed on Pam's face.

"What?"

Pam folded the banana peel over and placed it atop a napkin. "You know what I mean."

I did. I just wasn't ready to admit to it. To her or to myself. Instead, I changed the subject. "We should make a list of everything we know." I drew a paper napkin from the holder and a pen from my purse. "That way we won't get tongue-tied."

Pam shot me a look. "I would think you would like that."

"What are you talking about?"

"Getting tongue-tied with him."

My whole body warmed. "Pam!"

"Don't 'Pam!' me," she said, grinning. "I call it like I see it."

I pushed my back into my chair and folded my arms in front, fully aware my small act of defiance would get me nowhere. "I can't help that I have a little crush. It's harmless."

Pam laughed. "I haven't heard that word since junior high."

"What? Crush? Or harmless?"

Pam eyed me, stirring a few grains of sugar into her tea. "What do you like about him?"

I thought a moment before answering. I didn't really know anything about him. All I knew is that he'd been kind and patient...and had gorgeous eyes. "I think it's just a feeling," I said. "Kind of like..." My words trailed off. I couldn't, wouldn't liken it to when I met Jim the first time. How could I compare someone I'd just met and knew nothing about to the man I had been married to for ten years? And how could I compare someone I had a crush on to someone I had fallen out of love with?

I shook my head. "Dunno," I said. "He's just nice. It's been a long time since I've had an actual conversation with a man."

Pam set her cup on the table and tilted her head to one side. "The first time I met Marcus I knew, absolutely knew, I'd marry him."

"Really?"

Pam nodded. "That was probably my downfall. I should have ignored my gut...or rather my loins. I should have listened to my mother."

Despite all of our late-night talks during the separations, I'd never heard this story...not even when copious amounts of wine had been consumed. "What did your mom say?"

"She told me not to marry him." Pam laughed, but it held no humor, only irony. "She said that a man who loves women the way he loved me—flowers every date, candy, you know..." She rolled her hand, indicating excessiveness. "She said he won't stop at just one woman. Mom said it's best to look for a man who doesn't chase too hard—isn't too forward—doesn't make you feel like you're the only one in the room. She warned me about men like that—said they practice making women feel special. And you know what they say about practice."

She was right. Marcus had always been a huge flirt. When his attention focused on a woman, everything else seemed to disappear. To me, it had seemed staged, like Marcus had an act he performed whenever he wanted something. I'd never found him appealing...or even likeable. When we got together as couples, it was always Pam I was happy to see. Still, I'd kept my dislike of Marcus to myself all these years and would continue to do so. It wouldn't help Pam to know my feelings about him, and it would only hurt her.

"She was right," Pam said. "I'm glad I don't have a daughter who'll make the same mistakes."

Her words tugged at my heart. I hated to see her in pain. I wanted to tell her she wasn't to blame. Assure her Marcus was an asshole who didn't deserve her.

But I couldn't. She had a child with him, and he would always, *always*, be a part of her life...and more importantly, he'd always be a part of Gabe's life. Nothing could, or would, change that.

I reached across the table and patted her hand. "I'm sorry Marcus and Jim hurt us," I said. "But I'm glad we married them because that's how we got our babies. It's also how I met you."

Pam's eyes held a sadness that she rarely acknowledged. "I know." Her words had softened. She patted my hand atop hers, and I used my left hand to sandwich hers like kids with a baseball bat vying to see who'd go to bat first.

We both laughed, and the mood lightened.

"Okay," she said, "let's start that list of clues. We'll be seeing your boyfriend soon enough."

Chapter 19

With the notes of our research and observations in one hand, I strolled through the double glass doors of the police station, Pam a step behind. The jittery feeling of being sent to the principal's office hadn't disappeared, but neither had the girlish anticipation of seeing Daniels again. It all served to make me feel awkward and out of place, despite my bravado.

"May I help you?" The woman behind the tall wooden counter peered down at us. She had very long eyelashes and a severe braid twisted securely at the base of her neck. Above one breast her name tag read: M. Masters.

I angled my head upward, something I rarely have to do. "We're here to see Sergeant Daniels."

Pam placed her hands on the counter's edge like a small child at a candy shop. "He's expecting us."

M. Masters slid a clipboard across the counter. "Sign in."

Pam and I scrawled our names and slid it back.

"Have a seat," Masters said. "I'll let him know you're here."

We did as we were told, perching atop a hard metal bench, far below Masters's eye level. Neither of us said a word as we waited.

A few minutes later a side door buzzed and she appeared in the doorway. She waved. "I'll show you back."

A loud buzz erupted as the door closed again. Masters started down the hallway and we followed in single file. Despite her height—somewhere between Pam and me—she filled the space with her presence.

The tomb-like corridor couldn't have been less inviting. Stark, decor-less, harsh light. But we marched, following Masters's navy polyester uniform. Her footsteps were soft, despite the weight of her utility belt and weapons at her hips. Our own shoes slapped the linoleum, the echoes bouncing off the blank walls. At the end, she stopped and pointed to the right.

"See that door near the end that's open?"

We nodded.

"That's his office." She turned on her heels and headed back the way we'd come. "He'll see you out," she called out over her shoulder.

Pam and I padded down the hall, me clutching the list we'd prepared. We slowed as we approached, then poked our heads into Daniels's office. He sat behind an old laminate-topped, too-small desk, typing away at a laptop computer. He paused to motion us in. The scent of burned coffee filled the air.

"Have a seat," he said. "I'll be finished with this report in a minute."

We sat in mismatched molded plastic chairs, one orange, one avocado green, in front of his desk and waited. Plaques and certificates of commendation hung on the walls on each side of his desk. To the right, one recognized his contributions to the K9 unit, another honored his volunteer efforts in the Boys and Girls Club of Pierce County. Framed diplomas celebrated his graduations from Franklin College and Central

Washington University with degrees in Criminal Justice and Law and Justice. On the left, plaques congratulating him on five, ten, and fifteen years of service provided a timeline of his work with the Rainier Police Department. The name on each read: Anker "Dan" Daniels.

I studied the walls, especially the pictures of him accepting awards. In the first one he must have been somewhere around twenty. Just a kid with big green eyes and blond hair. The next showed a more mature man of around thirty. The smile had refined and his shoulders squared. Confidence shone in his eyes, and his hair had darkened and thinned a little. The last photo reflected a man with wise eyes, a soft crinkling at the corners when he smiled for the camera. He'd put on a little weight—how much was impossible to determine with his bulky vest—and his hair had begun to gray. He still appeared confident, but also humble. He'd probably been in his mid-thirties then. It had been an impressive career so far. And he was still so young. He must be good at his job. Very good.

I compared that last photo to the man before me now, hunched over his laptop. His hair had grayed a little more, but his eyes were as green as they'd been in that first photo. So handsome, so gentlemanly, so...I glanced at his ring finger. No wedding band.

Daniels leaned back, his chair creaking in its mechanism. Startled, I blushed at the direction my thoughts had taken me. I wrangled my attention back to the present moment.

He steepled his fingers and stared at what he'd written. Satisfied, he punched *Send*, lowered the monitor, and pushed the computer to one side.

"So we're all here to compare notes, is that right?" Daniels took a swig of coffee from a mug labeled "World's Greatest Uncle."

I set the list we'd made on his desk and ironed it with my hands. Without ceremony, he picked it up and read over what we'd written. I watched for surprise, but his face revealed no trace of emotion.

"Let's see if I have this straight." He set the list on the desk. "You believe the paneling was completed during a remodel back in the seventies and that John Doe was entombed at that time. You also believe that our John Doe is actually Gerald Jones."

"Yes," said Pam.

"You believe that, due to the weight of the aquarium, the John Doe, and the fluids, that more than one individual had to be involved."

"Yes," Pam repeated.

"You also believe that the former owner, Silas Morford, had something to do with this because he has a nickname that is used by the other tenants at the old folks' home. Is that right?"

Suddenly, I felt very, very silly. We'd allowed our imaginations to run away from us. I got the sense that we had added two and two together and gotten five. Why were we playing at being detectives? We weren't trained. My face reddened, and the heat radiated all the way to my toes.

Pam stared, her face blank. Her mouth opened and closed several times.

It wasn't like her to be speechless, and her quiet served to make me even more anxious. My thoughts raced, my tongue suddenly felt twice its normal size, and I couldn't think of anything to say.

When Pam finally spoke, her words were soft. "When you put it that way, they don't really seem like clues."

Daniels broke into a smile. "To be fair, you never really know what's important until the case is solved. Before that, things that are very important may appear innocuous. Things that are meaningless seem relevant."

"What about the ping-ponging of conveyance?" I said, suddenly braver. "What about quit-claiming the deeds?"

"What about it?" Daniels asked. He leaned back in his chair and focused his attention square on me.

His warm smile unnerved me. He took another drink of coffee. The dark brew inside had to be ice cold. I could see three dark rings inside when he tipped the cup, indicating time spent at each level. He'd been in his office several hours already.

I swallowed and avoided eye contact, staring instead at his chin. I began, stammering only a little. "It seems strange that the, uh, house changed hands back and forth, especially when the, uh, entombing took place during that time frame."

He pulled a manila folder from a stack on his desk and rifled through the papers inside. He pulled out the same parcel history I'd downloaded and looked it over. "The timing is interesting," he said. "But we still need the content analysis. We still don't know exactly when John Doe was laid to rest."

A little air escaped from Pam's and my collective balloon. He was right. It was all circumstantial. It didn't prove anything.

He set the paper down. "The deed transference between Huntington and Morford can be explained by the familial relationship." He shrugged. "Guy inherits a house from his uncle with the condition that the uncle can live in it as long as he is independent. Elderly people do it all the time. It saves on taxes. Then, when the uncle moves to a rest home, nephew moves in and lives there until the end of his natural life. With no heirs, the house reverts back to his only living kin. In this case, it happens to be the individual he inherited it from."

"But why give away a house if you're still going to live there?" Pam asked.

"It's called a life tenancy," Daniels said. "It allows an individual a way to take care of business and live at home as long as possible. This is done all the time with Alzheimer's patients." He winked at us. "This was all news to me, too, by the way. I found the same information interesting and did some digging."

He paused, staring over our heads. Before speaking again, he clasped his hands in front of him. "Here's a scenario: Uncle is sick. No one knows if he's going to make it. He wants to avoid paying taxes. He may also lose his house if he's in a home. He looks up the rules about how long in advance a gift to a family member can be made before someone dies so it's not seen as dodging taxes. He may also be worried about a contesting of his will. So he gifts the house to the kid, with the understanding that he'll continue to live there."

Pam and I looked to each other. Daniels's reasoning was clever, as well as solid.

"Look, Jan, Pam," he said, his tone kind. "I know this is frustrating. We need time to process the evidence. Give us time to investigate. We're doing everything we can to expedite the process…but it has to be done a certain way." He glanced at each of us in turn. "And it's best left to professionals. That means no more interference."

Pam and I nodded dumbly. I knew we shouldn't have been poking our noses into police business.

"Anything else that I can do for you ladies?" He rested his forearms on his desk and leaned toward us.

I chanced meeting his eyes. So warm. I felt pulled closer and pushed away all at once. Discomfort barely described the sensation of being near him.

"Not for me," Pam said, sporting her most devilish grin. "How about you, Janny? Is there anything Sergeant Daniels can *do* for you?"

I glared as best I could with a giggle bubbling up my throat. Surely she wouldn't let on to Daniels that I had a, uh, crush on him. Would she?

"No." I shook my head quickly. "No. We're good to go. Aren't we, Pam?"

Daniels observed the interplay between the two of us, but if he knew what was going on, he didn't show it. Instead he shot me another soft smile with his perfect peach lips.

I shuddered and rose. "Thank you for your time."

"No problem," Daniels replied. "You ladies have a good day."

I led the way, Pam following close enough so that I could hear her quiet chuckling. Once safely inside the Kia I turned to her. "Pam!"

"What?" Pam's voice was as sweet as cotton candy, her eyes wide with feigned innocence.

I squinted in an effort to subdue a nervous tic that had begun at the corner of my left eye. "That wasn't funny!"

"I don't know. It seems like something tickled you."

I allowed myself a short snicker. "Okay. You got me. Just don't—" Before I could finish, my cell phone rang.

"Ooh, that might be your boyfriend," Pam wiggled her eyebrows.

"Shhh!" I covered my cell. "He might hear you."

"You haven't even answered the phone!" Pam burst into laughter and then covered her mouth, muffling the sound.

The number displayed read: *Unknown*. The police department most likely had privatized numbers. I shot Pam a serious look. "Shhh!" and then pressed *Answer*.

"Hello."

"Stay away from Gerry." The voice, although deep enough for a man and obviously filtered through something that muffled her voice, sounded female. The line crackled from the poor connection.

"Excuse me?" My heart leapt into my throat. "What did you say?"

A slight pause ensued as the sounds of scraping came over the line. "You heard me."

My knees weakened and my back froze in place. "Who is this?"

She hung up.

Chapter 20

"What's the matter, Janny?" Pam reached for her seatbelt. "Who was that on your cell?"

I shook my head, holding my phone in front of my face. I stared hard, looking for answers. Within seconds, my screen saver appeared—the girls and me on a mini-hike near Mount Rainier. The caller's threat coupled with the girls' image heightened my anxiety. "I have no idea."

"What'd they say?"

I frowned. "She told me to stay away from Gerry."

"What!" Pam paused before snapping her seat belt in place.

"She told me to stay away from Gerry."

"You mean Silas?" The seatbelt slipped out of her hand and retracted, the metal clasp slapping the car door. "Are you sure? Who was she? Are you sure it was a woman?"

Closing my eyes, I heard the voice again. Raspy and deep and filtered. "She didn't answer me when I asked who she was. But I'm sure it was a woman—with a smoker's voice."

"Why are we supposed to stay away from him?"

"I have no idea."

"Check the caller ID."

I pulled up my call history. "Private."

"Star sixty-nine her." Pam leaned way across the

front seat and hovered over the phone screen.

"Wait. Let's think about this a minute." I set the phone on my lap. "Is it a good idea to chase after someone who just threatened us?"

Pam frowned and eased back into her seat. "Oh, right. It might make her mad."

"Yeah." I felt the worry line between my eyes grow deeper. Despite the suspicious nature of the call, the voice had sounded so old, so informal, I couldn't help but question her motive for threatening us...and what she could actually do to us if we didn't do as she said.

"Have you heard her voice before?" Pam asked. "Who do you think it was? Do you think she was serious?"

"I don't know. It happened so fast. I don't know what to think. On the one hand, who would joke about something like that? And who knows Silas, I mean Gerry, and us well enough to joke around?" I rubbed my head. "There's no logical connection. The only way we know him is as Silas. But no one at his convalescent center knows him by that name. They call him Gerry."

"Okay, let's think logically," she said, placing one hand on each side of her head. "The caller wouldn't necessarily have to know Gerry. She only knows his name. She does, however, know your cell number. Who knows your number and has heard his name?"

The pool of people who knew of Silas or Gerry and my cell had to be tiny enough to be considered a wading pool. Sergeant Daniels and his office knew him as both. Our realtor Sam knew him only as Silas, as did the escrow company.

"I can't think of anyone who would give out my

number," I said. "Daniels wouldn't—I think that's against the law. And Sam wouldn't, either, I don't think. Plus, he only knows him as Silas."

It has to be someone from ECC," Pam concluded. "Someone who heard us asking for him as Silas."

I caught my breath. "Allie!" I gasped. "We gave Allie my cell number."

Pam nodded. "Could have been her. And the ladies from Silas's—I mean Gerry's—room are probably the ones who called." She locked her door. "This is creepy."

I glanced around, half expecting a colorfully clad older woman to jump out from behind a car brandishing a cane or a bedpan as a weapon. "Do you think we should tell Daniels?"

Pam thought a minute before responding. "Definitely not. He'll think we're meddling again. He might also have to file a report, which will only slow things down more."

I hadn't thought about the possibility of this causing yet another wrinkle in the police timeline. "But it's a threat against us, isn't it?"

Pam chewed a nail. "Did they say, 'or else'?"

"No."

"Then it isn't really a threat. And if we stay away from Gerry, or Silas, or whoever he is, nothing will happen. Plus, Daniels will be pretty happy that we're keeping our noses out of it. And, if it was one of the women—my money's on Margaret—I hardly think we need to be afraid of them. What are they going to do? Run us over with their scooters?"

I tried to laugh at the image Pam created but couldn't. Her line of thinking screamed practical and logical, but I had misgivings. The thought of subjecting our children to possible, if not especially probable danger, Daniels had good reason to ask us not to get involved—it slowed his investigation. But he might know something more, something he didn't want to tell us. Or something he couldn't tell us that would jeopardize the case—or even put us in danger.

But the caller, too, wanted us to stay away for some reason, and it couldn't be because we were slowing down the investigation. That would work in her favor. She had to be afraid we would find something that would speed up the investigation. I felt spun around like a loose sock in a dryer.

"Let's get out of here." I inserted the key and revved the engine. "I need to think this over. My gut tells me we should tell Daniels. He might know who it was or be able to track down the person who made the call." I put the Kia in reverse and backed out of my parking spot.

"On the other hand," I said, shifting into drive, "it may be nothing. Maybe it was a prank phone call."

"Did she say your name?" Pam asked.

"No."

"That's a good thing. I think. Right?"

"I don't know. I hope so. The only way we're going to keep everyone happy, though, is to step aside."

We fell silent as we drove toward our condos. I offered to stop for more chocolate therapy, but neither of us was in the mood. What I wanted most was to go home and hide under my blankets.

"I know," said Pam, "let's go to Home Store."

I signaled and merged into the right lane. "Why?"

"We need a project," Pam said.

"But we can't get into the house. And we don't want to put anything on the credit card until we need it, or we'll have to pay more interest."

"This shopping trip is for us."

I shot her a questioning look, but heeded her direction and passed our turn off. I headed downtown. "What's the project?"

"A pass-through door."

I grinned, remembering our earlier discussion of removing the wall between our condos' closets. Installing a pass-through door would take most of the week. It would involve cutting into the wall, possibly rerouting wiring, installing a door and doorknob, plus a little trim work, maybe even a little touchup paint. In all, it would give us a few days off from the weird phone call and our growing list of problems. Most importantly, it would give Daniels some time to work his magic, remove the corpse, and get us back into the flip.

"Great idea." I snagged the first spot near a cart corral at Home Store.

An hour and a half later, with a brand new Sawzall, an unfinished door, and paint, plus screws, we headed back to the Kia.

"We need to hurry," I said, checking the time. "The kids get out of school in half an hour."

It wasn't until we'd loaded the back of the Kia with the bounty and attached the door to the roof rack that we found the note on the windshield.

Stay away from Gerry.

Chapter 21

Pam gasped.

I squinted. The note, a small red bar napkin that had been braced to the window with the wiper blade, had appeared out of nowhere. I stared at the message written in heavy black ink: *Stay away from Gerry*. Those were the same words the woman on the phone had spoken.

Wait! Was she following us?

Immediately, my pulse quickened. I scanned the area for nefarious looking thug types. I saw no one suspicious. In fact, I saw no one at all.

Since the coast appeared clear, I eased out of the Kia, and while keeping the door close to my side, reached across the windshield and grabbed the note. Then I pulled myself back inside, locking the door behind me quickly.

We studied the note. It had been written on one side of the napkin in what appeared to be female writing. Lots of loops and connected lines, but with a reduced mobility that resulted in jagged points at the tops and bottoms of the letters. The reverse of the napkin bore the logo, location, and contact number for *Devil's Wheelhouse Tavern*. Pam and I turned to each other, a cross between concern and confusion etching its way across both of our faces.

"What's the Devil's Wheelhouse?" she asked.

"Evidently, a tavern." I flipped the napkin back and forth studying both sides. "I think it may be time to call Daniels."

"Agreed." She took the note and studied the message and logo as I searched my purse for my phone.

"Wait!" she said. "Why would someone use a napkin with a logo to make an anonymous threat? It doesn't make any sense."

I paused and stared at it again. A heavy marker had been used, and the ink had bled into the fabric, sending spider web-like veins fanning in all directions. Creepy, but illogical.

"Let me see the back again."

Pam unfolded the napkin so we could see all sides at once, then turned it so that the picture was right side up. The logo was simple: a winking devil holding a trident.

"I think someone's pranking us." She shook her head. "But who would kid around like this? And why?"

"I don't know." I fired up the Kia. "But I'm a little creeped out. First a call on my cell, now this."

"Yeah. It's more weird than scary to me. It seems like a lot of effort for a joke. And if someone really wanted to hurt us, they sure as heck wouldn't leave a calling card. They'd want to surprise us."

I checked the clock and shifted into gear. "We can discuss it on the way to the school. I don't want to run to Daniels with every little thing, especially after that last meeting. I'm still embarrassed."

Pam grew thoughtful. "You know, something about this doesn't make sense. The caller was a woman with an older, gravelly voice. The note was written with a shaky hand. But the napkin is from a bar. How many old ladies do you know frequent bars? Especially bars like this appears to be?"

"It is weird." I checked my speed.

Pam chewed a nail. "I still think one of those little old ladies at ECC did this. But I don't get the tavern connection. And how did they get our number? How did they find us?"

I re-played the events in Gerry's room. They had seemed extremely protective of him. "Maybe Margaret likes their happy hour?"

Pam snorted. "I'm thinking maybe so. Even so, a bar like this seems like a bad choice. And it's so far away from Evergreen. It's gotta be at least thirty miles away." She held the napkin to the light of the window, examining all angles. "I hate to say it, but it could be two people. Two people who want us to stay out of their way."

Easing to a stop for a traffic light, I said, "I don't think so. I think it has to be the same person."

"Not if they're in cahoots."

"Cahoots?"

"You know, in it together."

I pondered that possibility until the light turned green again. When the light changed, I accelerated and spoke. "But maybe it wasn't Margaret. Maybe the person who's warning us knows something about the body."

"Wait!"

"What?" My foot hovered over the brake pedal.

"Whoever attached the note to the windshield knows we were at the station," Pam said. "They must have followed us from there to Home Store. How else would they know we were there?"

A heaviness settled over me as I realized the implications. I struggled to breathe. "Okay, let's review. They know we've visited Silas, AKA Gerry. And they know we're in contact with Daniels. What they don't know is what we know about the investigation or the body. The newspapers haven't reported our little surprise houseguest, and I doubt that the officers at the scene have blabbed it all over town."

"Right," Pam said. "When we talked to Gerry, we didn't tell him about the body. We only asked about renovations and Huntington."

My spirits lightened a bit. "And we could have been at the station for all kinds of things—it didn't have to be about the body. So no one knows that we've found the body—besides the police."

"And Sam," Pam added.

She was right. The realtor knew because we'd called him. "Sam wouldn't say anything—it could only slow down the sale of the home. Would he?" I asked.

Pam paused. "I don't know," she replied. "I'd hate to think Sam has anything to do with this, but you never know."

I pondered that a moment. It seemed unlikely, but the whole situation was confusing. "Okay. Hear me out. If the caller was responsible for the body, wouldn't she get out of town? She wouldn't just hang around, threatening us, on the chance that we'd be good little girls and go away. Besides, what good would it do to scare us off? We aren't the police, and we can't arrest her."

"What if she can't leave town because she lives at ECC?"

Good point. It hardly seemed likely that a person

who needed assistance to live would be able to skip town. "But if she's living at ECC, what is she doing following us around in a car?"

Pam shrugged. We were quiet for several minutes, a rarity for us.

Finally, just as I pulled into the school pick-up lane, Pam spoke. "We should call Daniels."

"Agreed. It would make me feel better—just to be on the safe side. We'll call as soon as we get home and the kids are occupied."

I slowed to a stop behind a gold Lexus and allowed the engine to idle. My thoughts wandered from the call to the note. Was Pam right? Did someone follow us to Home Store?

"Oh my God!" I exclaimed, scanning every mirror in the car and swiveling my head around. "Do you think they're following us now?"

Pam inhaled, the breath quick and sharp. She whipped her head left and right, mimicking my moves. "I don't see anyone. But I don't know what or who I'm looking for."

A flurry of worry set my nerves on edge. If someone had followed us, Margaret or someone scarier, she or he would know where my kids went to school. I swallowed against a lump that had formed in my throat.

"Call Daniels," I said. "But be quick. The girls will be out any second."

"Good thinking." Pam began punching in numbers, her cell phone beeping with each jab. A moment later she frowned. "I got his voicemail."

"Leave a message. Don't worry about telling him everything. Just say we need to speak with him." I glanced around again, looking for anyone who might be paying too much attention to us, but saw only a bunch of very tired-looking moms and dads, most wearing sweat clothes. "Tell him it's urgent."

The bell rang and Pam recited both of our cell phone numbers faster than an auctioneer at a foreclosure sale.

"Happy faces," she said, pasting on a smile. "How's this?" She turned toward me.

"Okay." I forced the edges of my mouth up. "Me?"

"Good."

We waited like that until the girls appeared and everyone belted in. We focused on asking questions about their days as we drove.

A block away from the daycare, Pam's cell rang. Daniels. Pam spoke to him, her answers cryptic. "Can we call you back this evening? What's a good time?"

A brief pause followed as Pam's expression grew intense. "That should work. We eat dinner around six o'clock." Pause. "Okay." She hung up and turned to me. "He'll be at your place between seven and eight o'clock."

Before I had a chance to respond, Emily piped up. "Who's coming to our house between seven and eight o'clock tonight?"

I exchanged looks with Pam. How could we keep this secret from the kids? They would see Daniels when he arrived.

"A friend of your momma's," Pam said.

I caught a glimpse of the girls in my rearview mirror.

"Then why did he call your cell phone?" Annie asked.

Pam's eyes widened. She was used to dealing with

toddlers, not curious little girls.

"He's a friend to both of us," I said.

Pam mouthed a quick *thank you*.

The girls stared at one another, their expressions serious. Soon, whispering ensued.

"You ask her." Annie's words were hushed.

"No," replied Emily, her voice a little louder. "You're older. You ask."

"Ask me what?" I parked and shifted out of gear.

Pam jumped out. "Back in a jiffy."

The two conferred behind hands covering their mouths, their voices mere whispers.

"C'mon, you guys." I forced my tone to be light. "What's on your minds?"

The girls continued their stare-down. My money was on Emily not breaking first. She had far more patience—some would call it stubbornness, despite her younger age. Sure enough, just as Pam reached the Kia and buckled Gabe in, Annie started speaking.

"Are you going on a date tonight?" she asked.

Chapter 22

"A date?" I braked, struggling with both the idea and how the girls came up with it.

Pam snorted in laughter.

"No, honey. He's, um, well..." *Police officer* sounded too formal, and *cop* felt inappropriate. *Sergeant* might work, as would *detective*, but that would release an avalanche of questions with answers that were just too complicated for their young ears.

Pam's eyes and mouth widened in unison. "He's...a...a..."

As mothers, we knew instinctively the track our conversation would travel. Still, I didn't want to lie to my kids. It set a bad precedent for their teen years. How could I expect them to be honest with me if I lied to them now? Diversion, however, usually worked in these situations.

"How was your day?" I asked. "Did you have indoor or outdoor recess today?"

"Outdoor," said Emily. "Who's coming to our house tonight?"

I sighed. They would see Daniels. He might even be in his uniform. Honesty would be the best policy, even in this situation. But I'd have to tread lightly. The only thing worse than lying to kids is getting caught in that lie by kids.

"He's a policeman." I shot a reassuring grin via the

rearview mirror. "He's going to ask us some questions about the house that we're fixing up to sell."

"What does he want to know?" Emily asked.

I glanced to Pam for backup. She nodded. It was a mother-to-mother truce that we'd confirm each other's story, even if it meandered into tiny white lie territory.

"He wants to know a little about the history," I said.

Pam piped up. "He wants to ask questions."

The girls' gaze ping-ponged from me to Pam and back again.

"Is he going to buy it?" Annie wanted to know.

"It's too early for that," Pam said. "But that would be awwwweeessssome." She dragged out the word.

"Yeah," I agreed. "We're still making it pretty."

"So he's not your secret boyfriend?" Emily again.

I frowned. *Secret boyfriend?* Where did that come from?

"No. I don't have a secret boyfriend. If I did have a boyfriend, he wouldn't be secret from you guys. I'd want you, both of you, to give him your seal of approval." I smiled broadly.

"Daddy has a secret girlfriend," Emily said. The words had barely fallen from her mouth when Annie shushed her.

Pam looked to me. We had had long discussions on how to handle news of the guys' dating habits. We knew they'd come one day. We'd talked about anger, and we worried that the kids would see things that they shouldn't. We talked about the kids' confusion and how we'd deal with it. We also talked openly about the twinges of jealousy we'd feel if the guys treated their next relationship better than they had treated the ones that they'd had with us.

I couldn't help but be surprised, though. Jim and I had made an informal pact not to bring significant others into the girls' lives until the other was truly significant. Neither of us wanted the girls to see a revolving door of boyfriends and girlfriends.

Wait.

Did this mean she *was* significant?

I took a deep breath, trying hard not to jump to conclusions, and slowed for a yellow light, a sudden feeling of nausea rocking my gut.

After a quick exhale, I asked, "If she's so secret, how do you know about her? Did she visit you last weekend?" I kept my tone casual, but my sights on the girls' responses in the rearview mirror.

A meaningful moment passed as they exchanged terse glances. And then, I understood: The girlfriend wasn't secret to them. The girlfriend was secret from me.

My body felt as though the ground dropped from below my feet and I struggled for breath. Had Jim told the girls to lie to me?

Pam reached over and gripped my arm but continued to face straight ahead at the road before us.

Emily, being only seven, may have forgotten. Annie had probably been trying to save my feelings from being hurt when she shushed her younger sister.

For seconds that felt like an eternity, I waited. Pam began to pat my hand but averted her gaze and stared out her window. My breath grew shallow and my head light. I fought tears.

Still, I waited for an answer.

Emotions boiled up my throat. I couldn't risk

speaking and having my voice crack, so I stayed silent. Sadness pooled as I thought of the girls' secret-keeping burden. Disappointment at Jim for asking them to promise not to tell me about Tiffany or Cindy or Bambi…or whatever the hell her name was. Rage as I forced myself to remain calm, when all I really wanted to do was pick up my cell and give him the tongue-lashing he well deserved.

A sharp beep from the car behind forced me to refocus on the road ahead and steady my breathing. Should I stay silent and pretend I didn't understand? Or should I prompt with more questions and get everything into the open? I could be wrong about what was actually going on. This could be innocent…although I doubted it.

I decided to err on the side of being proactive, and I'd do it in the most gentle way possible. After all, the girls would be exposed to Jim's romantic relationships sooner or later. It was up to us to set the tone.

Let the role modeling begin.

I took a deep breath and began. "Did you meet someone who is important to Daddy?"

Annie shot a glare Emily's way, and Emily buried her face in her hands. Sniffling ensued as she tried not to cry. The scene enflamed my motherly instincts, as well as my fury with Jim. Look what he'd done to our daughter.

Finally, Annie answered, "Kind of."

"I'm sorry, Mommy," Emily cried, tears flowing. "Are your feelings hurt? Daddy said your feelings would be hurt."

Anger spread like wildfire throughout my body. My fingers tingled and my toes burned. I was right.

He'd been keeping secrets, and he'd made the girls accomplices to those secrets. He'd also made them responsible for my feelings.

Very bad daddying. It bordered on abuse, the way I saw it.

How dare he!

I merged into the right lane and slowed the Kia a little. My stomach threatened rebellion and the queasiness oozed upward into my mouth. It tasted sour.

"Do you want me to drive?" Pam whispered.

I straightened my back and shook my head. "I got this."

This was no time to dawdle over anger and hurt and embarrassment. I had to summon the courage to respond appropriately to the girls. Not only did they need to see me being okay with the secret girlfriend, they needed to know they could always tell me what was on their minds. Especially when returning from their dad's house.

"Are you okay, Momma?" Annie asked.

It took every ounce of strength, but I shrugged and replied. "I'm right as rain, girls."

I looked to Pam. Her face reflected complete empathy. Her mouth pulled down at the sides and the crease between her eyebrows deepened. Even her normally upturned nose appeared to sag.

Okay. I wasn't alone. I could do this. I squared my shoulders.

"Mommy and Daddy will make special friends," I said. "You don't have to be afraid to tell me or Daddy anything you want. We're a family. We just don't live together. Not anymore."

"Will we ever?" Emily's voice was soft and low.

"Will we ever what?"

"Will we ever live together, like a family again?" Her big brown eyes reflected desire and doubt all at the same time. Next to her, Annie, too, awaited my answer. I'd never realized this was something they still wondered about.

I really wanted to tell her *maybe*. I wanted to tell her you just never know. But I couldn't plant those seeds of hope when I knew they wouldn't grow. It might be easier on me in the short term, but it would be far harder on them in the long run. Better to be honest now. Better to deal with all of the frustration and sadness that I knew the girls would have to experience…even if it broke my heart, too.

"No," I said. "I don't think we'll ever live together again. But you'll probably have a stepmom." I left out the possibility of having a stepdad. Right now I hated the entire male population and doubted I'd ever let any of them within ten feet of me or my kids.

"They will become part of your family, too," I continued. "It'll be different, but it will be okay."

Pam gave me a low five, her jaw clenched. Whether she was working to control her own anger or stop tears from flowing I couldn't tell. It may have been both. But I couldn't worry about that now. My girls needed me to reassure them that I was okay, and whatever it took, I would let them know I had a glorious life…with, or without, their dad.

"In fact," I added, "it's good if you like those special friends. Stepmoms and stepdads aren't new mommies or daddies. But they'll be there to help you and answer questions. They'll be like extra friends."

Emily peeked through her fingers. She didn't

smile, but her tears had dried. Annie huffed and crossed her arms.

A moment passed in silence before Annie spoke. "Her name is Vanessa. She's really pretty. She has blonde hair. She has a red bathing suit. She wears it all the time."

Oh, Lord. My smile froze in place and my gut lurched. Maybe I didn't want to know about her after all.

Hard as I tried, I couldn't shake the vision of a youngish girl skipping beside Jim: beautiful and wearing a skimpy red bikini that didn't have to hide child-bearing stretch marks because she didn't have any—stretch marks or kids. A new level of emotion had been breached, casting aside anger. Fury has a wicked stepsister, and her name is Jealousy. Pam rolled her eyes so hard I thought they'd fall out.

"Fabulous." I turned back around. The word did double duty. It confirmed I was okay for the girls. It also smacked of sarcasm for Pam's benefit. "Absolutely fabulous. Did she take you swimming?"

"No," said Emily. "We just sat around the backyard while she took a bath in the sun."

This time I didn't need to see Pam's expression because I was sure it had spread across my face as well. Precious. Absolutely precious.

"Cool." I turned on the radio. The awkward moment passed as I tuned to a channel the girls and Gabe would enjoy. Soon, the girls chattered away as though no beans had ever been spilled.

Mission accomplished. Now to work through my feelings…later that night, in my room, where the girls wouldn't have to see me sad.

We arrived home and greeted Moxie. The girls went to their bedrooms, looking for a book both wanted to read but neither had seen in a while. Pam joined me in the kitchen.

"Well, that was horrible," she said.

"I know." I put a hand to my forehead. "It had to happen sooner or later, I guess. I just didn't expect it so soon."

Pam glanced down the hall. "I can't believe Jim asked them to keep a secret from you. It's so wrong…in so many ways."

I filled a glass with fresh cold water from the tap and took a sip, then swallowed. "Maybe he wanted to spare my feelings. It's possible."

"I think you're way too nice." She shifted Gabe from one hip to the other. "No way could I be that nice if I'd just found out Marcus was doing the deed with someone like that." She shook her head. "You handled the girls' questions really well. I admire you so much."

I drained the glass of water in thirsty gulps, enjoying the cool sensation as it flowed down the back of my throat. "Thank you." I strengthened my resolve and refilled the glass.

"I hope I can be that brave when it's Gabe's turn to ask questions." Her words came out positive, but her frown reflected her concern. "Wait. Do you think Marcus has a girlfriend, too?"

I raised both eyebrows and took out a second glass from the counter, pushing it Pam's way. "Probably."

Pam took the glass, sprayed water into it and retrieved a bottle of baby aspirin from the cabinet. She poured a small handful of the pink pills onto the counter, then scooped them into one hand and threw them in her mouth. It was an impressive set of actions, given that Gabe occupied one hand. She swallowed the pills and a gulp of water before speaking. "Do you think Gabe understands?"

"No. I think that by the time Gabe knows what's going on, he will have watched the girls and me settle into these situations." I waved my hands in the air as if erasing her worries. "He'll know everything will be okay. He might even think it's normal."

"I hope so." She drew a finger through small puddles of water on the counter, connecting them. "I really hope so. Are you going to talk to Jim about this?"

"Oh, yeah. We'll be talking about this. But I'm going to wait until I cool down. We've got plenty of problems with the flip to think about besides bad daddying right now."

Chapter 23

At seven o'clock sharp, with dirty dinner dishes still in the sink and my mind far from the troubles of old lady stalkers, the condo doorbell rang.

It had to be Daniels.

Pam answered the door as I checked my reflection in the surface of the microwave. Tired eyes, pale skin. I pinched my cheeks and plumped my hair, then bared some teeth in a makeshift smile and joined the two in the living room. Daniels wore a pair of Levi's, a tan short-sleeve shirt, and a sports jacket over one arm. Casual, but professional. This must be how he dressed for the office when he wasn't in uniform.

The girls' quick steps and Moxie's tip-tapping punctuated my invitation to Daniels to have a seat. The girls stopped short at the end of the hall and surveyed him from around the corner, but Moxie plowed forward. I scooped her up before she could attack Daniels. Her legs continued trotting in the air and she began growl-humming.

"Annie and Emily," I said, motioning them in, "this is Sergeant Daniels."

"Hi, girls." Daniels waved.

"Hi," they replied in unison, still partly hidden by the wall. The room fell silent as the girls nudged one another. Finally, Emily asked, "Do you have a gun?"

Daniels nodded. "Sure do. But it's locked up for

safekeeping right now."

Annie cocked her head and stared at him. "You don't look like a police officer, and we're not supposed to let people in the house just because they say they are police officers. Can I see your badge?"

"Annie," I said. "Sergeant Daniels is a real police officer. He just happens to be wearing street clothes right now."

"You have a very good point. You shouldn't believe anyone unless they're willing to show you their badge." Daniels chuckled. "I'd be happy to show you my badge, if it's okay with your mom?" He looked to me, and my knees went to jelly. I'd have a hard time saying no to anything he asked. My face flushed at the thought.

"Of course."

The girls moved cautiously toward Daniels, who unclipped the badge he wore at his hip, and held it out. Annie studied the badge, but Emily was far more interested in staring into Daniels's eyes. I couldn't say that I blamed her.

A few seconds later, I asked, "Satisfied, girls?"

"Yes," Annie said to me. Then she turned to Daniels. "Thank you for showing me your badge."

"No problem." Daniels reattached it to his belt. "Anytime. And I'm glad you asked to see my identification. If a police officer refuses to show you his or her ID, you should run the other way as fast as your legs will carry you."

The girls sauntered off, clearly pleased with themselves. Before entering the hall, Emily did a quick about-face and saluted Daniels. He kept a straight face, but his eyes twinkled. He saluted her back.

Giggles erupted as they rounded the corner. Moxie's ears perked up. She scrambled to get out of my arms. When I released her onto the floor, she raced after the girls, skidding around the corner.

"Thank you," I said.

"No problem." He settled into the tan recliner and laid his jacket over his lap. "So what's going on?"

"You start." I looked to Pam. I knew if I spoke I'd stammer all over the place. Daniels's presence made me wiggly and giggly. Oh, Lord.

Pam faced him and explained. "We got a call from someone we don't know. She said to stay away from Gerry."

"Gerry? You mean Gerry, AKA Silas Morford?" Daniels brought out his notepad and pen from his jacket.

"Yes."

"Whose cell phone did it come in on?"

"Mine," I said, finding my voice.

Daniels focused his attention on me. "You said, 'she.' How do you know it's a woman?"

"Her voice sounded scratchy and old, but female."

"We think it's Margaret," Pam interjected.

"Who's Margaret?" Daniels's pen hovered over his pad.

"She's one of Silas's friends," Pam said. "But she calls him Gerry."

"And why do you think it's Margaret?"

"Because when we were up there, she and some other women came in, and she was sort of, uh, territorial with Gerry."

Daniels wrote down a few words. "Tell me what you mean."

Pam glanced at me, a non-verbal passing of the ball.

"Well, she seemed to not like the fact that we were there," I said.

Daniels looked up from his notepad. "And you went there to ask questions?"

I frowned. Uh-oh. Yep. We were meddling.

"We just went up to ask questions about the house." Pam's words were matter-of-fact, but she avoided his gaze.

Daniels raised his eyebrows. "Tell me about Margaret."

"We don't know if it was her for sure. I asked for her name, but she wouldn't tell me."

"Callers who are threatening others generally won't." Daniels drew a line across the paper. "Let's start at the beginning. Her voice was gravelly and raspy. Did it sound like a smoker's voice?"

"Yes!" I said, realizing that he was exactly right. "Like a woman who'd smoked for a super long time."

Daniels made a few notes, then repeated, "*A super long time*. So you'd guess she's older than forty, right?"

Right again. Man, this guy was smart. "Probably."

"Could she have been disguising her voice?" Daniels asked. "Speaking through a handkerchief or a sponge, maybe?"

I thought a moment. At the time it had sounded a little muffled, but it also sounded raspy. "I think so. The call was very short. And out of the blue. It's hard to say for sure because it seemed over before it even started."

"I understand." He nodded. "Give me the exact words again."

"*Stay away from Gerry*. That's all." I erased the air

in front of me. "But she didn't say, 'That's all.' She just said, '*Stay away from Gerry.*' "

"Got it. No return number on the screen?"

"No. It read *private*. Since we'd just left your office, I sort of assumed it was you. I thought there was something else you needed to tell us." I couldn't help but flush at the memory of Pam calling Daniels my boyfriend and how I shushed her before answering.

"May I see your phone?"

I fished it out of my purse and gave it to him.

He scrolled through the calls made and received. We waited, me hoping he didn't accidentally pull up any texts to or from Pam. There were many less than flattering messages about our exes on our thread. I made a mental note to delete our history.

"Did you try calling the number back?"

"We thought about it," Pam answered, "but we didn't know if we should. We thought it might be meddling."

"Appreciate that. Let's give it a try, shall we?" He jabbed at the phone a few times and held it to his ear. My heart jumped into my throat. What if she answered? What would Daniels say? What if she thought it was me calling?

A split second later, he ended the call. "As expected. No answer. No voicemail setup." He handed my phone back to me. "That doesn't mean much, unfortunately."

"What now?" Pam asked.

Daniels pocketed his notepad. "Not much. Unless you can think of something else."

"We also got a note," I said.

"A note?" Daniels cocked his head. "Tell me about

170

the note."

Pam retrieved the small red napkin. Daniels took it, reading it a few times while flipping the napkin back and forth. His eyebrows rose. "Devil's Wheelhouse." He folded the napkin once and asked, "Can I keep this?"

"Of course."

"What else?"

Pam shrugged. "That's all."

"So you think it was Margaret?" He rested his elbow on the arm of the chair and his chin on his fist.

His posture made me think he spent a lot of time listening to people. Welcoming, encouraging, nonjudgmental listening. Witnesses probably spilled a lot of beans in his presence. It made me admire him all the more. It also made me realize we weren't getting special treatment. A tiny feeling of deflation spread throughout my body, surprising me.

Pam answered. "It's the only person who makes sense."

"Let's think about this." Daniels said. "Who else knows you and Silas, AKA Gerry?"

"Our realtor, Sam," I began, "and the people in his office and the escrow agency."

"Which realty company is he with?"

"Rainier Mountain Realty." Pam grabbed her cell and scrolled through her contacts. "I've got his number right here."

Daniels recorded the information then turned to me again. "Who else?"

"No one," said Pam, "except your office."

He frowned and scribbled a little more. "How about the neighbors over near the Craftsman? Have you met any of them?"

"No one," Pam said. "That was our first day."

"What about your friends, or fellow contractors, even supply warehouses?" he asked. "Have you spoken with anyone not related to the house about the project? Maybe your ex-spouses?"

I could have slapped my forehead. Of course. We'd spoken to nearly everyone important to us about the house, plus a lot of people at the local Home Store. "Our folks know, and our kids, of course. They could have easily told their friends, who told their parents."

"All of our family know, too. Our husb—I mean, exes, do too," added Pam.

"Oh! We've also talked to carpet people, and some sales associates at do-it-yourself stores," I said. "But I doubt we ever mentioned the address or names, except for ordering purposes."

"Maybe a few people at our kids' school and at the daycare," added Pam, the lines between her eyebrows creasing deeper. "Wow. I guess there's a lot of people who know bits and pieces."

Daniels jotted notes. "Do any of the people you've spoken to have any ties to the house? Maybe they lived in the neighborhood at some point? Maybe their kids play with some kids from that neighborhood? Anything at all?"

I racked my brain. I couldn't recall anything—no nuance or surprising connection.

Pam replied, "I got nothing. Jan?"

I shook my head. "I'm not sure I would have realized anything that anyone had said as being odd. At the time, it wouldn't have seemed strange, more like a coincidence. Even a happy coincidence. Now, I feel more than a little creeped out. I hadn't realized how many people know about our flip."

Pam nodded. "We can call you if we remember anything."

"That's a good idea," Daniels said. He gave a little *ahem*, then continued. "Last question: Do either of you feel afraid?"

Pam and I sought out each other's eyes. In hers, I saw a little fear and a lot of false bravado. I felt the same way but didn't want Daniels to think we couldn't handle our own lives.

"A little," I confessed, "but nothing we can't handle. Right, Pam?"

Pam nodded a little too vigorously. "Right." She pointed to the hall closet and then the supplies on the floor behind the couch. "We're installing a pass-through door. If there's an emergency, we can get to each other, and the kids, lickety-split. That makes us both feel safer."

"We'll also have two lines of vision through the peepholes in case anyone knocks on either of our doors," I added. "And we always keep our doors locked."

Daniels got up and examined the closet we'd planned to renovate into a connecting doorway. "You're going to do this yourselves?"

Nodding, I said, "Yes. We've done things like this before."

He shot us a smile. "That's pretty clever." He returned to the living room. "And it's a great idea. It's good to see people taking initiative to keep themselves safe. As much as we'd like to be everywhere, we've got our hands full with major crimes."

I couldn't help but beam. He thought we were clever!

"So," he said. "Do you have any more questions for me?"

I tried hard to think of any questions that might keep him in my living room for a few more minutes but came up short. "No."

"Nope," Pam added.

"Okay," he said, "Give me a call if anything pops up."

I swung the door wide. Just as Daniels crossed the threshold, Pam cleared her throat. "Do you think we're safe—us and our kids?"

Daniels contemplated the question. When he answered, his manner was straight to the point and unapologetic.

"I think you're okay, so long as they don't know your address. This was designed to intimidate you. If the caller had wanted to hurt you, there would be no warning. Warnings put victims on edge which eliminates the element of surprise."

He shrugged into his sports coat. "Then there's the issue of the napkin. No one leaves a calling card if they want to stay anonymous. I think this little 'warning' was impulsive and not thought through. The person may even regret it now." He paused a moment and met each of our eyes in turn. "However, if you know who it is, or even *think* you know who it is, I would recommend an order of protection. That requires a name, however. So no filing yet.

"I'll poke around a little. Phone records can take forever." He held up the Devil's Wheelhouse napkin. "I'll check this out. People don't want to talk to cops.

But it's worth a shot."

Daniels paused a moment, glancing around the hall. "If you hear from mystery woman again, call me immediately. The same goes if you think of anything else—a connection, maybe. It may mean something's shifted. It may even have something to do with the investigation."

"Okay." Pam huddled with me in the doorway.

Daniels took a few strides down the condo corridor, his steps light on the carpet, before turning around. "Keep your eyes and ears open and your doors closed and locked."

He winked, my heart skipped a beat, and he was gone.

Chapter 24

We spent the next week holed up in the condo. We unhinged both of our closet doors, cut through the adjoining wall, then drywalled, taped, textured, and painted. Finally, we reset the doorframe into what was once the back of our closet and set the new door in place. Occasionally, Moxie wandered over and sniffed our progress. She always returned to her spot in front of the fireplace, however.

Once the structural components were finished, we installed brass coat hooks at kid reach level and an overhead shelf along both walls. On the floor we set wooden shoe racks. Standing back, we admired our efficient use of our mutual closet space.

"It needs light," Pam said.

"Agreed. I'll pick up a few battery operated, push-button lights that we can stick to the walls."

"Great idea." She exhaled gustily. "I think it's time for lemonade."

We plopped onto the couch in our work clothes, glasses of sweet lemonade in hand, Moxie between us. It was Friday afternoon, and still no word from the caller...or Daniels.

"This has been a good week." Pam swirled the ice cubes in her glass. Happy tinkling noises filled the room. "Even if we didn't see the light of day aside from taking the kids to school and daycare, it's still been a good week."

I reviewed our accomplishments. The girls had each gotten an A on their reports, and their papers had been dutifully attached to the refrigerator alerting the world of their achievements. Moxie hadn't had an accident in the house, despite the change in living environment and increased space to explore. And Pam and I had completed a fantastic addition to our condos that would enable us to rewall and sell them separately, or sell as one big unit for larger families. It had been a very good week.

"I'll drink to that." I raised my glass and clinked hers. I guzzled the tangy drink and wiped a few beads of sweat from my forehead. "I can't believe we have time to spare before picking up the kids."

"Neither can I." Pam sat quietly a moment. When she spoke again, her words were slow and measured. "I have an idea, and I want you to hear me out."

I paused, glass at my lips and stared at her over the rim. That's a phrase people use when they have a very bad idea that they want to convince you is a very good idea. "What?"

"Well," she began, "what if on the way to pick up the kids, we drove by the Devil's Wheelhouse?"

"Why?" I rested my glass on my work capris, creating a circular impression of condensation just above my knee.

She set her glass on a coaster on the coffee table and faced me. "I'd like to see who's there. I've been trying to figure out the connection between us and Gerry all week. I keep coming up with zilch."

I'd been puzzled, too. How did the caller get our phone number? Why did she even care if we met with

Gerry?

Then again, why would we poke at a hornet's nest again…especially when it appeared that the hornets were asleep?

"I don't know," I said. "What good would it do, even if we figured out the connection?"

"It would tell us if Margaret's really behind all of this. If we're right, we will know we don't have to be afraid." Pam bent her legs and rested her chin on her knees. "It could also help solve the case, which would be great since we haven't heard from your boyfriend all week. I'm getting itchy to start work on the house."

I frowned, uncertain. I had to admit I wanted to know if it was Margaret, too. My gut said the caller and note-writer couldn't have been serious, for all of the reasons Daniels had mentioned. But when it came to my kids' safety, I never took any chances. Never had and never would.

Pam must have sensed my flip-flopping. "How about this: We drive by and scope out the cars and the building. We won't go in. We won't ask any questions. We just look around. How does that sound?"

I glanced at the clock and out the dining room window. Plenty of time and sunshine streaming in. Not a cloud in the sky. And, with the closet project finished, spare time on our hands.

"It won't be dark for hours," Pam reminded me. "We won't even get out of the car."

Hmmm… Maybe the sense of accomplishment we both felt over the pass-through had made us bold. Maybe we had gone a little stir crazy in the condo all week. Maybe we just wanted to solve this mystery and get back to making money. But if Pam were game, so was I. I wanted to crack the case myself. And, I wanted to close the door on my worries.

My pulse skipped a beat realizing that Pam and I would be taking the reins back on our own lives, just like we did with the pass-through door. If our little drive-by did result in information, we'd also have a reason to see Daniels again.

I drained my glass and slipped on my shoes. "Let's go."

Pam's eyes widened. "Really? Okay! I'll grab my purse." She jumped up. "And, I'll go through our new doorway to get it."

She danced a little jig, making me laugh, and disappeared through the new pass-through. After I set our glasses in the sink and grabbed a soundly sleeping Moxie, we piled into the Kia.

Pam punched "Devil's Wheelhouse" into her cell phone map app, and we set off into the area of town that bordered the army base. The four-lane road gave way to two lanes. Another mile and the asphalt became pocked with potholes. The buildings grew shabbier and the streetlights larger.

"How much farther?" I asked. "This area's giving me the willies—even in broad daylight."

Pam glanced at her cell phone's screen. "The app says one more block." She squinted through the windshield. "But I don't see anything remotely resembling a restaurant or bar."

I checked the odometer. I'd give this little escapade one-tenth of a mile more, then hang a U-turn and admit defeat.

"There." Pam pointed to the right. "There it is."

I followed her trajectory. Sure enough. There,

sandwiched between the road and the freeway a vacant lot away, stood the Devil's Wheelhouse.

It appeared to be an old building painted to look like a boat, maybe sixty feet long and with its hull buried into the ground. The exterior was black and the door red. Circular-shaped peephole windows dotted the facade. The gangplank leading to the door had been fashioned out of ropes and wooden steps that appeared to be recently installed. At the top of the stairs, two red tridents framed the entrance.

On one end, the open bow held a few plastic molded tables and chairs in yellows and oranges and a few striped Sunbrellas. The other end, the stern, looked like a big black box with red, orange, and yellow flames leaping up its sides. The sign above the entry door read: *Good Food*. Despite its name and dubious location, it felt welcoming.

"Okay," I said. "I'm going to drive by as slowly as possible without attracting any attention. You look at every window and car and tell me what you see."

"Got it." Pam began reporting each person, place, and thing. "Yellow Toyota. Doesn't look familiar. White sedan. Never seen it before. Blue truck. Nope." She twisted in her seat to stare in the windows.

"A couple of guys with buzz cuts. They're wearing fatigues. Or at least the top half of fatigues."

"What else?"

"I can make out a bar in the background. Lots of bottles of booze."

The driver in the car behind me revved his engine, so I sped up and hung a right onto the next paved road. The car whizzed past. I executed a perfect three-point turn, then pulled out on the main street, cruising at a snail's pace. From this direction, we could see the gravel parking lot at a better angle. About ten cars had parked at odd angles with no lines to provide guidance. Mostly trucks filled the space, but a few smaller nondescript cars with body damage ranging from mild to significant had squeezed between.

"See anything I missed?" Pam leaned across me to stare out my window.

"Not at all. But keep your eyes peeled. I've gotta watch the road."

"Roger that."

I laughed. Being on heightened awareness had made us both giddy. I focused on the road ahead. Pam continued her play-by-play commentary.

"Woman. Tray in hand. She's delivering drinks in beer steins. I think it's beer."

"Good guess, Sherlock." I laughed. "It's probably happy hour. Do you see any more customers?"

"I'm looking, I'm looking." As we eased past the bow once again, she continued. "Nothing. A few people hanging out, looking like they're enjoying a cold one on a hot day. Nothing else. Everyone looks, I don't know, normal."

At the next light, Pam asked, "Can we drive by one more time?"

I glanced at the clock. We had time. Leaving now, with so little information, seemed like failure. When the light changed, I hooked the steering wheel left and reversed our path. One more sweep.

The bow appeared again, and then the gangplank and door, and finally the stern, but Pam saw nothing new.

"Wait." She motioned to the parking lot entrance.

"Turn in."

I hesitated, scanning the area. Nothing but trucks and SUVs in the lot. But from there, we'd have a better vantage point to see inside the tavern from the secondary entrance. I flashed my blinker and pulled in, driving slowly past the cars.

"Slower!" Pam whipped out her cell phone and snapped pictures of the cars.

"What are you doing!" My words came out hushed, in direct opposition to my blood pressure. "Someone's going to see you!"

"I want something to give to Daniels. Anything would help, right?"

I glanced around, on the lookout for anyone noticing us paying too much attention to their vehicles. Even I'd be annoyed at someone taking photos of my car and license plate, and I had nothing to hide. I focused on driving as if looking for a spot to park.

"Okay. I'm done," Pam said. "Let's put pedal to the metal."

She didn't have to tell me twice. I picked up my pace and sped out of there so quickly I sprayed gravel. I needn't have worried, though. No one seemed to be bothered by our surveillance.

As the road widened, my breathing came easier. Pam stared at her phone's screen, swiping at the pictures. Occasionally, she enlarged the picture.

"Uh-oh," she said.

"What?"

"I think I may have found the connection."

"What is it?" I asked.

Pam turned to me, her eyes worried. "One of the trucks has a parking sticker with the letters ECC on it."

"ECC?"

"I can't be sure," Pam said, "but I think it could stand for Evergreen Convalescent Center."

Chapter 25

I gripped the steering wheel hard. A truck at the Devil's Wheelhouse with an Evergreen Convalescent Center parking sticker felt significant. It wasn't so much that the two places were at least thirty miles apart. It was the likelihood of two people frequenting both places—one an old folks' home and the other a beer joint.

But what would Margaret be doing there? I just couldn't see Margaret bellying up to that bar, nor could I envision her driving a big truck.

Could our suspicion of Margaret be wrong? Could the caller and note-writer be an employee of ECC? And why would an employee want us to stay away from Gerry?

Wait! Maybe the person worked at Devil's Wheelhouse and was a visitor at ECC. My mind spun. Maybe Allie, the solitaire-playing receptionist was involved. I had way more questions than answers.

"What do we do?" My hands began to shake. "I know there has to be a connection, if we're right about the ECC sticker. And we know how the napkin note and Gerry link up. But I still don't understand why anyone would want us to stay away."

"I don't know either. But I guess we can rule out the realtor's office or Daniels's office as the leak."

"That could be a good thing. Whether it's Margaret

or someone who works at ECC or Devil's Wheelhouse, or someone who frequents both, it's still a female, and she's still old." I paused a moment, thinking it through. "Whoever she is, she's probably nearing retirement age herself. I'd say we don't have to be afraid of someone that old, but if she's going to that bar...well, I don't know."

We fell silent. Moxie must have sensed our distress. She yawned audibly, then poked her head over the back seat and stared at us.

"It's okay, Moxie. Almost there."

"She probably needs to go to the bathroom," Pam said. "Let's pull over at the park near the school."

I reached the park and leashed up Moxie. She leapt from the back of the car and immediately squatted next to the back tire.

"Do you think the caller knows that Gerry and Silas are the same person?" I asked as we huddled next to the Kia. "Do you think they know about the body?"

Pam chewed her fingernail. Clicking noises filled the air. "I don't know. Maybe she's old enough to be involved. Maybe that's how Gerry ended up at that particular retirement home."

"Wait. That was over forty years ago! How could she still be taking care of elderly people? She's one of them!"

"She could be a spry sixty-year-old," Pam said. "Maybe she lives there. Or maybe she has an accomplice. Maybe the accomplice is an employee."

I frowned. A friend of a murderer who has an accomplice? It seemed unlikely. Then again, it would explain a lot of things.

"Only one way to find out." Pam brushed

imaginary lint from her jeans.

I was almost too afraid to ask. "How?"

"We go back to ECC."

Moxie finished peeing and planted her front two paws on the back of the car. After a couple of jumping movements, she gave up, sat down, and stared up at me.

"Sorry, Moxie." I picked her up. "I know you can't reach."

I set her in the hatchback and unleashed her. She returned to her doggy bed, curled up, and closed her eyes.

Pam and I returned to our seats and buckled up.

"We can't go up there again," I said. "Daniels was very clear about that. Besides, Silas, I mean Gerry, clearly didn't want any visitors, especially if the visitors are us."

"Well, I didn't want our little visitor in the aquarium!" Pam removed her sunglasses and rubbed her eyes before sliding them on again. "We have to go back. It's the only way we're going to feel safe again. Plus, Daniels doesn't need to know...unless we tell him."

"How will we end up feeling safer?" I hung a right into the elementary parking lot and positioned the Kia at the back of the pick-up line. Kids of all shapes and sizes began pouring from the school's double doors. "Things have been a lot quieter since we've left him alone."

"Because we'll know who's up to all of this. Then we can go to Daniels. Tell him what's going on. He'll be upset that we went up there, but he'll be happy that we got the information. Then he'll lock her up. Everyone will back off. We can get back to work and put all of this behind us and focus on making some money." Pam brushed her hands as if finished with a dirty job.

I stared at her. "I don't think they're going to lock up someone for a threat. In fact, if she's as old as we think she is, I don't think they'll do anything at all to her. Maybe wag their finger in her face. Are they really going to throw an old lady in jail? That might be elder abuse." I took a breath before continuing. "Besides, getting the police involved might make her even angrier. And who knows how old her accomplice is—and what stake she or he has in harassing us."

Pam shook her head and began counting off facts on her fingers. "The way I see it is one, an old woman tried to scare us away from Gerry. Two, the napkin is from the Devil's Wheelhouse. Three, a truck with an ECC sticker was there. Like Daniels said, someone who writes a threatening, anonymous note, then leaves a calling card where they can be found is an amateur. So four, she's no one and nothing to worry about."

Pam was right. Either the caller had completely lost her mind, or she had a completely different motive to want us to stay away from Gerry.

But what could that motive be?

"I can feel it in my bones." Pam folded her arms in front of her chest. "This note—and the call—have nothing to do with the corpse. Think about it. The body's too old."

"Then we're back to Margaret."

"Maybe."

"But what is she doing at the Devil's Wheelhouse?" I asked. "And what is she doing driving a big old truck? It just doesn't make any sense."

"Maybe it's one of the other women. It may not make sense to us until we find out the reason. But then, none of this makes sense. The only thing that fits is that Margaret is involved somehow."

I chewed my lower lip in the silence of the car.

"Maybe we should have gone in there," Pam said. "Looked around a little."

"Where?"

"You know where."

I twisted in my seat, the belt snaking around my abdomen and holding tight. I faced Pam. "You are not saying we should go into the Devil's Wheelhouse, are you?"

She sighed heavily. "We could learn a lot…just sayin'."

My mouth dropped open and I stared at her until the girls burst through the school doors, their bright yellow rain jackets with the duck-bill hoods catching my attention. "Let's talk about this later. I might be willing to go back to ECC. But I have no intention of hanging out at the Wheelhouse."

"Should we call Daniels before we go?" Pam asked.

"No." I unlocked the doors. "He'll only tell us not to meddle."

"Got it." Pam pasted on a smile and folded her arms as if the decision had been made.

The girls piled into the Kia, followed by Gabe a few minutes later at the daycare. After a quick trip to the grocery store for take-and-bake cheese pizzas, turkey pepperoni for the top, and a bag of salad, we headed for home. We kept ourselves busy with salad tossing and pizza baking, and by the time we got the kids to bed, we were too exhausted to discuss it further.

"First thing tomorrow." Pam sidled through the pass-through, Gabe over one shoulder.

I scooped Moxie off of the living room floor and hugged her tight. "First thing," I replied.

Chapter 26

We arrived the next morning at Evergreen Convalescent Center. Yellow taxi cabs lined the circular driveway. I counted four taxis waiting and one signaling to exit.

"What's with all the taxis?" Pam asked. "Where could all of these residents be going?

"Beats me."

"Well, at least they're not hearses."

I harumphed a response.

I slipped the Kia into a visitor slot, and Pam and I settled back with our Americano coffees. The pungent aroma filled the car and I sighed in response. We needed a plan, and the freshly ground beans promised to sharpen our wits and boost our energy.

"Let's do good cop, bad cop," Pam suggested.

"The only problem with that is that we're not cops." I tested the temperature of the cup before setting it back in the holder. "Impersonating one is illegal. Plus, I don't know how to play either side."

"Good points." Pam removed the lid from her cup and blew across the surface of the coffee. A cloud appeared on the front window and slowly dissipated. "Besides who'd want to play the good cop? Not me. I'd wanna be the bad cop."

I took a short sip, burning the tip of my tongue. I set the cup back in the holder. "Why don't we be honest? Let's tell Silas-Gerry that we got a threatening call and a threatening note and then see what he says."

"Hmmm…straightforward." Pam considered that a moment. "That's a pretty good idea. It will catch him off guard. He'll either know nothing or everything. Either way, he'll tip his hand."

"Do you think we'll be able to tell if he's lying?"

Pam nodded and swallowed. "I do. If we walk in and he's surprised, we'll know he was in on it. He will have thought the warnings had scared us off and that we'd never be back."

"And if he isn't surprised? Does that mean he didn't have anything to do with the warnings? Or could it mean he doesn't remember us? Or that he's a really good actor?"

"Well, right. So my plan's not fool-proof." Pam swirled the coffee in her cup, sending steam wisps curling into the air between us. "Maybe we should go with your idea."

"You mean honesty?"

"Yeah, honesty, shmonesty. Whatever." She laughed. "Okay. We tell him about the call and note and see what he says." Pam set her cup in the holder and unbuckled her seatbelt. "Ready for this?"

I withdrew the key from the ignition. "Wait. What if he says nothing? Or denies everything? Should we ask him about the body?"

"Yes." Pam drew the word out as if still considering her answer as she replied. "We'll wait to see how he reacts about the call and the note first, though."

Reservations filled my head, but Pam seemed determined. "I'll let you lead this one."

Pam grinned and grabbed her purse. "Let's go."

After a quick check to make sure Moxie was still sleeping soundly in the back, we marched through the front door, fully expecting an absent greeting station. We were right. Wasting no time, we headed the way we'd come the first two visits. Pam led, me hot on her heels. Together, we dodged an obstacle course of wheelchairs and ambulatory residents pushing walkers. We turned right at the nurse's station without pause, and slowed only as we approached room two eleven. There, we held our breaths and listened.

Silence.

I peered around the corner first. No Silas. No Gerry. No one.

A momentary paralysis took over my body. We hadn't planned for this scenario, and it left me off-kilter.

"No one's in there," I whispered.

Pam peeked in. "Could he be in the bathroom?"

The bathroom door stood open, and the mirror's reflection revealed an empty shower. "No. He's gone."

Pam slapped a hand to her mouth. "You don't think he, uh…"

I mulled over the possibility that he could have passed since we'd last seen him. He'd certainly seemed plenty healthy a few days ago. But then… Fighting emotions that threatened to paralyze me, I looked for signs of habitation. Name tag at door. Personal effects in room. Check, check.

"I don't think so," I said. "He's gotta be around here someplace."

"But where?"

I swung my gaze back and forth to opposite ends of

the corridor. Several old people lined the halls. One propelled his wheelchair forward with his good leg, while the other curled in palsy. The others seemed satisfied to sit in place and watch the others move about.

"Let's take a look around," I said. "Maybe the magician's back and Silas is in the audience."

"Right." Pam snapped her fingers. "The activity room."

We strode along the corridor, Pam trailing behind me this time. Occasionally, I chanced a glance into the not-so-private rooms. Sagging flesh and hairless bodies lay atop beds with metal rails pulled high. Every once in a while, someone cried out, sending shivers up my spine.

Although it was clear that the residents were well cared for, I couldn't help but note the similarity between babies and the elderly. We go out of this world the same way we enter it. The only ones who escape aged bodies and the loss of movement are those who die young. Definitely not an attractive alternative. I shuddered and refocused my vision straight ahead.

An emergency exit blocked our way at the end of the hall. We turned on our heels and began backtracking. There had to be an activity room, and I would find it.

The nurse's station bustled with activity. A blonde woman in scrubs held a tray with tiny white cups, each holding an array of colored pills resembling miniature Easter baskets. Another woman with a tight afro spoke on the phone. A third headed into a backroom through a door labeled *Attendants Only*. No one even looked up as we approached. We could wait there all day and not get help.

I scanned our surroundings. Down one hall was the entrance and exit we'd used each time. The one behind us ended in an emergency exit. That left only one possibility. I turned to my right. "Let's go."

Pam and I walked with bravado a few paces before noticing the small sign that read *Activity Room*. The arrow pointed right. After a quick congratulatory wink Pam's direction, I pivoted and led the way down a short corridor that ended in double doors propped wide.

The interior of the activity room spanned an impressive twenty-by-twenty square. The left wall held a flat-screen television mounted at eye level. Images flashed of Peter Sellers as Inspector Clouseau flashed across the screen, but the sound had been muted, so the familiar super spy music was missing. In the corner nearest us, a mini coffee stand had been set up. It held a single-cup coffeemaker and several metal trees holding multiple capsules of coffee, tea, and cocoa. Multicolored cocktail napkins sat next to paper cups. From the scent of the room, someone had recently brewed a chocolaty cup of joe.

A long bookcase lined the right wall. Well-stocked with paperbacks and hard covers, it must have held at least a thousand books. Fake ivy crawled across the top shelf, blue hydrangea blossoms dotting the greenery. Directly in front of us lay a bank of white-paned windows that looked out over a tiny garden area. Flower pots bloomed in reds, pinks, purples, and yellows.

Several residents had found their way in here. Three were propped in front of the television, two men and one woman. One man slept, chin on chest, in a recliner. The other two appeared to be following along despite the missing soundtrack. Another resident sat in an easy chair near the book wall. She had her feet up on an ottoman and her walker positioned to one side. She read from a large book that covered her lap, thick glasses perched low on her nose. In the middle, just a few feet from the windows, stood a table with four chairs. Three women, each sporting elaborate hats, and a man wearing all white, surrounded the table. Each held playing cards with mugs to their right. The man sat at the same table, his back toward us. Even with only his hairline as a clue, I suspected the gentleman was the man we called Silas-Gerry.

"Pass," said one woman at the table, followed by "pass," and "pass," as the remaining two women spoke.

"Why, thank you, ladies," the lone man said.

The voice confirmed it. I looked to Pam and nodded.

Pam, brazen as heck, marched forward. I skulked behind, more comfortable with Pam in the lead.

Positioning herself to one side of him, she said, "Good morning, Silas. Or should I say, Gerry."

He set his cards upside down on the table and slowly raised his gaze. After glancing once at me, he settled his sights on Pam. "Ladies," he said, his voice steady as steel. "To what do I owe this pleasure?"

All three women cocked their heads to stare at us. I recognized Margaret from her sour expression and bright pink hat. None of this intimidated Pam. She plowed on.

"We were hoping to have a moment of your time," she said.

He made a sweeping motion. "I'm afraid you've

caught us in the middle of our weekly bridge tournament. Could you come back another time?"

"Come back another time," Margaret parroted. The other women at the table glared back and forth at Pam and me.

I straightened my posture and took over. "It's very important, Gerry."

He scooted his cards into a tight pile on the table a few inches from his chest. "Very well." He turned to each of the ladies. "Margaret, Joan, Linda. Could you please excuse us?"

The ladies began to move, rising slowly from their chairs, but not before giving us a scathing once-over. At my height, it's hard to feel intimidated by little old ladies, but I had to admit, I felt like a fourth grader under their gaze. I wondered briefly if any of them had been teachers.

Margaret made an exaggerated movement to lay a hand on Gerry's shoulder on her way out. "Will twenty minutes be enough, dear?"

"More than enough, my dear." He patted her hand, and she cooed a response.

When she turned to leave, she sent a look our way that would have melted a candle. Then the trio vanished out the double doors.

Pam and I sat in the vacant chairs.

"You're the ones who bought my nephew's house." He wove his fingers together and set them in his lap.

"Actually," Pam said. "We bought your house. You owned it when we bought it, and you owned it before quit-claiming it to your nephew."

I gulped. Pam wasn't wasting any of those minutes.

196

"All of that is accurate." His tone didn't waver, but his eyes narrowed slightly like a cornered animal. "But I hardly see why you're here again if you already know all of that."

"We're here for a different reason this time," I chimed in.

"That's right," Pam added. "We're here because someone wants us to stay away from you."

He smiled for the first time. "I can't imagine why anyone would want you to stay away from them." He paused to allow his real meaning to land before raising an eyebrow. "But if that is the case, why are you here?"

His message was clear. He didn't like our company. I swallowed hard. This was not going well.

"That's what we want to know." Pam pushed her back into the chair. She folded her arms in front of her chest. "I mean, we know why we're here. But we don't know why someone else wouldn't want us here."

Confusion etched Pam's face as she rambled, and her arms slackened. Before she could clarify her words, he spoke.

"Perhaps, my dears." He picked up his cup and took a slow sip before continuing. "People don't enjoy your company."

His insult landed square on my shoulders, and I felt myself shrink, my eyes cast downward. We may have thought we could use the element of surprise, but clearly, he could hold his own in any conversation. He held all the, um, cards.

That's when I noticed the napkin under the cup: A cocktail napkin in green with the "Devil's Wheelhouse" name and logo on front. I scanned the table. The other napkins at the table—one pink, two blue, but all the same size as the green one had been flipped upside-down. The remaining green napkin in the center of the table held the same words and logo.

I pointed to the napkins. "What do you know about the Devil's Wheelhouse?"

Gerry set his cup down, obscuring the logo on the napkin. "Why do you want to know?"

"Because the threat was written on one of those napkins," Pam replied. "And the police have it now."

A flicker of indecision played across Gerry's face. He sighed and smiled before responding. "One of the orderlies moonlights there. He brings us extra napkins and straws. Occasionally, he brings us a bottle of bourbon." He held his fingers to his lips in the universal shhh sign and winked.

"Which orderly?" Pam asked.

He cocked his head as if measuring the wisdom of revealing any additional information. "Tony."

"Which one is Tony?" I fired back.

"Oh, you can't miss Tony. He's huge—nearly six-six and built to plow fields. Big one, but gentle as a lamb. As they usually are. So kind to all of us."

A memory of the man mopping the floor on our second visit flittered behind my eyelids. The name tag over his well-developed pectorals had read *Antonio*. He probably went by Tony.

But why would he want us to stay away from Gerry? And his voice definitely wasn't female.

"Is he related to you?" I asked.

Gerry shook his head.

"Is he related to anyone you know?" Pam asked.

He shrugged. "He simply works here, cleaning up after us and bringing goodies to us. He's a lovely man."

He tipped his cup and took another short sip.

"So who would want us to stay away from you?"

His eyes twinkled just a bit, as if he were enjoying our curiosity—and his ability to withhold information.

"I have no idea." He set his cup down. "Is that all I can do for you ladies?"

Pam and I exchanged looks. I was out of ammo, and by her expression, I judged her to be, as well.

"Well, I won't keep you any longer then," he said.

Taking the cue, we rose. "Thanks for your time," Pam said.

He nodded and picked up his cup again.

We headed for the door, but we got only two steps before Pam cocked her head and spoke again. "Out of curiosity, what did you do for a living?"

He sighed and set his cup back in its saucer with a clank. "I was a teacher."

"What'd you teach?" I asked.

At first, he simply stared at us. I knew he heard me, though. It piqued my curiosity. I stepped closer. "What subject did you teach?"

"Is this the last question?"

He was hedging, but what else could I say? "Yes."

He huffed and shifted in his chair. "Chemistry. Now, if you ladies will excuse me."

Pam took a leap back. "So you'd know all about how to preserve things, right?"

Gerry's face grew pained, and he winced.

Pam leaned in so that her face hovered less than a foot from Gerry's. "Making you uncomfortable, Gerry? What if I said I thought you probably know how to preserve entire bodies—entire human bodies?"

Gerry remained mute, his chin firm, but I saw the

twinkle in his eye turn to stone.

Pam moved in even closer. I wanted to pull her back from harassing an elderly person but couldn't force my feet to move. The proverbial beans appeared to be ready to spill.

"Ladies." Gerry's voice was hoarse. "I don't know what you're talking about. But since you won't excuse me, I'm going to have to ask for your help. Please go down to the nurse's station and ask for Tiffany. I'm in need of her assistance."

"I bet," Pam said. "I bet this is just a big ploy. Tell me what you know about the body in the closet!"

I made the cutting movement at my throat, but Pam didn't notice. She continued her stare down as Silas grimaced.

The room silenced only momentarily. Within seconds, the telltale splish-splash of fluid hitting a hard surface reverberated through the space. There, below Gerry's wheelchair, a yellow puddle began to form.

"I want answers!" Pam cried out, clearly oblivious to the pants-wetting incident.

Quickly, I grabbed her arm, apologized, and promised to find Tiffany.

"Not yet," she said.

I cast Pam a quick glare and pointed at the puddle. She covered her mouth in surprise. We both headed for the door. "We'll be right back with help," I called out over my shoulder.

"Yeah. Don't go anywhere," she added.

Without a look back, I jerked Pam forward and we race-walked out of the room.

Chapter 27

I nearly flew down the hall of the ECC, still pulling Pam's arm. She struggled to keep up, taking a step and a half to every one of my long strides. Of course, the bustling nurse's station stood vacant. They were probably out delivering all those little Easter baskets of colorful pills we'd watched them measure out earlier. With nothing else to do, we alternately paced the length of the counter or rested our backs against it, shifting our weight back and forth. We scanned the hallways, anxious for anyone to arrive. Finally, after what seemed like an eternity, the backroom door clicked open. We swung round. Allie.

"We need Tiffany!" I said. "Silas, I mean Gerry, needs her."

"What?" Allie placed a knee on her chair and leaned across the counter.

"Gerry needs Tiffany," I said. How much clearer could we be?

"Oh, I remember you guys." Allie sighed and settled into her chair. "Just a moment." She withdrew her cell phone and sent a quick text message.

Anger shot through me. Before I could summon the words to tell her what I thought about her social networking habit when old people needed assistance, she spoke.

"I'm sorry." Allie matched our franticness with

calm. "There's no one here by the name of Tiffany."

What was this place? An alternate universe? Why doesn't Allie know anyone we know is here?

"Could you issue a call for Tiffany?" Pam lowered her voice a full octave. "Gerry said that's who he wanted. Maybe she's new. Maybe you haven't met her yet." She paused a moment, staring at Allie and her lack of response. "Please?"

Allie smiled and picked up the phone. She probably discovered long ago that the best way to deal with hysterical relatives is to give them what they want—regardless of the validity of their request. There may even be a policy for that kind of thing. After punching a few numbers, she issued a call for Tiffany. Its echo sounded through the halls a split-second later.

"Thank you," Pam and I said together.

"You're welcome," Allie replied. "So how long should we wait for this person who doesn't exist to arrive?"

Without missing a beat, Pam responded, "Let's give her five minutes."

"Okay," Allie logged onto her computer. "Five minutes and then I'll call for someone else."

The fluttering of cards emanated from her computer's speaker, proof of yet another round of computer solitaire. She shifted her attention to the screen and clicking noises ensued.

Pam and I turned our backs to her, rolled our eyes at each other, and settled in to wait.

Slowly, the minutes ticked by, each of us checking our cell phones repeatedly. No Tiffany. My uneasiness over leaving poor Gerry alone and in need of attention ate at me. I have never been one to let my kids "cry-it-out" when they were babies. Now, I got that same angsty feeling, listening for him to holler out, knowing he was sitting in a pool of his own pee. Sweat slickened my armpits, and I nearly danced from foot to foot.

After six minutes, I rubbed my forehead. "I don't think Tiffany is coming," I whispered.

"Let's give her one more minute before asking her to call someone else," Pam whispered back.

I nodded, understanding her reluctance. Frankly, it was embarrassing to be constantly harassing Allie, especially when she had the upper hand...and appeared to be right about everything, most recently the non-existence of Tiffany. But she was the only employee around. And why would Gerry ask for someone who didn't exist?

Three minutes later, I didn't bother conferring with Pam. She had to know, as I did, that no Tiffany was going to show up. I swiveled back to Allie, but before I could open my mouth, she picked up the receiver.

"I'll call someone now."

Pam and I scurried back down the hall. Over our footsteps we heard the request for assistance to the activity room. I didn't understand why he asked for the non-existent Tiffany, nor did I know if we would get back there in time to help him—or even if there was anything I wanted to help with. Adult diapers seemed best left to the professionals. But I certainly wasn't prepared for what we found...or rather, didn't find.

Gerry.

He was gone.

Chapter 28

Everything else in the activity room looked the same. The ladies had returned and sat down, each staring at the cards in their respective hands, the television watchers faced the big screen, the reader stared at the book. Even Gerry's wheelchair awaited, puddle cooling below. Only Gerry wasn't in it.

"Where's Gerry?" Pam asked.

Margaret raised her head from her hand long enough to glare, then returned her focus to the cards.

"Maybe she can't hear you," I whispered.

Margaret spoke, her eyes never meeting ours. "Gerry excused himself. You women must have tired him out." Under her breath she added, "Thanks a lot."

The other women looked at everything but us.

"But wait." I waved my hands in the air. "How'd he leave without his wheelchair?"

Margaret raised an eyebrow. "Gerry doesn't *need* a wheelchair all the time. Only when his leg is bothering him." She returned to her bridge game.

"Okay," Pam said. "Well, thanks a lot. You've been *super* helpful."

If any of the women caught the sarcasm in Pam's voice, they disregarded it. Instead, they began their round. Margaret led with a nine of clubs.

Their nonchalance irritated me, but it angered Pam to the point that the tips of her ears turned red. I took a step closer to her in case she erupted.

Pam opened her mouth. "For your information—" She wagged a finger Margaret's direction, "we know you're the one who called us and wrote that mean note. We don't know how you got our number or how you followed us, but we know you did it."

Margaret's frown deepened, but she didn't speak.

"We have kids, you know." Pam placed her hands on her hips. "You could have scared them, too."

The women glanced at Margaret, their demeanor reflecting surprise, but no one said anything.

"And another thing," Pam began, "I don't appreciate the way you always glare at us. We're just trying to make a living…"

Everyone fell silent when a young, tall, African-American woman wearing a pink smock and pants with a butterfly pattern arrived. Her name tag read Jessica.

"Someone here need help?" she asked.

"It was Gerry," Pam said. "But he's gone now."

"Okay," Jessica said, her tone cheerful. She paced around the room asking all the residents how they were doing. She righted the one who had fallen asleep, his head lolled to one side, and plumped the pillow behind the back of the woman who was reading. "Are you enjoying your book today, Melva?"

Melva raised her eyes long enough to nod, then returned to her book.

Back at the door, Jessica paused. "Is there anything else I can help you with?"

I wanted to ask her where Gerry was. How he managed to leave without his wheelchair. But I didn't know how to explain that we'd lost him because he outsmarted us.

Before I could speak, however, Jessica's smile collapsed, and she moved to one side, peering at something behind us. We followed her line of vision out the windows. There, in the garden area, just beyond the cement patio and a few wheelchair-bound residents soaking up sun, stood an open gate.

She moved closer to the window and held a hand to her brow, shielding her eyes from the glare. "That's odd. We better get that gate closed." She dashed off, her rubber soles squeaking on the corridor floor.

Pam and I pressed our noses against the warm glass and squinted in the direction of the gate. Sure enough, it swung slightly in the breeze, revealing a long narrow cement walk path leading away from ECC. Farther down, nearly out of sight, a lone man rode a motorized scooter. Even from here, I knew whose white jacket that was.

Gerry.

Slowly, but surely, he was escaping.

Chapter 29

Pam pressed her hands against the glass and focused on the scooter. "Oh no!" Gerry was making a slow, but sure, getaway. He rounded the corner as we watched, and then he slid from view.

"We need to go!" I tugged on Pam's arm a little harder, keeping my eyes on the scene transpiring outside the big picture window in the activity room. "Gerry's getting away."

Jessica reappeared, this time on the patio. She glanced around as if taking stock of the residents soaking up the morning sun, then hurried over to the gate. After a quick look round, she stepped through the gate and took a long look in all directions. A moment later, she swung the gate closed, then latched the high and low locks.

"Come on!" Pam twirled on her toes and began sprinting toward the door. "We need to find him!"

I raced behind her. As I passed the ladies playing bridge, each member of the trio laid her cards on the table and twisted in their chairs to get a better look at the commotion outside.

"Oh, my," Margaret said.

Pam's pace made it impossible to catch up. She ran straight down the hall toward the entrance, dodging oxygen tripods and slowly moving, scantily clad residents. Once, as she whooshed past, an old man's robe flapped open, revealing a very wrinkly backside. I picked up my pace and caught up with her once outside the doors.

"What do we do now?" Pam's gaze darted around the grounds. "Should we try to find the path?"

I inhaled deeply, trying to catch my breath. "I don't know. Does the back connect to the front? Let's go around the side and see if we can pick up the path. He could get hurt, and it's our fault that he's out here in the first place."

"Don't remind me!" Pam sprinted to the left.

I took a giant gulp of air and chased after her.

She disappeared around the corner and doubled back by the time I caught up.

"Nothing there." She started for the right side of the building, never breaking stride.

Again, I attempted to chase after her but became sidetracked by the cabbies. Several had gotten out of their yellow taxis and huddled together, clearly enjoying the show Pam and I were putting on. I waved weakly as I tried to follow Pam's long strides. Even though I'm a foot taller, I had trouble keeping up. I didn't feel out of shape. It's just that Pam is so darn energetic.

A moment later, she spun on her heels and sprinted back to me.

"There's no way around." She leaned over and placed her hands on her knees. "It's all fenced off."

"I'll go back in and alert the staff." I tossed the car keys to her. "You get the car and bring it round to the front. Maybe there's an exit off the back. Maybe we can find him on the street somewhere."

Pam caught the keys mid-air and started off in the

direction of the Kia. I hot-footed it inside.

Allie didn't seem surprised to see me or hear my story. She simply finished yet another text message, then put out an all-call.

"Don't worry," she said. "I'm sure he's here someplace. We have a lot of Alzheimer's patients, so our doors are routinely locked and checked. Jessica has probably already found him. Occasionally, the really clever ones talk a visitor into opening the door for them, though. We appreciate your report."

I thanked her, then ran back the way I'd come, my now sweaty hair sticking to my neck. I startled several residents who remained perched along the hallway. Allie had no way of knowing how sure I was that the man outside the gate was Gerry. But I was dead certain.

Pam tooted the horn as soon as I emerged. I flew into the Kia and buckled up, and Pam shifted into gear and put pedal to metal. "Where should I go?"

"Let's start by making a big loop around the building. Look for streets that hug the ECC."

"Got it." She swiveled her head and hung a right. "Where could he possibly be going?"

"I have no idea." I checked the side mirror. Pam was moving along at a good clip. I had no doubt a cop would pull her over. All we needed was to be stopped and then try to explain why we were pursuing an old man on a Little Rascal.

Pam leaned forward and peered out the front window. "He can't get very far on that thing, can he?"

"Not sure. I don't know how fast they go, or how far they go before running out of juice."

An intersection loomed ahead, the light changing from green to yellow.

"Shoot!" Pam slammed to a stop.

Pam unbuckled and shifted the Kia into park. "Quick! Change places. You drive and I'll look for Gerry. If we find him, I can chase him down."

Frantic, I unbuckled and ran around the front of the car as Pam raced around the back. Just as I closed the driver's side door, the light turned green. I buckled and shifted into gear in one motion and took off.

"Think logically," I said. "If he went right here, he'd be headed toward the freeway. If he goes straight, he'd be going in the direction of downtown. To the left leads to an industrial area."

We stared each direction, across asphalt and sidewalks, short trees and mini-strip malls. We searched for signs of him...or brake lights that might signal traffic congestion.

"Let's go straight and see if we can pick up his trail," I suggested. "He must be creating a distraction on the road."

"Good point."

I accelerated and the little Kia roared to life. I drove in the middle lane in downtown Renton, keeping an eye to the left while Pam watched the right. We'd gone two blocks before Pam shouted, "There!"

Tearing my eyes from the road ahead, I saw what she saw, just a few hundred feet past her outstretched finger: Gerry, across the median. On the shoulder of the road. Humming along at a decent pace.

"He's going to get hit!" I said.

"Make a U-turn," Pam insisted. "We've got to catch up to him before he gets hurt."

I merged into the far far-left lane and waited for a break in traffic. As soon as I saw the lull, I pulled into a gas station. I passed between the islands, cars on either side, and exited, reversing our direction and never missing a beat.

"Good one, Janny," Pam called out.

"Thanks!"

We sped along, both of us craning our necks, trying to glimpse Gerry again. I knew, however, that the freeway veered south a bit ahead. I had grave concerns that he'd already made it that far.

"I don't see him anywhere." Pam pressed her nose against the passenger window, the glass fogging from her ragged breath.

"Neither do I. Let's get on the freeway."

"The freeway? Why would he get on the freeway in a Little Rascal? That would be so dangerous!"

"It's the only direction left to look."

"Okay," Pam said. "Do it."

Two intersections later, we barreled down the highway. Half a mile after that, a blue dot with white hair appeared on the right side of the road. It moved faster than I would have expected, but we caught up in no time in the car.

"That's him," Pam confirmed as we neared. "Get in the right lane. We'll see if he'll stop for us."

I merged and slowed my approach. Not only did I not want to startle him, I didn't want him to maneuver the scooter into traffic. The prospect of driving him over the edge terrified me.

"I'm going to follow behind." I checked my mirrors. Cars were slowing around us, trying to get a good look at the scene. "You deal with Gerry, and I'll deal with traffic."

"Good idea," she said, rolling down her window.

"We need to get him back to the ECC before he kills himself on that thing. We'll be held responsible."

I slowed to a crawl. As we neared, Gerry whipped his head round and spotted us, then twisted the handle to accelerate. The scooter revved and his pace quickened. I eased off the brake a little to keep up. He couldn't possibly imagine he would outrun us in that thing, but maybe he figured he'd have to try.

Pam rolled down her window and hollered. "We're sorry! Slow down! You're going to get hurt!"

Another quarter mile passed as we continued our slow-speed chase down the interstate. Each time Pam spoke to Gerry, he either ignored her or flipped her off and alternately braked or sped up to avoid us.

More cars were slowing to get a good look at us and Gerry. More passengers from multiple vehicles rolled down their windows to get better views. A few had arms outstretched, cell phones in hand, videotaping the entire scene. Gerry's response was consistent. He either ignored their catcalls and honking, or he flipped them off as he did us.

"That'll be on Youtube within minutes," Pam said.

"For sure. I hope we aren't starring in the little videos, too. I wouldn't want Daniels to see this." I swung my head round but didn't see any lights flashing. "I can't believe the cops haven't shown up yet."

"Yeah. I can't believe people will take their cells out to take pictures but not call the police," replied Pam.

With no signs of Gerry slowing, I asked, "How long should we follow him?"

"I don't know. Maybe until the battery runs out? Then we can take him home." Pam paused, squinting ahead. "Wait! What's that?"

I looked ahead. Debris on the shoulder. "Uh-oh. If he hits that, he'll teeter right or left. Just in case he comes our way, I'd better back off and leave some space in front of us."

"I hope the others back off, too!"

I rolled down my window and tried to wave off the other cars. No one budged. Gerry's shoulder show was too hard to ignore. If possible, there were even more cell phones focused squarely on him.

"Try to reason with him," I said. "Just keep telling him we're sorry."

Pam leaned out her window even further. "Sorry, Gerry, or Silas, or whoever you are! Please pull over! You're going to get hurt!"

Gerry glanced at us once, then back at the debris growing steadily closer. A split second later, he turned his head, flipped us the bird, and swerved to the right, straight down the embankment.

Chapter 30

I slammed on the brakes as Gerry disappeared over the edge. The Kia screeched to a complete stop on the shoulder just in front of the debris. Pam jumped out of the car and chased after him, vanishing over the embankment almost immediately. After a cursory glance at oncoming traffic, I flung my car door open, shoved it closed behind me again, and raced around the Kia.

A zillion thoughts raced through my mind. Why did he run? Is he okay? Is it our fault if he does get hurt? Where were the police?

I reached the edge and peered over. Fortunately, the embankment wasn't very steep. Unfortunately, Gerry was at the bottom of it, separated from his Little Rascal by several feet. From the looks of things, he'd been thrown from it and landed in a heap of assorted grasses. He wasn't moving.

"Omigod, omigod, omigod." Pam scrambled down the hill toward Gerry.

I sidestepped down the hill as quickly as I could in the gravel. Each foot caused a mini avalanche that sent a landslide of tiny jagged rocks Gerry's direction. I leaped forward to get to a different location and continued crab-walking down the hill, using both hands to stabilize my movement.

Pam reached Gerry first and cradled his head in her

lap. "He's breathing," she screamed. "Call nine-one-one!"

I fished my cell out of my pocket, punched in the numbers, and began describing where we were. "There's a casino on the right—I don't know if it's east or west—it's to my right. And my car's at the top on the side of the road. A Kia, with a dog in the back. There's a gravel embankment. We're down at the bottom. He doesn't look good. Please hurry!"

The operator asked, "Is he alive?"

"Yes. He's breathing." I moved closer, inhaling dust and fumes, and stumbled over one scooter wheel. "Wait! His eyes just opened."

"Can he speak?"

"Gerry," I said, finally reaching him and Pam, "can you say anything?"

"Ouch!"

"He can speak! He can speak!" I hollered.

"I'll dispatch emergency personnel," the operator said. "If you can have someone at the top to direct their attention, we'll get to you sooner."

"Okay." I ended the call. "You need to go up to the top and flag them in. I don't think I can make it up that hill as fast as you."

She eased out from under Gerry, holding his head stable. "Here, slide over here and support his neck."

I scootched over and did as Pam asked.

"Thank you," Gerry said, once I was in place and his head rested in my lap.

Pam jumped up and retraced her pattern back up the hill, leaving wedge-shaped divots in the gravel slope.

"I'm afraid I'm going to die soon." Gerry closed

his eyes.

"No, you aren't. You're okay. EMTs will be here any second."

"No, I'm in too much pain. And very sleepy. This is the end." His eyes flickered open, then closed again.

"Gerry, hang in there! Please, we're sorry. We shouldn't have harassed you! We should have left you alone." I began to cry. Big fat alligator tears dripped directly onto Gerry's face.

He scrunched his nose and focused a very vacant gaze my way. "I want to confess. Just in case there's judgment, I want to confess."

My tears abated and I sniffled. "Confess what?"

He paused a moment, then closed his eyes again. "The body. I want to tell you about the body."

Chapter 31

"Gerry?" I softened my voice to conceal my anticipation. Who would have thought I'd find out the truth about the corpse in a ravine on the side of a freeway?

When he didn't respond, I prompted him. "Who was he?"

"Who was who?" His eyes snapped open, his expression blank as fresh snow. He had either lost his train of thought, or he lied better than anyone I'd ever met, including my ex-husband, Jim.

"The guy in the closet. In the aquarium," I whispered. "Who is he?"

"What closet?" His gaze moved from me to the sky as if searching for answers.

I had grave reservations about pressing a man in pain for information...but he was the only person in the whole world who could give it to me. Or so I thought. Plus, if it kept him awake, that would be a good thing.

I took a deep breath. "The closet in the house you sold to us," I reminded him. "The cedar closet. You wanted to confess."

I paused a moment, watching for tell-tale signs of memory. "Is it the real Gerald Jones?"

He lay still a moment, the only movement the wind in his wispy white eyebrows.

"Is it Silas Morford?" I asked, hoping for a nod or

eye twitch. "Is it Thaddeus Huntington?"

His lips parted. "I'm dying. Oh, Lord, I'm dying." He shuddered and grasped his heart. "My pulse…so weak. My heart…"

I searched for obvious signs of trauma. No blood pooling on his white pantsuit. No bones jutting from his skin. Nothing. There could be significant internal injuries, of course, especially in someone his age who just tumbled down a hill at a decent rate of speed. Or he may be having a heart attack…or a stroke.

I inhaled sharply, realizing there wasn't anything more I could do for him, other than hope the medics hurried. Closing my eyes, I summoned my First Aid skills. If he stopped breathing, I would do chest compressions. If he had a seizure, I would move everything away from him. The most important thing I remembered was to keep him lucid and conscious.

"You're going to be fine, Gerry," I reassured him. "Just keep talking. It will help."

"I didn't kill him. I didn't kill anyone," he said. "It wasn't my fault. Thaddeus…Thaddeus, my boy. Where are you? Help me."

I froze in place. Now we were getting somewhere.

"Who's Thaddeus? Is he your son?"

He attempted to move and released a muffled cry.

I adjusted his head a bit higher.

"Better," he said. "Better."

"Good." I scanned the embankment. Still no signs of Pam or the medics. I had a fleeting worry about Moxie in the back of the car. I hoped Pam was keeping an eye on her.

Gargling noises erupted from deep in his chest. He gulped, his jaw working hard under the skin, then he opened his mouth. "He was sick…so was I. So sick. My brother. Couldn't work. Thaddie…Thaddie helped. But he was so young."

"It's Silas in the aquarium, then?"

"It's me…It's him," he said, tears forming on his lashes. "Silas Morford. And Gerald Jones. It's both of us. It's both of me."

I struggled to make sense of what he was saying. How can someone be both people? Was it identity theft, or a case of delusion due to age, pain, or some combination of the two?

"I'm sorry, but I don't understand." I smoothed the hair off of his forehead.

"I'm him." He coughed, a loose, wet cough. "He's me."

Clear as mud. "Start at the beginning," I said. "We've got plenty of time. Start when you were born."

The muscles in his face relaxed. His eyes lost focus. Had he gone to sleep? Had he passed out? Was he simply deep in thought?

He didn't die, did he?

I placed a hand at his temple. A flutter of pulse reassured me that he was still alive.

"Gerry? I mean Silas? Whoever you are, stay awake. Keep talking until the medics get here."

His eyelids fluttered and his mouth formed a slow smile.

"Tell me about your brother. What happened to him?"

He shook his head. "He died. I took him. Couldn't leave him. They would have killed him." He gulped. "I promised Mama I'd watch out for him. My whole life. He couldn't move from that bed, but I took care of him."

I lowered my voice. "I believe you."

He grabbed my arm, his grip weak. "I had to protect Thaddeus...He had no one. His mother...his mother..."

"Thaddeus was Silas's son?"

"No, no, no." Gerry's chest heaved. He seemed exhausted.

"Thaddeus is your son."

His emotions broke. Slow, controlled sobs erupted at regular intervals, as if they been shed many times before. White spittle gathered in the corners of his mouth. "He died...my son...my son."

I struggled to fill in the blanks. So Silas and Gerry were brothers. That was clear. And Thaddeus was Gerry's son, or at least I thought he was. Were Silas and Thaddeus both dead? Wait. Thaddeus had passed away recently. That was the reason for the deed transfer. That left only one conclusion.

"It's Silas in the aquarium," I said. "Isn't it? And Thaddeus was your son."

He gulped, his small Adam's apple bobbing. White spittle spilled out of his mouth and flowed onto his chin. Even I knew that was a sign of poisoning.

Uh-oh.

"Gerry," I said. "Did you take something before you left Evergreen? A pill maybe?"

His mouth worked open and shut a few times, but no sound came out. The saliva continued to bubble up and out.

Frantic, I called to Pam. With the freeway noise, I could barely hear myself. I knew she'd never be able to hear me.

"Gerry?"

Nothing.

"Gerry?" I worked to keep the shrill from my voice, but I had serious concerns that Gerry would choke on his own vomit.

Still nothing.

"Gerry, I'm going to turn your head. I don't want to hurt you, so please relax."

I paused just a moment to see if he would do it himself or maybe object. Still nothing.

Gently, I turned his face to the side. Foamy clumps dribbled from his mouth, landing on the ground next to my knee.

Gerry coughed, spewing forth a stream of sour-smelling viscous froth. He opened his eyes.

I leaned over to meet his gaze. "You're going to be okay. Hang in there."

"I need to confess…"

I didn't know if he really would meet his maker soon, but I knew he'd taken something to hasten his departure.

"I'll hear your confession," I said, "but first I need to know what you took."

"Val—"

"Valerie?"

He shook his head.

"Val?" I asked, then realized. "Valium?"

He nodded.

"How much?"

"Bottle." His voice grew weak. "Just like Silas."

"Silas took a whole bottle of valium?" I didn't understand how someone confined to a bed and needing care could take even a pill without help, let alone an entire bottle.

Gerry stared out at the green weeds reaching for the sun, then shifted his gaze to the sun. "No…"

And then it dawned on me. "Did you give Silas the valium, Gerry?" My words came out as a whisper.

His eyes moistened with fresh tears. "He had so much pain. Nothing to do." He gulped and shuddered. "I helped him. Helped him. Gave him his and mine."

He had given his brother two bottles of valium? That meant he had helped his brother commit suicide. That was illegal, of course. He could have even been tried for murder. That would have left Thaddeus without a guardian. But where was the mother?

So many questions whirled in my brain, and yet, they all paled in comparison to the realization that Gerry had tried to kill himself in the very same way that Silas had killed himself.

My heart ached for him. For all the troubles Pam and I have experienced in the past year, never had I had to consider helping someone end their life. That must have been awful.

But a nagging question remained: Why pretend to be Silas?

I toyed with the wisdom and ethics of asking him any more questions in these circumstances. What would be the use? I knew who was in the aquarium. I knew how he had died. And I had a pretty good idea that the reason he was entombed was to cover up the crime. A crime, according to the law, but maybe not a moral crime.

Then again, if the valium won, this might be my last chance.

And if it wasn't my last chance, Gerry would

probably clam up again.

His confession would mean an end to the investigation, an end to being locked out of our flip, an end to our financial woes.

I stared down at his face, growing grayer with each passing moment.

A siren pierced the air, and Pam appeared at the crest of the ridge. Her back toward me, she jumped and waved her arms, then pointed down toward us.

It was now or never.

"Gerry, the medics are nearly here. Hang in there." I adjusted the cradle of his head. "Just one more question. Okay. Just one." I paused, waiting for a response, and saw a slight flutter of his eyelids. "Why are you pretending to be both Silas and yourself?"

Gerry didn't respond immediately. He waited until the medics were halfway down the hill before opening his eyes.

"They're here, Gerry," I said, my voice an octave higher with relief. "You're going to make it!"

A female medic dropped to her knees beside us. "How are you, sir?" she said.

Gerry shifted his gaze from her to me and said, "Well, money, of course, my dear." Then he closed his eyes and all hell broke loose.

Chapter 32

Hours later, long after Daniels had arrived at the scene and ordered us to leave and wait for him at the station, Pam and I sat in front of Daniels's desk, Moxie sleeping soundly in my lap. I couldn't leave her in the car any longer. Our butts had long ago molded into the shape of the plastic '70s-era chairs, but we didn't dare move. We didn't know if Gerry had passed away from his overdose. We didn't know if we were going to be in trouble for meddling. We didn't know if we would be held responsible for his injuries or possible death. We didn't know if this would set back our rehab plans for the Craftsman even further. And we certainly didn't know when Daniels would be back.

"I think we should call the guys," Pam said. "We're cutting it too close to pick up the kids."

I'd been thinking the very same thing. I pulled out my cell, sent a quick, general text, and pocketed the phone again. A few moments later, my phone buzzed. Confirmation that they would pick up the kids. A moment later, a ping announced another text. Jim.

—*Everything okay?*—

I flashed the screen to Pam.

"Don't say anything," she warned.

"I won't." I punched out: —*Yes. Just a little behind schedule.*— That was out of the ordinary for me, and I hoped he wouldn't pick up on it.

—Okay. Do you want to pick up from my place or should I bring the girls by later?—

—I'll text as soon as my meeting is over.—

—What meeting?—

I ignored the question. I couldn't explain without giving away too much information or spurring more questions. And my lies were crap. I repocketed my cell.

With the kid pick-up taken care of, Pam and I continued to sit in silence, as if for the principal...and possible punishment.

Neither of us spoke. I found myself staring at the plaques and commemorations recording Daniels's career, impressed at the man who would decide our fates soon. The feeling of being responsible for pushing an old man over the edge—literally—haunted me. I knew we hadn't done the actually shoving, but we'd upset him so much that I knew we shared the blame.

Just when my nerves began to settle down, the sound of leather-soled shoes spanking the hallway grew nearer. Moxie's head rose and she blinked several times. "It's okay, Moxie." I snuggled her closer and wrapped my jacket around her body.

Pam turned to me and spoke out of one corner of her mouth. "Times like these I'm glad Daniels is your boyfriend and not mine."

Heat rose from my chin to my temples, and I scowled at her. It was bad enough to be waiting to be told if you were in trouble with the law. It was quite another thing to have a secret crush on the man making the decision and having your bestie joke about it.

We faced forward as Daniels came into the room, closed the door, and sat at his desk in front of us. "So, ladies, before I ask how your afternoon is going, let me reassure you that Gerry is going to be fine."

Pam and I each breathed a sigh of relief. I felt my entire body's muscles release at once, and I had to stop myself from tearing up. Pam sniffled and rubbed her nose.

"Thank goodness," I said. "Did they have to pump his stomach?"

"Did he break any bones?" asked Pam.

"No, and no," Daniels said. "He didn't take enough to do any real damage. A little charcoal and some rest for the overdose. And even though he took a tumble, he's tougher than he looks. A few bruises. That's about it. He'll be fine."

"I don't understand." I was surprised. "How did it kill his brother but not him?"

"Whoa, whoa, whoa," Daniels waved his hands. "What are you talking about?"

"Gerry told me he gave Silas an overdose of valium. That's how he died."

Daniels cocked his head. "When did he tell you that?"

"In the ditch. We were waiting for the medics, and he thought he was dying. He said he needed to confess."

Daniels leaned forward and steepled his fingers. "Let's start from the beginning. What did he say?"

I was still a little worried that we were responsible for some of Gerry's actions. I didn't know how much Daniels knew, and I definitely didn't want to lie to him. But I didn't think it would hurt to find out how much he knew about all of our interactions with Gerry and the women at the convalescent center before we spilled our guts.

I tried to think of a witty, yet non-committal response, but came up empty.

Fortunately, Pam broke the silence. "We went to the rest home again today. I was mean to him."

"What do you mean you were mean to him?" Daniels asked.

"We...I...we just wanted..." Pam's voice broke, and she sniffled, rubbing her eyes. "You tell him, Janny."

Daniels transferred his attention back to me again. Caught off guard by his green eyes and perfect peach lips, I fumbled with my answer.

"Um..." I attempted to collect my thoughts. If I wanted to paint ourselves in the best possible light, I'd have to think quickly. It's already been established that I don't lie well. Especially not under pressure. And this office felt like a commercial grade pressure cooker.

"We went to the convalescent center this morning to see Gerry." I stroked Moxie thoughtfully. "Or Silas. Or, both actually because we didn't know who he truly was."

"What happened there?" He settled back in his chair, probably sensing my hedging. Clearly, he knew he could wait me out.

"We had trouble finding him."

Daniels didn't speak. He just continued to wait.

I cleared my throat. "Eventually, we found him in the activity room. He seemed shocked to see us, but then he asked his friends to leave." Remembering Margaret, I added. "Oh, and it *was* Margaret who wrote the note. We could tell from her response."

If I had expected congratulations for confirming our earlier suspicions, I was mistaken. Daniels didn't even register surprise.

"Right," he said. "On a napkin Antonio donated. He moonlights as a bouncer at the Devil's Wheelhouse. He takes overstock, including napkins, to the old folks' home. From what I understand, he also occasionally brings them booze…which they aren't allowed to have." He grinned, clearly amused at the geriatric rule-breaking.

My balloon deflated. I thought we'd been clever to get proof. But he told me everything we knew, plus a little extra, in one breath.

"We're not sure who actually put the napkin on the car," I said, following the chain of thought. "It might have been Antonio."

"Nope," Daniels said. "Margaret again. She hitched a cab the minute you two left. I checked the cab companies' records. She followed you, placed the note on your car, then returned home to ECC before anyone missed her. Seems you brought out a big jealous streak in a little old lady."

"Jealous?" Pam frowned. "Why on earth would they be jealous of us?"

"I'm guessing because men are pretty scarce at her age," Daniels replied. "Especially kind old men with the ability to remember a woman's birthday, which he made a habit of doing." He paused, chuckling. It sounded like ice cracking in the small room.

"I don't understand," Pam said. "I mean, I get that she saw us as moving in on her, um, territory. But why go to such lengths to scare us off. It seems…over the top."

Daniels shrugged. "It may have been on impulse. There are a lot of cabs there, just waiting for a fare. Few of those old folks use rideshare apps, and it's probably a good thing that they don't, since they'd be easy targets. Legitimate cab companies could make a killing there, without ever worrying about putting their own people in danger of pick-ups in less desirable areas."

"But it's so expensive to take cabs!" Pam said. "It must have cost her a couple hundred dollars to follow us, pay the guy to wait while she put the note on the car, and then return."

Daniels dipped his chin. "Well, that is one pricey place to retire. Margaret's probably loaded. I did some research and the cab company told me their average fare is ten bucks to the store one way. But get this—the old folks pay for time waiting and always tip heavily. Sometimes, they pay the cabbies to go in and reach the cookies on the high shelves and cart the groceries back to the car. They can make several hundred a day for helping out the residents."

"Oh," Pam and I reacted at once.

"Maybe we're in the wrong business," Pam muttered under her breath.

"Maybe we all are," Daniels replied. "Anyway, I spoke to Margaret. Told her to knock it off. She won't be bothering you again."

Well, that explained why she wouldn't talk to us in the activity room.

"So what happened next?" He returned his gaze to me.

"Which time?" Pam piped up before I could speak. "When we were at the ECC? Or when Janny and I were on the side of the road?"

"Why don't we start with the home?" he replied, turning to face her. "You go first, then Janny can tell

229

what she remembers."

If Pam noticed that he'd called me Janny, she didn't react. I did, though, with a quiver that ran from the top of my head to my toes...and every spot in between.

Pam took a deep breath before speaking. "When we were at the center, I kind of told him I knew he knew something about the body." Pam fidgeted in her seat. "And I might have gotten a little aggressive. I didn't mean to upset him. Well, I did mean to rile him up a little, but just a little. Not too much. I certainly didn't intend to harass him to the point of...of...of running away." She diverted her attention to her yellow tennis shoes.

"So something tweaked him. Do you remember what it was?"

"Not really. He wouldn't tell us anything." Pam sniffed again, and I feared tears were on the horizon.

I spoke up. "He's pretty clever."

Daniels nodded. "Yes, he is. I'll give him that."

We sat with our mouths shut, allowing Daniels to direct the conversation. "What else? Do you remember anything more, Janny?"

"Actually," I began, my words slow as I remembered the conversation, "I remember when he got upset. It was right after he told us he had been a chemistry teacher."

Pam nearly jumped out of her seat. "Oh, right! And so I said, 'So then you know how to preserve things.' "

I nodded. "That's when he peed, I mean lost control of his bladder, and told us to go get Tiffany." I turned and faced Daniels. "And Tiffany doesn't exist."

Daniels frowned. "He wet himself?"

My shoulders hunched forward. Something about discussing bodily eliminations with a good-looking man felt more humiliating than all our sleuthing pratfalls combined. "Uh, yes."

"It was a ploy," Pam added.

"A ploy?" Daniels focused on Pam.

Pam's head bobbed up and down. "Absolutely. That's how he got away."

"So while the two of you were looking for the non-existent nurse, he hopped from the wet wheelchair to a dry scooter?"

Pam and I nodded vigorously.

"So then you began looking for him in the car?"

"Uh-hunh," I confirmed.

"Why?"

Pam and I looked at each other before I spoke. "We both felt like it was our fault."

"Okay. So you spotted him, tried to reason with him, and he went over the embankment," Daniels concluded. "Is that right?"

"Pretty much," Pam said.

Daniels shot a smile her way. "Got it. I think I have the main points now. Let's cut to Janny's part of the story."

I shook my head to clear my thoughts. "What do you mean?"

"Once you were in the ditch with him."

"Oh." *Duh.* "He began talking. He said he wanted to make a confession. But his sentences were so jumbled, I couldn't make sense of anything."

"What did he say?"

I stared at the corner of his office a moment before responding. I wanted to get this exactly right. "First, he talked about the body and called Thaddeus his 'boy.' He also said he was both Silas and Gerry, but later I figured out he really is Gerry. Silas is his brother and Thaddeus is his son. He told me about the valium. Oh! He also said he had promised his mama to take care of Silas."

Daniels nodded. "That works with what I know. Evidently, Silas was institutionalized back in the fifties for being *simple*." He shook his head. "That would not have been a good time to be cognitively challenged."

"No," Pam and I said together.

"My gut tells me this is about money, though."

"Yes!" I actually jumped out of my chair. Moxie leaped to the ground and blinked up at me, surprised and confused. I picked her up again before she realized she didn't know where she was.

"He said something about money. Money was the reason he did everything."

Daniels smiled. Feeling self-conscious at my exuberance, I snuggled Moxie close and sat again. Moxie circled in my lap but refused to lie down. Instead, she sat on her haunches and stared into my face.

"See, that place is pricey—nearly six grand a month, and that's for the non-Alzheimers, full mobility wing. It's all-inclusive, but that's one big nut every month." Daniels rubbed his chin. "His pension and Social Security add up to about half of that. But if you add Silas's Social Security and Disability, it leaves him with a few hundred dollars to spare. Enough to buy the several old ladies a birthday gift once a year." He grinned.

Pam's hand flew to her mouth. "He's double-dipping Social Security."

Daniels nodded. "He's double-dipping, and he's been doing it for a very long time. Probably forty years. That's most likely why he put the house back into Silas's name when Thaddeus passed. It made it appear that he was really still alive."

"Whoa," I said.

"Whoa is right," Daniels agreed. "So what do you both think? Any more questions for me?"

Pam and I looked to each other. She shrugged. I returned my gaze to Daniels. "Just one," I said, unsure if I should even ask. "How did you know we went to the ECC?"

"Allie texted me. I knew you'd go back, even though I told you not to…more than once." He glanced at each of us before continuing. I cringed a little and pulled Moxie closer. "So I gave her my number. Told her to text next time you showed up."

"Oh," I said. "Wait. How did you know we'd go back?"

"Because if it was my house, I would have."

If that had been intended to be some sort of validation, it did little to soothe my sense of shame. It was like Daniels could read our minds. My heart jumped a beat, thinking of the fantasies I'd had of him in recent weeks. Did he know I had, as Pam says, a crush on him? Had he thought of me in the same way?

As it turned out, I wouldn't have a chance to ask, even if I'd been so inclined.

His cell buzzed and he checked the screen. "That's all for now. Gotta go. Gerry's awake."

Chapter 33

Pam and I ran from the station, a yapping Moxie under my arm. Once inside the Kia, we locked the doors and allowed ourselves ten minutes to vent and cry. Moxie sat between us, alternately pawing at our hands and simply staring at each of us, ears in worried-back position.

"I never wanted to hurt him." Pam's words came out nasally.

"Neither did I. I feel so bad. He's just an old guy."

We sniffled a few more minutes, repeating ourselves occasionally, then rode in hushed silence to Jim's house. Pam texted him from my cell so we wouldn't have to go to the door. Jim would pick up on my emotional state immediately—and I really didn't want to relive any of the day.

Sadness turned to disbelief that threatened to morph into anger when we reached his home. A brand new, shiny marine-blue boat sat in his driveway.

"Did they buy a boat?" Pam asked, shielding her eyes from the sun.

"I have no idea." I stared at the hull and guesstimated the length and cost of such a luxury. "I don't think I want to know."

"Well, I do." Pam unbuckled and exited the car without closing the door. Moxie, sensing adventure, leapt out the passenger side before I could grab her.

234

"Pam!" I said. "Moxie got out!"

By the time the dog caught up to Pam, Jim had come out and was standing on the front porch. He wore a white short-sleeved T-shirt and orange Bermuda shorts, his hands in his pockets.

"Whose boat is that?" Pam demanded, stomping across his front lawn.

Jim stared at her. He was either surprised to see her or didn't know how to respond. None of that mattered anyway. Moxie interrupted any conversation they would have had by running up to Jim and biting him on his ankle.

"Damn it!" He grabbed his foot and hopped around. "That thing bit me!"

Moxie circled Jim, lunging occasionally for the remaining ankle.

"Moxie!" I screamed. No use. She couldn't hear me from this distance. And given recent history, she probably didn't care. I unbuckled and jumped out of the car. Tear-stained face or not, I couldn't let Moxie terrorize anyone…not even Jim.

"Hey," Jim screamed. "Hey, get that thing away from me!"

Pam remained calm and grabbed Moxie.

I sprinted up the driveway. "I'm so sorry! Is it bleeding?"

Jim squatted and peeled back his sock. A tiny red mark the size of a bothersome mosquito puncture lay exposed. "Yes. He bit me!"

"First of all," Pam replied, "Moxie's a girl. And chill out. She only has three teeth. It can't be that bad." As if to prove her point, Pam pulled back Moxie's lips, revealing a gum-filled mouth.

Moxie growl-hummed.

"Well, it only takes one, and one of them got me." He rose and stamped his foot a little as if increasing circulation to the injury. He paused a moment to glare at Moxie. "I'll go get the girls. They're out in the pool."

Despite the overabundance of adrenalin in my system, a new flood spilled into my bloodstream. "They're in the pool?" I cried. "Alone?"

I blasted past him, raced across the great room and out the back door. There, next to the pool, Marcus reclined in a lounge chair. Aside from the mass of body hair that had been neatly manscaped into a diamond on his chest, he wore a gold chain necklace and a bright red Speedo that left little to the imagination. Really. The girls were splashing happily in the pool, however, and Gabe lay sleeping in his playpen under the shade of a tree.

Placing a hand over my thundering heart, I breathed deeply. The events of the day had done me in. I felt exhausted and overwhelmed and emotional. I burst into tears. Big, long sobs that racked my body. I sat down on a nearby recliner to steady myself.

When I looked up, seven sets of eyes, ranging from very concerned to very confused, focused on me. I spoke to the girls first. "Momma's okay. I just had a bad day."

"It was rough, guys," Pam chimed in, helping me to my feet. "But it's better now. In fact, we decided to get Juicy Burgers for dinner. How does that sound?"

We hadn't decided that, of course, but the result was effective and immediate. The kids jumped up and down, their wet bathing suits throwing droplets in all directions. Relief flooded my body. Moxie responded by wiggling in Pam's arms. Marcus scowled and backed away, wiping the drips from his tanned body.

"I'll go wake up Gabe," he said.

The girls were wrapped in towels, Moxie was transferred to me, and Gabe giggled and climbed into Pam's arms.

Jim walked us to the door. "Can I talk to you for a minute, Jan?"

Pam nodded to me and threw a glare Jim's way before turning. "Okay, guys, everyone follow me."

The girls trooped after her. I waited until they were out of earshot, then turned to Jim. "What do you need?"

"Well, this may not be the right time to talk to you about this."

"Just say it. I want to get home."

He cleared his throat. "It's about child support. I'm a little over-extended right now, and I may need a few more days to get all of the money to you."

On any other day, I would have read him the riot act. It was pure selfishness that put his kids last on the list. Today, however, was the exception. I didn't have the energy or the willpower to argue. I simply glared at him, unflinching. "When will I have it?"

Jim hemmed and hawed a moment. "Maybe a week?"

"One week." I glanced at the boat and then back to him. Immediately, he blanched. He knew I knew it was the boat that had overextended his finances. "One week," I repeated.

He gulped. "I promise. One week."

Chapter 34

The next day as the girls and I sat at the breakfast table, Daniels called. "Hey, Jan. I've got news. Good news this time."

"Good news?" I rose from the table quickly. "Awesome. Hold on while I head over to Pam's."

"Did you finish that pass-through?" he asked.

"We did." I swung the door wide. "I'm passing through it right now."

He laughed. "I'd like to see that sometime."

My tummy jumped a bit. It may have been the extra fiber from the steel-cut oatmeal I'd recently added to my diet regime, but I doubted it. I waved to Pam who sat in her kitchen, feeding Gabe in his highchair. "It's Daniels. He's got news."

She motioned me over. "Put him on speaker."

I punched the button and set the phone on her kitchen table so we could both hear.

"First," Pam said, scooping a spoonful of peaches into Gabe's open mouth, "I want to apologize. I never meant, well, we never meant to come on so strong. We're just so antsy right now."

"I understand. You might have been a little too much for him, but you didn't force him to take off. More likely you caught him off guard. Pushed a few of his buttons. I don't know what he was thinking. What I do know, however, is that we're ready to remove the body from your house."

"When?" asked Pam, handing Gabe his tippy cup.

"Monday. We decided to go with the drain and pain method. We'll siphon the fluids and Silas out, preserving the evidence as part of the process. Then we'll dismantle the aquarium, preserve the sides and sealant, and haul it out of there on our backs."

"Wow. That's a lot of work." I paused a moment, thinking. "Does that mean you won't need to take out a wall?"

"No. We'll take everything out the front. The door may have to come off, but we'll replace it when we're done."

Pam and I high-fived. Gabe squealed and raised a hand covered in peach goo, flinging it about. Pam grinned and grabbed a wet rag.

"Don't count your chickens just yet. Before we release the house, we need to push everything through forensics. We need to scan for more bodies and close the scene."

"But why?" asked Pam. "We know what happened. We know who did it, and we know who the body is...was."

"Formalities," Daniels said. "My chief doesn't like surprises later. It's all backup in case Gerry changes his story. And he will."

"Oh," Pam and I said in unison.

"What I'm telling you, though, is you'll be back in within a week."

"A week?" Pam jumped atop her chair and did a jig. Gabe squealed louder this time, his eyes dancing and fists pumping in the air.

"That's great!" I said.

Daniels interrupted our revelry. "One more thing."

Pam got down off the chair, and my heart fell. I spoke, "What?"

"I need a little more information."

I shot a quizzical look at Pam. We'd told him everything we knew. Every last sordid detail. Every last embarrassing thing we'd done…even the things he'd asked us not to.

I swallowed hard. "What do you need to know?"

"The asking price."

"On the cottage?" I felt my eyebrows furrow. "Why do you need to know that?"

"Well, I may be interested in buying it."

"Buying it?" Pam said. "You want to buy a house that had a dead body in it?"

"Well, the body will be gone by the time I move in, right?" He laughed.

I laughed, too. My shoulders released from tension I didn't realize I'd been holding, and the muscles along my spine eased. I hadn't realized how anxious and uptight I'd been, or for how long.

"Let me get this straight," Pam said. "You want to buy our house after we're done with it?"

Daniels cleared his throat. "I think so. It all depends on the price."

Quickly, I began throwing numbers together in my head. We'd gone over a lot of the changes, based on how much there was to do and what we could do given the additional expenses caused by the corpse. All of our decisions had been held, however, until the body was gone and we knew the extent of the damage.

"We'll crunch some numbers and get back to you on that, Sergeant." Pam's voice quivered with excitement but held a professional tone.

"Okay. Let me know. My credit's good."

"Are you sure?" Pam said.

"About my credit?"

Pam laughed and began verbally stumbling over herself. "No, sorry, I meant about buying the house."

"Yeah. I like the area. It's a good location and there's an extremely low crime rate in that neighborhood." He chuckled. "Your call is the first call we've had to that neighborhood in a couple of years."

Pam and I grinned at each other.

"It sounds like a good fit," I said.

"It might take us a week or so to figure everything out," Pam said. "Once we get inside we'll have a better idea. But we'll definitely give you first option to buy."

"Sounds good," he replied. "Talk to you then."

I ended the call. "I can't believe he wants to buy the house!"

"I know. I wouldn't want to live there after seeing that guy." Pam shook her head. "I'd see him every time I opened the closet door, or even thought about going to that closet. I'd probably have to re-wall the whole thing just to get it out of my mind."

"But then you'd lose the bedroom, and the property becomes a one-bedroom, one-bath house. That would ruin the sales price."

"You're right. I'm glad the, uh, history of the house doesn't bother him."

"You know what it means if he buys it," I said, rising.

"Quicker closing and faster cash flow?"

I nodded. "It also means we don't have to worry about disclosure, because he already knows about it."

"And," Pam added, a glint in her eye that I hadn't seen in far too long, "it also means we pay less commission to Sam because we found our own buyer."

Less commission meant we could pay all the extra holding costs. It was so perfect I couldn't quite believe it.

Plus, I realized with a little flutter inside my rib cage, it meant I'd get to see Daniels again. I felt my skin tingling in anticipation, then remembered all the caveats he'd issued. There were still a few hurdles to clear.

"All that's left is keeping our fingers crossed," I said.

Pam shot me a quizzical look. "About what?"

"About the scanning process. The only thing that could mess up everything is if they find another body. About the removal. About everything."

Silently, I reviewed all the possible locations a John Doe, or Jane Doe, could be hiding in the little house, about the possibility of ruining the wood floors with fluids, about everything.

"Do you think they will?" Pam covered Gabe's ears. "You know, find another body?"

I took a deep breath. I just didn't know. More importantly, I didn't see how we could absorb any additional costs—or surprises. In fact, I didn't want to even imagine it. "I guess we'll soon find out."

Chapter 35

Throughout the weekend I had visions of skeletons stashed under the floorboards and wedged behind refrigerators and hot water tanks. I'd push the negative thoughts away, but they found their way back at night in dark and gloomy dreams featuring snowy-haired corpses and saggy skin. The nightmares had their roots in everything we had experienced—the ECC residents, the call and the note, the Devil's Wheelhouse, and, of course, the body in the closet. It didn't matter, though, as everything rode on the scans that would be completed the following week.

So when Daniels called a week later with the good news of no more bodies, twinges of trepidation shook my body. Pam and I were eager to get back to work, but we both admitted to nerves. We hadn't been in the house since we'd found the body. Would we be jumpy in there alone again? And what about the removal process? What damage had the forensics team done? We wouldn't know anything until we were back inside. The result was a shared anxiety as we picked up the kids from school and day care before heading over to get inside the house.

We told Jim and Marcus that we were meeting with a potential buyer, and they agreed to babysit and promised to feed them a nutritious dinner. Jim even expressed surprise that we'd found a buyer so fast. I didn't respond to that. Every cloud has a lining, I guess.

I didn't even feel guilty for telling them a half-truth: We were actually meeting with Daniels. He would give us his final decision on whether to buy the cottage or not once we'd shown him the numbers and plans.

Since the kids were safe with the guys, I buckled up and waited until we merged onto the main road before speaking. "I hope there's no evidence of the body or the aquarium, or anything."

"Me, too," said Pam. "But mostly, I hope the smell's gone. That was obnoxious."

"Truthfully, I'll be happy just to see an empty closet. I know we can get rid of any odor once the, uh, source, is gone. We can open the windows, scrub till we're blue in the face, and use massive amounts of air fresheners and essential oils."

"Good plan." Pam made notes on her legal pad. She'd taken to hanging a pen on a chain around her neck for easy access. "So did the guys ask any questions about what we were doing?"

"Hunh-unh. I think they're both minding their p's and q's. I discussed the 'secret girlfriend' situation with Jim the other day, and Marcus walked in on it." I grinned. "I've never seen anyone back out of a room so fast."

"OMG!" Pam tucked her notepad into her purse and looped her pen onto her necklace. "Tell me everything."

I took a breath. "I told him, in no uncertain terms, how I felt about him and his secret girlfriend. I told him how harmful it was to our relationship that he broke our promise to each other to keep our children out of our dating lives until the person was truly significant. That means engagement or impending engagement."

"Did he pull the old 'We're not married so you can't tell me what to do' song-and-dance?"

I shook my head. "No way. I reminded him that we were still partners in the job of raising our children. That comes first. That will always come first."

"What'd he say?"

"He agreed." I shifted gears to speed up.

Pam squealed. "Good for you, Janny. I'm proud of the way you stuck up for yourself and the girls."

"Thanks, but that's not all. I also told him exactly what I thought of him asking our kids to keep a secret from me, their mother."

Pam twisted in her seat until it strained against her torso. "Tell me exactly what you said. Word for word. Don't leave anything out."

"I told him that if he ever asked the girls to lie to me again, I would go back to court to add stipulations to the custody arrangement."

Pam's eyes widened and she clasped a hand over her mouth. "Really? Would you really do that?"

I nodded, my jaw firm. "I would. If I believed his home environment wasn't suitable for the kids. I really would."

"Wow…" Pam fell silent for a moment. "What'd he do then?"

"He got really quiet and really pale." I thought back to the scene, picturing the surprise and shame written all over his face. One thing I admired about Jim—when he was caught, it showed. And when it showed, he usually owned up to it and changed his ways.

I lowered my voice. "I feel a little bad about playing the custody card, but it had to be done."

"What'd he say?"

"He said it wouldn't happen again. He apologized and told me that *she* had dropped by, even though he'd told her he was busy that weekend. Apparently, *she* has a jealous streak and thought he might be cheating." I rolled my eyes. "I don't know if he told her the circumstances of our divorce, but if he did, I can understand why she'd be checking in on him. If the situation were reversed, I'd certainly be making surprise visits."

"Me, too." Pam frowned. "Actually, if a guy I dated confessed to having an affair on his first wife, especially when she was pregnant, I'd run for the hills."

I nodded. "We both would. But we're older, and smarter."

"True dat. So then what happened?"

"He said she wasn't in his life anymore. They broke up a week later."

"Do you believe him?"

I shrugged and shifted gears. "I don't know. So long as he doesn't bring her around the kids, I don't really care."

"I wouldn't be surprised if she did break up with him," Pam said. "In fact, I hope they have a lot of breakups after what they've put us through."

I grimaced. Revenge wasn't my style, but I had to admit to a certain satisfaction in knowing that there were consequences to their actions. I glanced at Pam, sure my next words would shock her. "And then, I have to admit, I felt a little bad for him."

"What!"

I averted my eyes. "I know it makes me a big softie, but for the first time I saw him in a completely different light. Sure, he has a big new house and a new boat and a new truck. But the house is empty. There's hardly any furniture, and what he does have is just thrown in there. And there are no people in his house."

"Oh." Pam's tone was subdued. "You mean his house is not a home?"

"That's exactly what I mean. And he's there, all by himself, most of the time. He's lost his wife, his kids, his home. It's pretty sad, really."

"I hadn't thought about it that way. But you're right. I would hate to be separated from my kid."

"And then there's the burden of knowing that your actions—yours alone—caused you to be living in those circumstances—" I took another deep breath, exhaling before I continued. "Well, I can see why he'd try to fill up his life with other stuff."

"Compensation."

I nodded. "So I told him that I knew he hadn't hurt the girls—or me—on purpose." I paused to collect my thoughts. "I told him that he was a good dad and that I knew he was doing the best he could."

"That was really nice of you. Really generous," Pam said, her words nearly a whisper. "What'd he say?"

I paused, getting a handle on my emotions. "He cried."

Pam gasped. "Really? Like real tears?"

"Yes." My voice quivered.

We rode without speaking the rest of the way, Moxie's snores in the hatchback breaking the silence. The weather had been mild, so after parking, we cracked the windows and peeked in at her. She lay curled into a ball, sound asleep. From one corner of her mouth, her tongue lolled. Next to her, the food and water bowls held ample amounts. The money we'd invested in spill-proof bowls had been worth it.

"She's out." Pam turned and faced the Craftsman. "Okay. We're here. Here goes nothing."

I swallowed a lump of tension that had wedged in my throat and squared my shoulders. "I feel the same way. But I'm ready. More than ready. In a couple of weeks, we'll look back at this and laugh."

Pam raised one eyebrow in skepticism. "Right." She looped her shoulder bag over her head so it rode diagonally across her torso. "I guess it's now or never."

I grabbed her arm. "Let's go."

Chapter 36

We strode with purpose up the sidewalk to the cottage's open front door. Along the way, I surveyed the landscaping. A few brightly colored flowers on the path, some fresh bark, and a good mowing would work wonders.

Daniels greeted us in the living room. "Hello, Jan, Pam. Welcome back."

I grinned despite my earlier feelings of anxiety. Finally, we were back in our little house, our little fixer-upper. We could begin moving forward at last.

Pam and I joined him. The house seemed older, a bit shabbier than when we'd last been in it. The wood flooring a little less shiny, the paint a bit more patchy. I sniffed hard at the air, but the scent of formaldehyde had disappeared. A good sign.

Despite feeling like we'd experienced several layers of disappointment and potential disaster with this house, I now felt a renewed sense of potential. It would be up to us to keep from fogging the proverbial rearview mirror and continue focusing on the positive.

"Follow me." Daniels motioned us forward.

We linked arms and trailed him to the bedroom, our footsteps echoing in the bare hall. Once we'd crossed the threshold, I sniffed the air. The room smelled strongly of lemons. What a relief from the scents of formaldehyde and whatever else had leaked out of the aquarium.

Drawing a deep breath, I turned to look toward the closet. The rest of the paneling had been removed and stacked in the far corner. The entire space lay exposed, like a closet that had been recently spring cleaned.

Satisfied, I chanced a peek at Daniels. He wore jeans and a white cotton button-up shirt under a sweatshirt. Only the sleeves and collar showed. He'd probably come straight from the office and hadn't wanted to risk getting his clothes dirty.

He stepped ahead of us. "Don't touch anything. This is just a look-see to put your minds at ease. We're doing a thorough, but efficient, and most importantly, clean, job."

"Thank goodness." Pam braced one hand on either side of the closet and peered inside. "You know, a little elbow grease and creative use of space, and this closet will be better than new."

I sighed in relief and stuck my head in above hers. I examined every inch of the interior. The faux cedar formed the back and both sides. Below, the original hardwood floor and its lustrous finish revealed what the bedroom's floor could look like. I imagined what a little sanding, prepping, and staining would do for the grain in the wood. Excitement flickered in my brain.

"That's what the floors will look like when we get done with them." I pointed to the closet. "And we'll paint the interior paneling a nice, fresh white."

Daniels turned and smiled at me. In a flash, I truly believed what I'd been saying about everything being okay. We'd finish the flip, hand over the keys, and collect our check. And maybe, just maybe, I'd bring Daniels some of my special Black Forest cheesecake cupcakes as a housewarming gift.

He closed the gap between us and followed the trajectory of my finger. "Gorgeous." He was so close I could smell his minty breath. Impulsively, I stuck my hands in my pockets. I couldn't trust myself not to grab his sweatshirt and plant a kiss on his perfect peach lips. It was an urge I hadn't felt in a very long time, and it took me by surprise.

Pam stepped back. "I'm amazed there aren't any watermarks or anything."

"This room will be perfect as a spare bedroom," Daniels said. "I don't have kids of my own, but I've got four nieces and four nephews who come to visit."

"Four of each?" I asked.

"Eight?" said Pam. "You have eight nieces and nephews?"

He smiled and nodded. "Sure do. Three brothers. One had three boys, another three girls. The last had one of each and they left it at that."

I laughed. "Are you sure all you'll need is a two-bedroom house?"

"Yeah, two will do it. This will be my first house. I want to ease into home ownership. Get my feet wet, so to speak," he replied. "I only get two or three of the rugrats at a time, anyway. I doubt I'll ever get all eight at the same time."

"I hope not! Even their parents stopped after three. They'd never ask you to take on all of them at once."

"You'd be surprised at the shenanigans they pull on their bachelor brother." He winked. "I'll get a couple sets of bunk beds and a chest of drawers, then install shelves in the closet for games and sports equipment. Aside from that, I'm not sure what I'd need to do.

They're pretty small kids. They can't take up much room."

Pam snorted, but I held my own response in. No sense spoiling the surprise of how much room a little kid takes up. He'd learn soon enough.

"You could hang curtains at the window," I said. "Or even install a mini-blind. If you put a throw rug on the floor, it will keep their tootsies warm at night."

Daniels stared at me, his expression soft. "Hadn't thought about their, uh, tootsies." He grinned. "But that's a good idea."

I flushed. This time, rather than fueling the fire with a sassy comment, Pam came to my rescue.

She cleared her throat. "You could easily put two sets of bunk beds in here." She paced off six feet by three feet on both sides of the room. "It doesn't leave a lot of space, but since they don't live here, they won't need much furniture."

Daniels nodded, momentarily distracted. He examined the spaces Pam outlined, taking giant strides to measure as she did. He rubbed his chin in thought. "Can I get your opinion on the kitchen, Janny?"

"Sure."

Casting a last look around the bedroom, searching for tell-tale signs of damage, I felt satisfied that the room was good as new. Or in this case, better than before—no body or aquarium.

"What I'm wondering about," he said, once we arrived in the kitchen, "is the lighting. I don't like tube lighting."

We all craned our necks, staring at the ceiling. Long, fluorescent tubes had been encased in a clear plastic fixture. Definitely ugly.

"That's an easy one," I said. "We can replace it with anything you'd like. All you need to do is go to Home Store and pick out a replacement."

Pam drew her notepad out of her purse and unhooked her pen from the chain. "If you're serious about buying the house, we could incorporate what you want in the remodel, then adjust the price accordingly. If something's too expensive, we can dial it down."

I nodded. "Your suggestions would give us a direction to go in and help us determine what all we need to do to make you happy with the end product."

Pam poised her pen over the pad. "Why don't we do a quick walk-through? You tell us what you absolutely must have and what's on your wish list. Then we can come up with a fair price."

"We'll also price out the upgrades," I added. "That way, you can finance it over the long run, and get everything you want now. Interest rates are still reasonable, so it's like getting more for less."

"That's a great idea." His blue-green eyes met and held my own. "Let's start now."

I knew his words were about the house, but I felt like he meant more than that. I couldn't wait to find out if that was true.

Chapter 37

Pam read over Daniels's wish list in the car. There were only three items labeled "musts": better lighting in the kitchen, extra outlet in the bathroom, and new refrigerator. The appliance currently in the kitchen had yellowed with age.

"These are easy," I said, mentally calculating the costs of the items. "I bet we can even swing a new stove, too. What else?"

"Extra half bath, or a washer and dryer in the utility room."

I considered. "That's pricey, but we can do it. The plumbing's already there, and we'd already accounted for something with that space in our original budget." I closed my eyes and pictured the rectangular alcove off of the kitchen. "You know, if we put a stackable washer and dryer on the left, closest to the hot water location, we could add a toilet and pedestal sink to the right."

"Oh! Good idea." Pam jotted a note on her pad. "Two birds, right?"

"Yep. What's next?"

"Covered walk path from kitchen to garage."

"Do-able for the cost of lumber, cement, and screws. I don't think we'd even need blueprints. Just basic fencing requirements which I know by heart."

"Agreed," Pam said. "The only thing left is an updated vanity and new toilet in the main bathroom."

"Hmmm…we're going to have to price those items out. Let's have him pick them out so we can determine the cost," I said.

"Oooh-la-la. Maybe the two of you could go together to *discuss* it."

I frowned at her, but it turned into a smile. An invitation to go to Home Store with Daniels sounded wonderful. I refocused on the task at hand. "Is that it?"

Pam inhaled deeply. "You won't believe this."

I shot her a quizzical look. "What?"

"Carpet in the bedrooms."

I groaned. "Why would he want to carpet the bedrooms? Those wood floors are gorgeous! I thought we'd talked about all of that during the walk-through."

"He said he likes to keep his tootsies warm, remember?" Pam wiggled her eyebrows.

"I remember." I blushed at the memory of our conversation. "Okay. The customer is always right. On the upside, that means we don't need to refinish the floors—carpet's cheaper. It also means we can defer some of the money to other things he wants."

"One more thing," Pam said, a glint in her eye. "But it won't cost us a penny."

I cocked my head. "What?"

"You."

I glanced her way. She grinned so hard her molars showed.

"Pam!"

Her laughter filled the car. "You know it's true. I know it's true. A blind person could see it's true."

Could she be right? Did Daniels have a crush on me, too? My heart leapt a little in my chest. Immediately, I pushed the feelings aside.

I shook my head. "I don't want to talk about it. I'm not ready for any of that."

Pam shrugged and stared at the road ahead. "I hear you, sister. I can't imagine ever wanting to be in love again. Too hard. Too much hurt. It's easier to be alone. But still, if there's magic in the air…"

She was right. There's no such thing as love without the risk of pain. Loving others doesn't come easy, but when it works, it really works.

"I think relationships have a cosmic balance scale," I said. "You have to weigh out how much pleasure the person brings to your life, despite the pain loving them brings, versus the pain of never feeling that incredible surge of love for another human being but feeling safe."

Pam wrinkled her nose. "I've never thought about it like that. It's kind of like knowing when a good thing has turned bad. If only men were like bananas, it'd be easy to know when to throw them out."

I giggled.

"I'm not there," she said. "I don't think I'll ever be."

"I'm not there, either." I reached over and patted her hand. "But I'm closer to it now than I was six months ago. That's progress."

"Maybe there's hope for me, then."

"Of course, there is. It'll all fall into place when you're ready."

She nodded. "You know what won't fall into place on its own?"

I grinned. "The house?"

"Yep. Let's make a trip to Home Store and start working out a budget."

Chapter 38

Less than a month later, we put the finishing touches on our cute little Craftsman. We'd maxed out our PB & J credit card with electrical and plumbing contractors' fees, as well as some hefty bathroom and lighting purchases from Home Store. Because Daniels had wanted to roll the entire cost into one loan, we'd furnished him with top of the line appliances: refrigerator, stove, and dishwasher, as well as a stackable washer and dryer unit in the newly refurbished half-bath/utility room combo. Holding a paint brush and tiny plastic bowl of Santa Fe Tan paint, Pam and I moved through the house, scanning for thin spots. We dabbed here and there, finally finding ourselves back in the living room.

"I can't believe we finished," she said.

I sighed. "It's been a whirlwind. But we did it."

"Let's give the exterior the once over."

"Good idea."

We tossed the paint brushes into the garbage and grabbed our iced coffees from the kitchen counter. I took a sip. The ice had melted and the coffee weakened. The sugar-free caramel syrup worked wonders to wake up my taste buds, however.

"Boy, it's hot out today," I said, as we exited the house.

"No kidding." Pam fanned her shirt.

"Let's do this." I wiped my brow. "We're due at escrow in less than an hour."

We inspected the landscaping from several angles. The flower beds we had cut in on either side of the walk path bloomed in yellows, oranges, and whites, and purple hydrangeas framed the door. I took a breath and savored the sweet scent of summer.

"I kind of hate to see it go," Pam said.

"I know what you mean." I held my hand up for a high-five. "But I'm very ready to trade in this project for a stack of cash."

"Well, that day has finally arrived." Pam slapped my hand, then took one last swig and crushed her cup. "Let's put pedal to the metal."

"Just a sec." I raced back inside and checked on the Black Forest cupcakes I'd stashed in the refrigerator, then flicked off the lights. At the door, I pulled up my loose jeans.

Pam eyed me then locked the door. "How much weight have you lost, Janny?"

"About six pounds." It didn't seem like a lot, but for someone whose weight had refused to budge, it felt fantastic.

"That's a pound and a half a week!" Pam grinned. "Good for you."

"Thanks. It helped that we've been too busy to eat for the past month."

"That and all the physical labor."

I pulled the waistband of my jeans out to show Pam. "Between the toning and reduced calories, I think I'm almost a size smaller. Back to where I was when Jim left."

"That's amazing." Pam smiled. "You're amazing."

I beamed and revved the Kia's engine. "Thanks!"

We cast one last look at our Craftsman cutie and waved.

"Good-bye," Pam called out. "I might miss you."

"Good-bye," I said. "I hope I don't have to miss you."

"What do you mean by that?"

I hunched my shoulders around my ears. "I guess...I mean...you know."

"Oh." Pam nodded. "Daniels."

"Yeah."

"I thought you weren't ready," Pam said as we left the neighborhood.

I pulled onto the main drag. "Me, too. Then, the other night I realized once we close escrow I may never see him again. It made me so sad it surprised me. The next day I made the cupcakes. The worst he can do is not contact me."

"Oh." Pam drew the word out and stared at me.

"I mean, I guess," I stammered, then shook my head. "I don't know. Let's just get through today, get some cash in our accounts, and worry about all of that later."

"There's something else I've been wanting to talk to you about anyway," she said. "I found another, uh, project."

I slowed for a yellow light. "What kind?" But before she could open her mouth, I added, "Wait! Let's pay off all of our debt and set aside three months' rent on our condos rather than tying up all of our money next time. These past two months have been hairy and scary."

"Agreed," she said. "We may not have to, though."

"Are you thinking we should buy a cheaper home next time? It will probably need more work done to it. That requires more cash."

"Not if it's a killer deal."

I groaned. "Nice word choice. What do you mean?" I slipped into a convenient parking spot in front of the strip mall. "Are you thinking a condo or duplex instead? You don't want to venture into commercial property, do you?"

She shook her head, sending her blonde bangs flying into her eyes. Neither of us had found the time, or the energy, to go to the hair or nail salon. I glanced at my nails. The ends were hooked and jagged, and only the pinkie and ring finger on my left hand had a smudge of tutti-frutti polish in the center. We were looking pretty raggedy.

"What then? Contracting or remodeling for others?" I asked.

She brushed the hair out of her eyes. "I'm thinking something entirely different. There's an interesting property that's been sitting a while."

"What's wrong with it?"

"Well…" Pam began. "It's an unusual property."

I withdrew the key and unbuckled, then faced her. "What do you mean, 'an unusual property'?"

One side of Pam's mouth turned up. "It wasn't a house originally."

I frowned. I'd heard of shipping containers being re-fabbed into homes. Was that what she meant? "What was it originally?".

Pam's grin broadened. "A church."

"A church? As in Sunday morning services?"

"Yep. Except no one's been doing sermons there

for a while."

"How long is a while?"

"About thirty years."

"Thirty years?" I repeated. "Why?"

Pam dug out a printed email from her purse. "I asked Sam to do a little research. He said the pastor there passed away and the church board disbanded rather than conduct another pastor search."

"So who owns the property?"

"The church foundation, but without a name associated with it, no one. It's in foreclosure."

My spirits lifted. "A foreclosed property with no residents? And no one has any vested interest? That sounds promising."

Pam erupted in a nervous laugh. "There are only two of the board members left, and, apparently, or so the story goes, neither one will set foot in there. They've released all interest and dissolved their relationship with the property. Whatever proceeds there are after the back property taxes are paid will be forwarded to the larger church body—it's an international council, I think."

"How odd. Wait a minute—why won't they go inside? Is it dangerous?"

"I guess that depends on who you talk to."

I set the keys in my lap. "Okay, Pam, you're hedging. Give it to me straight. What the heck is wrong with the property?"

Pam's eyes grew wide. "They say it's haunted."

Chapter 39

After agreeing to discuss the haunted church later, we signed the escrow documents and exchanged the last of the keys for a cashier's check. We deposited the check, then grabbed a slice of blackberry pie at our favorite hometown restaurant to celebrate. Later, as we headed for the school, Daniels called.

Pam answered. "I got you on speaker. How's everything?"

"Great. I'm in and looking around at my new digs."

"How do you like the appliances?" I asked. Even though he had picked them out, he hadn't seen them installed in the house yet. I also wanted to see how he'd respond to the cupcakes I'd left for him but didn't dare ask. Would I come off as too forward? Needy? Maybe I misread the entire situation.

"Not to sound like a broken record, but great." Echoes came over the line: his voice, then footsteps. I pictured him walking around the living room, the only room we were able to convince him to leave uncarpeted. "I've got a bunch of guys who followed me over. They'll be here any minute. I promised them a pizza if they help me move my stuff in."

"Sounds like fun," Pam said. "We left a couple more keys in the drawer next to the sink. It'll save you a trip to Home Store to get copies."

"Wow. You guys thought of everything." His voice

sounded light, happy. "I should hide one outside somewhere. Although I could probably leave the doors unlocked if I wanted to. Like I said, there's hardly any crime in this neighborhood." He laughed.

Pam and I shook our heads. We neared the school, and I positioned the Kia at the back of the pick-up line.

"We're really glad you like it," Pam said. "Is there anything else we can help you with?"

"Uh, sort of." The sound of suction from a new refrigerator door opening came across the line. "Thanks for the cupcakes. Who made them?"

"Janny did," Pam said. "She's an excellent baker." She wiggled her eyebrows at me.

"It's nothing." I hurried my words. It's impossible for me to not make light of my efforts. "We plan to do it for all our buyers. Do you like cupcakes?"

"Absolutely. I love chocolate. I think I'll have one right now."

We waited, but Daniels didn't continue. He was probably stuffing a bite of chocolate cake with cherry whipped cream frosting into his mouth.

Pam raised her hands in the air, signaling impatience. "Anything else?"

"Um," he stammered a little, his words muffled by what I assumed to be cake.

I couldn't help but smile. It had been a long time since I'd made this recipe for a man, and his obvious enjoyment brought me...well...joy.

A moment passed as Pam and I simply stared at each other, waiting. Then, Pam's mouth formed an O. She pushed the phone into my hands and whispered, "He wants to talk to you." In a voice louder than necessary, she added, "Hey, I'm going to head into the school and get the girls. Janny will take you off speaker phone and handle any other questions."

A gusty exhale came over the line. My stomach knotted up. He either wanted to tell me something really bad that he'd discovered about the house, or Pam was right and he wanted to talk to me—just me. My pulse jumped into my throat as I held the phone to my ear.

"This is Janny," I said, my words fluttery. "I hope everything is okay at the house."

"It is. It is."

Pause. I warred silently with myself. Should I say something? Should I wait for him to say something more?

I knew what I wanted to do. I wanted to ask him out. My six-pound loss and the cash in my pocket had made me braver than I'd ever felt in my life.

But I'd never asked a man out. And I couldn't help feeling like it was better if the guy asked the girl out for the first date. Call me old-fashioned.

Then again, it could be the fear of rejection.

Voices, then the thumping of feet came from the background.

"Hang on a minute." He pulled the phone away from his mouth to speak to his buddies. "Couch goes in here next to the window. Gimme a minute to finish this call."

More footsteps, then a faraway voice asked, "Where's the beer?" Again, the sound of a new refrigerator being opened and closed. "Dude, those look good."

"Don't eat those!" Daniels said. "Those are mine. You'll get pizza later."

"Okay. Okay. Get off the phone. We ain't gonna unpack your stuff by ourselves while you sit around eating cupcakes."

Daniels laughed. "Gimme a minute."

Closing my eyes, I imagined him walking the hall toward the back bedroom. A door closed and he began to stammer. "I was wondering if you, uh, might like to, well, grab a, I don't know, bite to eat sometime."

A swarm of butterflies took flight in my stomach. Had he really asked me out? What do I say? How do I accept?

"Okay." Even to my ears it didn't sound convincing. Or enthusiastic. "Okay!" I said again. This time it came out too excited. I closed my eyes and braced my forehead with the hand not holding the phone. "Okay." Better, but now I'd said it three times. Arrgh.

"Great," he replied, his voice relieved. "How about tomorrow night? Maybe six o'clock? I can pick you up at your place. We'll go down to the waterfront, have a bite to eat, then maybe take a walk afterward if it's warm enough. I like to walk along the waterfront, do you?" His words were hurried. Whether he'd rehearsed them or was simply trying to finish before his friends barged in, I couldn't be sure.

But it didn't matter.

"That sounds fantastic," I said.

"I'll see you then."

Chapter 40

Daniels proved to be as punctual in his personal life as he was in his professional world. When the doorbell rang, Pam whispered, "Have fun," and corralled the girls through the pass-through door. She'd volunteered to babysit and answer any questions they asked by maintaining my story that Daniels was the man who bought our flip and was now a friend.

Once the door had closed firmly behind them, I ushered Daniels in, and after a quick greeting, he pointed to the pass-through. "That is so clever." He walked over to the frame and examined the trim. "I'm impressed that you knew how to do that. And you finished the project so well. The edges are so clean."

"Thanks," I said. "It's not perfect, but it works really well for our needs."

"It looks pretty good to me." He turned. "You look really pretty, too. Are you ready to go?"

"Thanks, and yes." I straightened my spine, which pulled my new push-up bra back into place under the black cotton jumpsuit I'd bought for the occasion. I pulled the door open, glad I'd worn flat sandals. At least my feet would be comfortable tonight.

I locked up behind us and we walked out of the building to his car. Like a perfect gentleman, he opened my door before getting in himself.

"So how's the house?" I asked when he slid in

266

beside me. "Are you all settled in?"

"Close." He put the car into reverse and began backing out. "I've got my bedroom situated and the refrigerator stocked."

"The necessities," I said. "Any cupcakes left?"

Daniels laughed. "Not a chance. I tried hiding them behind the beer, but the guys found them and devoured every last one."

I giggled. "They are good, if I say so myself."

"Yep." He shifted into drive. "Now all I have to do is hang my flat screen on the living room wall and move the couch in front of it."

"How about the kids' room?"

"Bunk beds. Two sets. Enough for all of them." He laughed and pulled out onto the road, picking up speed as we headed for the freeway. "The kids came over to inspect the room and each left a toy. I think they're holding their place."

"Was there enough room in the closet?" I asked. "Do you like the organizer?"

"It's awesome. I wasn't expecting it." He flashed a grin. "I can store all of their board games and most of the sports equipment in that space. Like I said, there isn't much need for clothing storage. Just bedding and extra blankets…and, of course, the toys they left."

"That's great. I'm glad you like the house."

"I really do. And what's more, I like the circumstances that led me to find it."

My nose wrinkled. "It doesn't bother you that there was once a, um, body in there? Not at all?"

"Nah. It's gone. And after the thorough sweep we did, I know there aren't any more surprises. I bet the average homeowner can't say the same."

"Good point. The same thought went through our heads after we found him. I think Pam walked around the entire condo twice thumping on walls and listening for thuds that meant the space wasn't empty." I laughed at the memory.

"Ha! I bet she did. She seems very driven." He cast a look my way. "You both do."

I smiled, waited a beat, then asked, "And Gerry? How is he?"

"He's fine. Immediately recanted his story, as expected, but we know the truth. Putting him through the legal process won't help, though…given his age. He won't be able to pay anything back, and ECC can't force him out under Washington state law, even if he runs out of money. So his Social Security has been cut in half and will probably be garnished, but he'll stay there until…well, you know."

I gulped. "I guess it all turned out for the best."

"Probably," he said. "It's not the worst result I've seen."

"I bet. By the looks of the walls on your office, you've probably seen a lot of crazy stuff. Probably the worst people can offer up. And you've also helped a lot of people."

"Part of the job." He grinned and exited the freeway. "And I love the job. It's been good to me. I try to make the uniform proud."

"I can tell."

"Enough business talk. Where do you want to eat? I was thinking of the waterfront. It's such a nice day we could sit outside."

"Anywhere is fine. And I love the waterfront."

He glanced at me as he turned onto Soundview

Road, which ran along the water's edge. "I'm really glad we're doing this," he said. "I think you ladies are pretty amazing. There aren't a lot of ladies who would try to flip houses for a living."

My breath caught in my throat. In all of our years together, Jim had never said he thought I was pretty great. He'd called me pretty, and always told me I was a good mom. But Jim's perception of me had been flavored by everything we'd been through…as well as my limited involvement in the company business. He didn't know me like I was now.

To Daniels, however, I'd revealed more—a fully independent woman, capable of juggling family, career, and unexpected hurdles. I grinned at my accomplishments. I liked seeing myself through his eyes.

I faced him and my smile softened. "Thanks. I think you're pretty great, too."

Daniels parked, killed the engine, and turned toward me. "Are you ready?"

My breath caught in my throat, and I thought carefully about my answer before speaking.

"Absolutely," I said.

A word about the author...

Lori Pollard-Johnson is a retired educator and current wife, mama and grandma. She writes from a lakefront cabin in Washington and a sun-filled porch in Arizona, and has been published in fiction, nonfiction and poetry, in Vegetarian Journal, Seattle, Black Belt, Bridal Connections and The Binnacle, in addition to two children's novels, one Young Adult novel and two cozy mystery novels. When she's not writing, she's playing with her grandbabies, braiding rugs, perfecting her shavasana, swimming, practicing her releves, hiking, renovating fixer-uppers, reading, or watching javelinas dance through her backyard.

Thank you for purchasing
this publication of The Wild Rose Press, Inc.

For questions or more information
contact us at
info@thewildrosepress.com.

The Wild Rose Press, Inc.
www.thewildrosepress.com